Savannah's friend Tamara Grimaldi was fourteen when her mom was murdered, and the body dumped along the side of Interstate 65 in Indiana. Since then, Grimaldi has kept an eye out for her mother's killer, first as a homicide detective in Nashville, and now as the chief of police for the city of Columbia, Tennessee.

When a new body with the old MO shows up along I-65 in Maury County, it looks like there might be a break in the case. But trying to find a serial killer who has been active for two decades, along an interstate that stretches from the Gulf of Mexico to the Great Lakes, is easier said than done.

Even though this time, there are indications that the culprit might be found closer to home...

Between the serial killer's first and last victims, an old, related cold case Grimaldi sniffs out, and the new stalker Rafe has picked up, Savannah has her hands full juggling friends and enemies, corpses and clues, in the book early readers have called "the best one yet."

OTHER BOOKS IN THIS SERIES

SURVIVAL CLAUSE

Savannah Martin Mystery #20

JENNA BENNETT

SURVIVAL CLAUSE

Savannah Martin Mystery #20

Interior design and formatting: B. Gallagher
Cover Design: Dar Albert, Wicked Smart Designs

One

It started, as such things often do, with a phone call.

"Where are you?" Tamara Grimaldi's voice asked.

My husband, whose phone it was, answered, "On our way home from dinner. Just leaving Beulah's."

Beulah's Meat'n Three is a favorite of Rafe's, and he's a favorite there, seeing as he once had a fling—a very brief fling, a long time ago—with the owner.

Grimaldi hesitated. "Savannah's with you?"

"And the baby," Rafe confirmed, with a glance at our four-and-a-half-month old daughter in the backseat.

Grimaldi hesitated again. And must have decided that the circumstances outweighed him being saddled with the two of us. "Get to Broad and Green as fast as you can. Tucker's got a kid on the ground and is sitting on him."

Rafe's lips tightened and he dropped the phone in my lap. The tires screamed as he made a tight U-turn, barely even slowing down, before jamming his foot on the gas pedal. The Volvo—because we were in my personal car, not the Chevy that was his loaner from the police department—lurched forward. I fumbled the phone up to my ear. And I'll admit I was a little breathless. "Where are you?"

Subtext: *Why can't you go to the corner of Broad and Green and deal with Sergeant Tucker yourself?* She was Tucker's boss. Rafe wasn't, and Tucker has zero respect for Rafe even aside from that.

"Murder scene," Grimaldi said. "With Sheriff Satterfield."

That explained it, then.

Or maybe not. If the Maury County sheriff was at the murder scene, surely the chief of the Columbia police didn't have to be?

But now wasn't the time to worry about it. The Volvo was zooming up the highway toward Columbia at a heart-attack-inducing eighty miles an hour, and Rafe was weaving in and out of traffic, narrowly dodging the other cars.

"Tell me about it later," I told her. "If these are my last few moments on earth, I want to enjoy them."

Grimaldi snorted, and Rafe shot me a look. "I know how to drive, darlin'."

"Eyes on the road," I told him, as I dropped the now-silent phone in the center console. Grimaldi had gone back to her murder scene. "Want to tell me what's going on?"

"You heard everything I heard."

He zipped around a slow-moving Cadillac that looked like my mother's. I peered out the side window. Yep, there she was, staring wide-eyed at me. She'd recognized my car too, of course. The shadow next to her was either her best friend Audrey or maybe my sister Catherine, since Bob—Mother's gentleman friend and the guy she's living in sin with—was at Grimaldi's murder scene.

Or more likely she was at his. But either way, he wasn't with Mother in the car.

I gave her a wave as we shot past and back into the right lane, just before we got flattened by a big, black truck with bug lights on top. The driver leaned on the horn, a deep, angry bass.

"Sergeant Tucker is over at Broad Street and Green, and he's apprehended somebody," I paraphrased from the phone. "That's his job, isn't it? Won't he be upset if you show up and take his drug dealer away from him?"

Tucker worked narcotics, so this wasn't clairvoyance on my part. Or prejudice, either.

"I ain't aiming to take nobody away from him, darlin'. Just make sure he doesn't kill the guy."

"Why would he…? Oh."

Rafe nodded. "Yeah. Tucker's old school, and not fond of young, black thugs."

No. Rafe had been a young, black thug himself back when Tucker had arrested him, at eighteen, for assault and battery.

In Tucker's favor, Rafe had started it, and he had definitely both assaulted and battered the victim before Tucker got there. I'm sure my husband would be the first to admit that Tucker had had every right to arrest him.

"He didn't…" I began, "um…?"

He glanced at me, and as usual, read my mind. "Back when he arrested me? He mighta twisted my arm a little extra hard when he was trying to restrain me. Pretty sure I remember taking a couple of punches while he was trying to peel me off Billy."

My eyes narrowed, and his lips curved. "I'm sure I wasn't making it easy for him."

Probably not. "But now—?"

His hands tightened on the wheel and the car shrieked on two wheels around the corner of Broad, but his voice was just as calm. "I don't think he's trying to hurt this kid. Might rough him up a little if the kid fights back. But if he had a history of that, it'd be in his file."

"And it isn't?"

He shook his head. "I had a look. Part of my job, after all."

Yes, it was. As far as most people in Columbia knew, Rafe was working for the local PD as an investigator, after being fired from his job at the TBI—the Tennessee Bureau of Investigations—in January. Unbeknownst to those people, he still had his job with the TBI, and was on loan to Grimaldi, and the two of them were working on cleaning up the Columbia PD after the previous chief had been hauled off in the back of a squad car. So far, they had mostly cleared one investigator of suspicion, and had taken another away for murder. Tucker was still an unknown. We knew he didn't like Rafe much, but there were good reasons for that—Rafe had, indeed, not made it easy for Tucker to peel him off Billy Scruggs back then, and then he'd had the audacity to come back to Columbia as a colleague and the new chief's pet investigator. So it was understandable that Tucker was resentful. But that didn't mean he wasn't honest.

Up ahead, we saw a squad car parked at an angle across the street, lights flashing, and a knot of people. Some of them were holding cell phones. I could see the blue of the screens in the gathering dark.

Rafe pulled the Volvo to a stop, and pushed his door open. "Stay here," he told me, even as he had one foot on the ground. "Don't get out of the car."

I shook my head, but he had already slammed the door and was on his way across the blacktop to where Sergeant Tucker did, indeed, have one knee on the back of a prone figure that was face-down on the street, unmoving.

Two officers hovered nearby. They weren't actively helping Tucker, but they weren't actively interfering with him, either. They gave off a vibe of hand-wringing, like they didn't like the situation much but didn't quite know what to do about it, and about their superior officer. One of them had a hand on his weapon and one eye on the crowd that had gathered, but since no one was threatening to come any closer, he didn't actually move. The other man had half an eye on Tucker and the other on us. When he saw Rafe get out of the car and come toward him, like the wrath of God descending—if that isn't too religious an analogy—I could see his shoulders brace. His partner glanced at him, then at Rafe, and squared his own. A couple of the phones in the crowd swung toward my husband, and I understood what—or some of what—Grimaldi had been worried about.

Tucker hadn't noticed Rafe's arrival. Not until Rafe grabbed him by the collar of his uniform and lifted him off the offender.

If that gives you the impression that Tucker is small and weightless, I can assure you he's not. He's a solid guy with a slight paunch, who probably weighted in at around two hundred.

Rafe, though, is six-three or a little more, and he has big shoulders and the kinds of muscles you usually see in ads for Hanes briefs. Most of those muscles were hidden under a T-shirt right now, but they function well in addition to looking pretty, so he had no problem shifting the generation-older, stocky Tucker. His biceps and triceps flexed and bunched when he plucked Tucker's form off the skinny body on the ground, and set him down, a little more forcibly than necessary, a few feet away. But other than that, he didn't evince any particular effort.

Tucker staggered as his feet hit the ground, and Rafe took the opportunity while the sergeant got his bearings to reach down again, and haul the victim to his feet. A buzz spread through the crowd, like from an angry beehive.

The kid turned out to be just that, a kid. Sixteen, maybe seventeen, in an oversized T-shirt and workout pants. Not too dissimilar to what Rafe must have looked like when Tucker hauled him off Billy Scruggs at eighteen, minus the injuries. There didn't seem to be much wrong with this boy, other than some dirt on the front of his shirt and pants, and a few minor scratches from where he'd hit the pavement. He was clearly happy to be let up, at least until he got a good look at who'd done the letting. Then his eyes widened and he gulped. "I didn't do nothing!"

Rafe didn't respond. Or at least not with anything more than an arched brow. "See that blue car over there?" he asked instead, nodding to where I was sitting. The kid's head bobbed up and down, and so did his Adam's apple. "Go stand by it."

The kid's eyes must have flickered, because Rafe added, "Don't run. There are four people here with guns, and you don't want one of'em to get the idea that he can shoot you in the back because you're trying to evade arrest. Just stay where I tell you."

The kid swallowed again. When he moved toward the Volvo, it was slowly and carefully.

Tucker, meanwhile, had gotten his balance back, and with it some of his bravado. "Who the bleep d'you think you are," he yelled at Rafe, "coming here and interfering with my apprehension…!"

I couldn't hear Rafe's response. He moved close enough to Tucker that he could practically whisper in the older man's ear. Tucker tried to move back as Rafe came forward, but Rafe wrapped a hand halfway around Tucker's arm and kept him in place so he could lean down and talk to Tucker in a voice that didn't reach me, and more importantly, didn't reach any of the cell phone cameras trained on the pair. I had no doubt that most of those phones were set on video, and that some of them might even be live-streaming this encounter right now.

Whatever Rafe said, was effective. Tucker turned red, and then pale, and then red again. But when he wrenched his arm out of Rafe's grasp and stepped back, he didn't follow it up with a punch or a push, or even anything verbal.

"Go on home," Rafe told him. Calmly. There might have been an edge there, but not enough of one to make him sound threatening. Or any more threatening than he usually does, at any rate. "I'll take care of this."

Tucker hesitated. He glanced at the kid, and he glanced at

the other cops. Finally he glanced at the crowd, and that seemed to make the decision easier. Looking surly, he brushed past Rafe, close enough to bump him with his shoulder, and headed for his car.

Rafe didn't bother to watch him go, just turned his attention to the other two cops.

"We were just providing backup…" one them began as the cameras turned toward them. Tucker slammed his car door, and a moment later, the engine revved before the squad car took off up the street with a roar of the engine.

Rafe took advantage of the noisy interlude to have a quiet word with the two officers, neither of whom I knew personally. Maybe they were attached to Sergeant Tucker's unit and not traffic. But they knew Rafe, and were obviously willing to take orders from him. Or suggestions, at any rate. By the time Tucker's car engine had faded in the distance and everyone's attention had shifted back to them, they were both nodding pleasantly. "Yes, sir."

Rafe nodded back. As he turned toward me, or more likely, toward the kid who was still standing like a statue next to the right fender, the other officers headed toward the second squad car. It might have been me, but it looked like they weren't wasting any time doing it. You couldn't call it an escape, exactly, but it came close. I could practically feel their relief at being able to get away without anything worse happening.

"Nothing more to see here," Rafe told the onlookers as he walked back toward the Volvo.

"What're you going to do to him?" someone piped up from the back of the crowd. There were maybe eight or ten people standing there altogether, and I counted the glow from at least four phones.

"Who are you?" someone else called out.

I held my breath as Rafe stopped and turned toward them. He held still for a beat, maybe to make sure they were listening, or else because he was trying to decide what to say.

Or maybe just because it made for good television.

In the end, he went with the truth. "My name is Rafael Collier. I work for the Columbia PD."

He pulled his badge out of his pocket and lifted it. And then he waited for the rumbles to die down before he added, "That's my wife and my baby girl in the car. We were on our way home when Chief Grimaldi heard about what was going on, and wanted somebody to take a look. When I'm done here, I'm gonna take my family home and put my baby to bed. But first I'm gonna talk to the kid over there about what happened to him."

"How do we know you're telling the truth?" someone wanted to know.

I'm sure Rafe wanted to roll his eyes. I rolled mine, since no one was filming me. Rafe probably didn't, since he had several cameras trained on him. His voice was vaguely irritated, though. "You don't. But you can watch me do it. And if I do something you don't like, you can put my face all over social media. You're prob'ly gonna do that anyway."

Probably. And while part of me was a little worried about what might come of it if they did, the other part rejoiced in the fact that it would make it even more impossible for him to ever go undercover again. He'd spent ten years doing undercover work before we got married, and I'd happily take anything that would stop him from doing it again.

Even unwanted social media attention.

The cell phones swung toward the car as Rafe headed that way. I wondered whether they could see me through the windshield, and decided they probably couldn't. But I'd refrain from picking my nose, just in case.

Rafe stopped in front of the young man, by now quivering like a young birch. "Name?"

The kid opened his mouth, and had to clear his throat.

"Curtis."

I waited for Rafe to ask him his last name, but he didn't. "What happened, Curtis?"

"I was in the store down there," Curtis said, pointing down the street with a finger that shook. "It was me and a couple of friends. And we… um…"

He trailed off, flushing.

Rafe sighed. "What did you take?"

"Nothing, man!" He shook his head frantically, and his hair, twisted into spirals on top of his head, swayed. "I didn't take nothing. But my friends, they grabbed some chips and sodas and stuff, and then they ran. I didn't even know they were gonna do it, man! And they left me there…"

He wound down again, sounding sincerely baffled that his friends would do such a thing. I winced. Rafe probably wanted to.

"Lemme guess," he said now. "Your friends got away, you got caught, the owner called the cops, and Tucker showed up. When you said you didn't do nothing, he didn't believe you."

Curtis nodded.

"Did he ask you for the names of your friends?"

Curtis winced. "No. Guess we didn't get to that part."

Rafe nodded. "I ain't gonna do that, either."

Curtis looked relieved, until Rafe continued, "You're in enough trouble already. Besides, by the time I tracked'em down, the evidence'd be long gone."

Curtis nodded, looking glum.

"I'm not likely to be as understanding next time, though," Rafe added.

Curtis looked up at him, and he elaborated. "If I get another call like this, and I find out that you've let your friends talk you into another trip to the market, whether you steal something or not, I'm not likely to be understanding of you putting yourself in this situation again. You're either lying to me—"

"No, sir!" Curtis shook his head. "No, I ain't."

"—or your friends planned this without telling you, and then they left you holding the ball while they ran away. Either way, I don't wanna come back here and find you again. You understand me?"

"Yes, sir." Curtis nodded vigorously.

"And maybe think about getting some new friends, since the ones you've got don't seem like the ones anyone oughta have."

Curtis looked glum.

"You need a ride somewhere?" Rafe wanted to know.

Curtis blinked, and it took him a second to respond. "No, sir. My granddad'd kill me if I came home in a police car."

Rafe nodded. He's had some experience with grandfathers who beat their grandchildren, so he knows what that's like. "Go on home, then. And stay outta trouble."

"Yes, sir." Curtis took off running. The buzzing from the crowd got louder, and then softer again.

"Show's over," Rafe told them, and reached for the door handle.

Only to stop when a voice asked, "What about my merchandise?"

The speaker was an older man, middle-eastern in coloring. When Rafe turned to him, he looked like he might have wanted to quail, but he squared his shoulders. "They stole from my market!"

"*He* didn't," Rafe pointed out, indicating Curtis, who was now a block away and fading fast. The kid should be on the track team at school, if he wasn't already. "You the one who called the cops?"

The man nodded.

"I can't arrest him when he didn't do nothing. It's not his fault that his friends shoplifted and ran."

The market owner looked obstinate, and Rafe sighed. "Here." He pulled out his wallet, extricated a twenty, and passed it over. "That oughta cover it."

The older man tucked it away. The crowd buzzed again, the anger turning toward the shop owner now.

"Go on back to your market," Rafe told him. "You got enough money to pay for what was stolen. And you shouldn't leave the place unattended."

The shop owner turned and trotted away, and I think it was spurred just as much by a desire to get away from the crowd as the need to see if his place was all right.

"Anybody else got something they wanna say?" Rafe inquired. When nobody spoke up, he grabbed for the car door again. "Go on home. We're done."

He folded himself into the car and snapped his seatbelt in place. And drove away, careful not to get too close to anybody. The cell phone cameras stayed on the car until we were out of sight, and it took that long for Rafe to let out the breath he'd been holding.

"Shit."

"Tense situation," I said.

He rolled his head back and forth, loosening the no doubt tight muscles in his neck, and then he glanced at me, his lips curving. "Coulda been worse. In the past, I'd be the one on the ground."

With Tucker's knee in his back. "Did you ever…?"

"End up on my face on the pavement with some cop's boot on my neck? More than once, darlin'. Lucky for me, none of'em had an itchy trigger finger."

Lucky, indeed.

"You handled it well," I said.

"Easier when you've been the one on the ground," Rafe answered. And shook his head. "Stupid kid."

"Do you think he was telling the truth? About his friends

taking off and leaving him?"

"I don't imagine he'd be stupid enough to let himself get caught if he'd known what was gonna happen," Rafe said, maneuvering the car back in the direction of home, for the second time that night. "He'd have been outta there with the others if he'd known. And I don't imagine what's-his-name..."

"The store owner?"

He nodded. "—woulda let him get away if he'd had anything in his pockets that oughtn't have been there."

Probably true.

"So justice was served. More or less."

"If you wanna call it that," Rafe said. "Curtis went home. The guy got his money back. I'm twenty bucks poorer, and my name and face'll be all over social media tomorrow. But it coulda been worse."

Very easily. "What's going to happen to Tucker?"

"Not much," Rafe said. "He was only doing his job. The kid wasn't damaged. Tucker wasn't killing him, or even hurting him much. I don't see him doing that even if I hadn't shown up."

"So Grimaldi—?"

"Didn't want the bad press," Rafe said, leaving the lights of Columbia behind as we headed south on the Pulaski Highway toward home. "The optics—" his tone made quote marks around the word, "are bad any time a white cop has a black man on the ground. And with what happened last month..."

I nodded. What had happened last month, was the discovery of a small, local, white supremacist cell that held target practice in Laurel Hill Wildlife Area in the next county over, and that had staged a mass shooting right near the square in Columbia. The leader was in prison now, and so was his right-hand man, but the discovery of a neo-Nazi group operating out of Columbia hadn't made the optics, as Rafe called them, any prettier. Especially not since said neo-Nazi group's big gesture had been to shoot up a gathering of black people that were celebrating the raising of a monument at the site of the 1946 Columbia Race Riots. Including Civil Rights era icon Mordecai Lawson, who had marched on Selma and Washington with Doctor King.

The Reverend Lawson was fine, by the way. Healthy and hale and back in Memphis, where he lived.

"So Grimaldi wanted you to make the situation look better for the cameras," I said.

Rafe smirked. "I'm sure she figured I'd get some personal satisfaction out of being the one to deal with Tucker, too."

No doubt. "Did you?"

"It didn't suck," Rafe said.

I settled more comfortably into the seat now that we were outside the city limits and it looked like we'd make it home this time. "Any idea what murder scene Grimaldi's at? Have you heard anything about it?"

"Not a word," Rafe said, "but I'm sure I'll find out tomorrow."

I was sure he would, too.

As it happened, though, we didn't have to wait until tomorrow. About thirty minutes after we'd made it home, while I was upstairs feeding Carrie and singing lullabies, I heard the crunch of gravel and the sound of a car engine outside the house. Then the sound of a car door shutting, steps on the floor of the porch downstairs, and the doorbell ringing through the house. Rafe, who had made it out of the shower by then, stuck his head through the doorway to Carrie's nursery. "I'll get it."

I nodded. "I'll be down in a few minutes. She's almost asleep already."

He disappeared from the doorway, and I called after him, "Put your shirt on before you answer the door."

He didn't respond, but I heard a chuckle float back on the air.

He padded down the stairs on bare feet, and across to the front door. And I recognized Grimaldi's voice, the timbre and inflection, even if I couldn't hear what she was saying.

By the time Carrie was tucked up in her crib, and I had rearranged my clothing, they had migrated to the kitchen, where Rafe had put on a pot of coffee—coffee?—and lined two mugs up on the island.

"Where's mine?" I wanted to know.

He gave me a look. "You need your sleep, darlin'."

"I guess you two aren't going to get any?"

I headed for the fridge, where I pulled a carton of milk out. If I wasn't going to get coffee, I might as well make myself a cup of hot chocolate. Dairy's good for the baby.

"We'll get some," Grimaldi said, "just not in the next couple hours."

"Did Rafe tell you what happened with Tucker?" I poured the milk into a mug and stuck it in the microwave to heat.

Grimaldi nodded. "And I saw the live stream."

Live stream? "Really?"

They both nodded. Neither of them said anything else. I looked from one to the other of them as my milk rotated in the microwave. "So what's going on? Are you going to talk to Tucker now?"

"Tucker can wait till tomorrow," Rafe said, pulling the coffee pot off the coffee maker and tilting it over the two cups.

"What, then?"

"That murder scene I came from," Grimaldi said, and my heart sank to the bottom of my stomach.

"Oh, God. Who do we know who's dead?" My mother? One of my sisters? My brother? A friend?

"Nobody," Grimaldi said. "It's not who, it's what."

"What do you mean, what?"

"Dead woman," Rafe told me. "Found a couple hours ago at the truck stop down by the interstate. No identification on the body. No idea who she is. Or was. But not anybody we know."

Good to know. Although how would he know that, unless— "Have you seen a picture?"

He nodded.

"Can I see, too?" Just to make sure it wasn't someone I knew, that he didn't.

He glanced at Grimaldi, who shrugged. "She's been dead just a few hours," she told me, while she opened the camera program on her phone. "Best as we can figure."

"OK." Nothing to worry about, then. No maggots or anything. I took the phone she handed me and looked at the picture. Dark-haired woman in her thirties, and no, no one I'd ever seen before. Or if I had, I didn't remember.

I handed the phone back to Grimaldi. "What does she have to do with us?"

And I didn't mean to sound cold, but Grimaldi was a homicide detective with the Nashville PD before she took over the Columbia police department. And Rafe has certainly seen his share of dead bodies. So have I, tagging along behind him. It's always sad, but if she was no one we knew, it didn't seem to warrant this kind of reaction.

"Murdered woman," Grimaldi repeated, as if this should mean something to me, "left at the truck stop off Interstate 65."

She waited. It took me a second. I admit it. And then, finally, I got what she was—or rather, wasn't—saying. "You mean..."

"Yes. The I-65 serial killer is back."

The I-65 serial killer who had murdered Grimaldi's mother when Grimaldi was just a kid. The serial killer Grimaldi had been wanting to pit wits with for going on two decades now.

"And this time," she added, her voice grimly satisfied, "he

left the body in a place where I get to investigate it."

Two

"If it's over by the interstate," I said, "won't it be Bob Satterfield's body to investigate?"

Grimaldi looked at me, and I clarified. "You're police chief of Columbia. The interstate is outside the city limits. Therefore, it isn't your investigation. Or your body."

"The sheriff called me," Grimaldi said.

"He's giving you his murder investigation?"

"Not exactly."

Rafe had put the coffee pot back and was watching her with both hands wrapped around his mug, one brow elevated. "Lemme guess. He called you because he wanted me, and you decided to invite yourself along."

"Something like that," Grimaldi admitted.

Rafe's lips curved. "How'd he like that?"

"He seemed fine with it. But I had to promise I'd bring you back with me."

Of course. "He wants Rafe as a representative for the TBI," I said, and they both nodded.

"The woman ain't gonna be local," Rafe said. "The killer picked her up somewhere along the way. Mighta been Nashville, mighta been farther north."

"Or south," Grimaldi added, "if he was trying to throw us off."

And had dumped her on the opposite side of the interstate

than the direction he was traveling. He'd been going south, obviously. Or at least he had dumped the body on the west side of the highway.

Rafe nodded. "Mighta been inside the state, or in Kentucky. Or Indiana or Alabama. Either way, it's outside county jurisdiction."

And into the TBI's. "So you'll be taking over?"

"It depends," Rafe said. "First McLaughlin has to agree to it."

"But he will. Won't he? I mean, you're here. Surely it makes more sense to let you deal with it than send someone else down when you're here already."

"I imagine he will," Rafe said. "And if it turns out that the victim was picked up inside the state, then I'm all we need. If she came from outside Tennessee, I'll have to coordinate with folks from there. Or the FBI, if some bright soul has the idea to call'em in."

Grimaldi grimaced.

"I guess you're hoping she'll turn out to be local," I said, looking from one to the other of them. "From inside Tennessee."

"It'd make it easier," Rafe agreed. "The feds sometimes try to take over. And they can be..."

He hesitated.

"Pushy?"

His lips curved. "I was thinking 'condescending bastards,' but pushy works, too."

I nodded. "So first you have to figure out who she was and where she came from, and then you can go there and start looking around?"

"Something like that. And on that note—" he turned to Grimaldi, "I'll go get ready."

She nodded. I busied myself with the hot chocolate while he walked through the kitchen and down the hall. Over by the door, Pearl the pitbull looked up and slapped her tail against the fabric of her pillow a couple of times before she settled back down. The bullet wound on her flank was still pink and puffy against the silvery gray fur that was just starting to grow back around it.

"Good girl," I told her, and turned back to Grimaldi. "How do you feel?"

She opened her mouth, probably to claim she had no feelings whatsoever, but she closed it again without speaking. And took a few seconds to settle her thoughts before responding. "I'm not sure. I've been tracking this guy—or his victims, more accurately—since I came on the job almost a decade ago. They were always left somewhere else. Now that he's put one where I can actually investigate it, I'm almost afraid to believe it."

I nodded. I could well believe that. "Worried you won't be able to solve the case?"

"No." She sounded surprised I'd even ask.

"He probably isn't local, you know. You might be able to investigate the crime—" If Bob Satterfield allowed it, since it was his jurisdiction, "but if the murderer isn't local, you won't be able to catch him."

"I'll find a way," Grimaldi said.

"As you said, he might not even be in Tennessee." No reason to think he was. He could be based anywhere along I-65, from the Gulf of Mexico to the Great Lakes.

That included here, of course. So he might be from here, huge coincidence or not.

Grimaldi nodded when I said so. "That would be nice. But not very likely, I'm afraid. Whoever dumped the body was at the trailer stop. If he lived nearby, he had no reason to stop at the truck stop. He could just go home."

"Unless he wanted to get rid of the body," I said. "He wouldn't want to take it home. It'd be hard to explain away, if he doesn't live alone."

"Eighty percent of serial killers are unmarried," Grimaldi said.

"That means twenty percent are married. He could have a wife."

Grimaldi shrugged.

"And he has to be from somewhere. I don't think the truck stop is enough of a clue, though. He could have stopped there simply to get rid of the body. Or to do whatever it is he does to them…"

"Rape," Grimaldi said distantly, "mutilate, and strangle."

I blinked. And it took me a second or two to get my voice to cooperate. "What do you mean, mutilate? What does he do?"

"Carves a number on the body," Grimaldi said. "Or a numeral, I should say."

That wasn't as bad as I'd feared, honestly, although it was bad enough. And quite chilling. I could almost feel the ice cubes drop into my stomach as I asked, "You mean, he numbers the victims?"

She nodded.

"In Roman numerals?"

"Yes," Grimaldi said.

Well, that made a certain kind of sense, anyway. Roman numerals are all straight lines. Much easier to carve than curved Arabic numbers. Which, I'm sure, was why the Romans did it that way in the first place. Made it easier with all those marble monuments.

"Which number is he up to?" I wanted to know, and I'll admit that it took effort to keep my voice steady.

"Eighteen," Grimaldi said.

"XVIII."

She nodded.

"He's killed eighteen people?"

"He or they. There might be more than one murderer."

Maybe. That's a lot of murders for just one person. On the bright side— "At least you know that those are all the victims."

"Not necessarily," Grimaldi said. "We know that those are the victims he's claimed. But there might have been earlier murders. While he was practicing, finding his style. Before he decided to start counting."

Ugh.

"And there could be others he just didn't claim, for one reason or another. But we can say with certainty that these eighteen are his. There might be more, but there can't be less. Not if they were all marked in the same way. No one else would have known to do that."

We stood in silence a moment. I took another sip of chocolate, but instead of tasting rich and creamy, it filled my mouth with bitterness. I put the cup down. "Your mother…"

"Number three," Grimaldi said.

I saw the three straight lines in my head, and swallowed hard. "At least you know for sure that she's one of them. Once you find him, there won't be any doubt that he did it."

Grimaldi nodded, just as Rafe's footsteps came down the stairs and then along the hallway toward us. He stopped in the doorway and looked from Grimaldi to me and back. "Everything all right?"

"As right as it can be," Grimaldi told him, as she put her mug on the counter. "Ready?"

He nodded. "Sorry, darlin'. I'll be home as soon as I can."

"Take your time," I told him. "Pearl and I, and Carrie, will be fine here."

He nodded, and dropped a quick kiss on my lips before turning to the door. "Let's go."

They went. I followed them out to the foyer, where I watched Grimaldi's official SUV roll down the driveway to the road before I locked and bolted the front door and headed back to the kitchen to clean up the mugs.

It was late when he came back. I was up again with Carrie, for her middle-of-the-night feeding, when I saw the headlights move across the wall as the car turned into the driveway, and heard the crunch of tires on the gravel. A car door opened and—with a low-voiced comment—closed again, and then I heard footsteps on the porch and the key in the door.

He gave me a quick wave from the doorway, and mimed that he was going into the bathroom to rinse off. I nodded, and watched him shut the door behind him. A few seconds later, the shower kicked on.

He was in bed when I tiptoed across the hallway and into our room. (Mother might have been living in sin with the sheriff, but I hadn't felt comfortable enough to move my husband and myself into the master bedroom yet. In my mind, that was still my parents' room. So it was sitting empty at the end of the hall while Rafe and I slept in what had been my room as a girl, across the hall from Carrie's nursery in Catherine's old room.)

He was lying on his back with his arms under his head when I appeared in the open door. He turned to look at me, and the corners of his mouth turned up, but he didn't say anything. I floated across the floor and slipped under the comforter next to him. "You OK?"

He turned and pulled me in. "Fine. You?"

"Everything's good here." I tucked my cold toes between his feet. The air conditioning can be freezing in the middle of the night when you're not wearing slippers. "Carrie's back to sleep. And nothing else happened after you left."

He didn't respond, just kept his nose buried in my hair, breathing deeply. Trying to get the scent of death out of his nostrils, maybe. I've smelled it, and it's hard to get rid of. I was under no illusions as to why he'd needed another shower when he came home, just a couple of hours after the previous shower.

His hair was still a little wet, and I ran a hand over it. It was like the slightly rough, slightly silky nap of a Persian rug against my palm. "Was the crime scene bad?"

"I've seen worse," Rafe said. And added, "So have you."

Perhaps. I've seen some things that keep me up at night if I think too hard about them. And I know for a fact Rafe has seen a lot worse than I have.

"This wasn't too bad," he told me. "She was killed somewhere else and dumped there, so there was nothing to the crime scene other than the body. Not much blood, all of it dry. Death was from strangulation. She was naked, so whatever she'd been wearing when he picked her up, he took with him."

"Or dumped it somewhere else," I suggested, while I marveled, with half of my mind, at what constituted pillow talk in our family.

He nodded. "Or he dumped it elsewhere. But not there. Tammy's crime scene crew checked inside the dumpster—glad I wasn't assigned that job—and everywhere else we could think of, and there was nothing that looked like it was related. They have to take it all back to the lab, to check it for fingerprints and DNA, just in case the killer happened to toss out a Styrofoam cup or empty his ashtray at the same time he dumped the body—"

Another job I wouldn't want to take on. Not, in this case, because it would be unpleasant—although sorting through so much icky, smelly trash probably wouldn't be fun, either—but because it would be tedious and would take forever and at the end, probably wouldn't result in anything useful. But it had to be done, and I guess it was good that there were people out there willing to do it.

"I'm glad it wasn't too unpleasant," I told my husband, who was starting to act drowsy. His eyes were at half mast and his breathing was getting deeper. "Go on and get some sleep.

You'll have to be up again in a few hours."

"Team briefing at nine." He snuggled a little closer. "You sure you don't wanna…?"

"Positive," I said. "I'd rather wait until you're more awake."

"Tomorrow morning."

"No problem," I said, and held him as he drifted off to sleep.

He was up bright and early the next morning, and when I use the word up, I use it advisedly. I woke to him nuzzling the back of my neck and the area behind my left ear, while his hand was busy under my nightgown.

"Careful," I murmured as I turned to meet him. "It's been a few hours since Carrie's last meal—"

He silenced me as soon as I'd turned around enough that he could reach my mouth with his own, and that, as the saying goes, was all she wrote. He sauntered off to the shower with a distinct jaunt to his step, and I burrowed back into the mattress and tried to get comfortable again. But then Carrie woke up, and by the time Rafe came out of the shower, I was wrapped in a robe and sitting in the rocking chair in the nursery feeding my daughter.

He dropped a kiss on the top of her downy head, and a longer, more leisurely one on my mouth—he tasted minty fresh; I did not—before he told me, "I'm gonna go get the coffee started."

I glanced at the clock ticking away on the wall. "Didn't you tell me you have a briefing at nine?"

It was barely six-thirty now.

"Team briefing," Rafe corrected. "I gotta be there sooner."

"For the super secret, inner circle briefing that only you and Grimaldi and Bob Satterfield get to attend?"

His lips curved. "Something like that. Mostly I need to find out if Ben McLaughlin has authorized me working on this, or whether somebody else is gonna come down and take over."

"He wouldn't be that stupid." I shifted Carrie from one arm to the other. "I only met him once, but he seemed like a reasonable guy. And it doesn't make sense to send someone else when you're already here."

Rafe gave a shrug. "Guess we'll find out."

"Leave me some coffee," I told him.

He nodded. "What've you got going on today?"

I made a face. "Another trip to the house on Fulton, to make sure everything's done and ready so we can get the place back on the market."

A couple of months ago, my sister Darcy, my best friend Charlotte, and I had bought a fixer-upper together. Or rather, Darcy had put up the money while Charlotte and I had put in the sweat equity, and what expertise we had in home renovation.

It wasn't much, but after a rocky start—a dead body in what was intended to become the new master suite—we'd persevered until the house was finished. And at that point, not only had someone gone inside it and vandalized the place, but someone else had set off a bomb outside and done damage to the structure.

Rafe and Grimaldi insisted it hadn't been a bomb, and technically speaking they were right. It had been a cardboard box full of something called Tannerite, that blows up when you shoot at it. People use it for target practice, I'm told. Apparently it's more exciting when the target explodes in a cloud of orange or blue smoke when you hit it.

In this case, someone had put a box of Tannerite outside our front door and shot it, and if it hadn't been a bomb, it had acted like one, blowing out part of the front wall and floor and roof. Our poor house had come away from the experience with a gaping hole in the middle of it.

Those particular repairs were beyond Charlotte's and my capabilities, so we had hired a construction company—at more cost to Darcy—to fix the damage for us. Meanwhile, Charlotte and I had spent our time on the interior of the house, fixing the cosmetic vandalism by replacing broken glass and smashed tile and repairing drywall and applying new paint.

At this point, we were almost back to where we'd been before Rafe—and by extension I—got tangled up with the white supremacy group that had been responsible for some of the damage. We'd only been on the market a couple of days the first time. Long enough to garner a little interest, but not long enough to get a purchase offer. At this point, we were in danger of missing out on the hot spring market. I wanted the house listed for sale ASAP.

I wanted it off my hands, to be honest, before something else could happen to it. By now, I was almost ready to believe the house was cursed. We'd had nothing but trouble with it since we bought it, and even before that, the previous owner was besieged by bad luck. Up until and including the moment he wound up dead in our master bedroom conversion.

"Good luck," Rafe told me. I gave him a suspicious look, but he seemed to mean it sincerely, without any hint of sarcasm.

"Thank you." *I think.*

"No problem." He turned toward the door again. "I'll make sure there's plenty of coffee."

"Thank you." I was going to need it.

A few minutes later he called up the stairs that he was leaving, and then I heard the back door close, and a minute later, the sound of the police-issue Chevy making its way past the front steps and down the driveway. I got Carrie ready for the day and wandered downstairs, where the coffee was fresh and hot. And strong.

By the time I made it to Columbia and Fulton Street, it was

after nine, and Charlotte was already there. She had finally got rid of the minivan her ex-husband had used to abduct her and their two kids—another long story—and was driving a new-to-her Jeep Grand Cherokee with plenty of room in the back for the car seats.

They were empty, though, because Mrs. Albertson was taking care of the children while Charlotte was busy renovating. It was for her sake, more than for my own, that I wanted to get the house on the market and sold as fast as I could. We had Rafe's income, and we were living for free in Mother's house. But I wanted to get Darcy her money back, and give Charlotte the opportunity to buy or rent a place of her own if she wanted one, or at least to pay her parents rent, so she'd feel more independent, and not like she was a failure living back in her childhood room.

She opened the door to the Jeep with her phone in her hand; glossy brown hair bouncing around her excited face. "Your husband's all over Facebook!"

I winced. I know it was what I'd wanted last night. Another nail in the coffin of Rafe's undercover career. But that still didn't make me feel good. "No kidding."

"No," Charlotte said, almost dancing toward me. "Look at all the hearts and heart-eye emojis!"

She thrust the phone under my nose. I grabbed her wrist and pushed it a little farther away, so I could see the screen without going cross-eyed. The video was dark—it had been dark on Green Street last night—but... "Yep. That's my husband."

And those were definitely little hearts and heart-eye emojis accompanying comments like, *He can arrest me anytime!* and *I need to be stopped and frisked immediately!*

I rolled my eyes. "He stood there and pointed to the car and said, *'That's my wife and baby in there.'* I'm sure it's part of the video."

Charlotte looked like she wanted to laugh, but she contented herself with a grin. "It is. I watched the whole thing, and it's definitely in there."

"Then why are they talking like that?"

"Because he's hot?" Charlotte suggested.

Of course he was. But since it had taken her as long as it had to admit it—because at first she could hardly believe I'd get involved with our hometown black sheep—I just sighed. "I hope they don't drive down here and try to get themselves arrested. Rafe has more important things to do than dodge women."

"I'm sure he's used to it," Charlotte said and dropped the phone in her pocket. And of course that was true. He was used to it. This was just blowing up on a larger scale than either of us had seen before.

But as long as they stayed where they were, and didn't come to Columbia to get in his way, it'd probably be all right.

I turned to the car and hauled Carrie and the baby seat out of the back. And turned toward the house. "So far, so good."

Charlotte nodded. "I just got here, so I haven't gone inside. But the new roof and front door look all right."

They did. You could hardly tell that the roof had been patched at all. If you didn't know that a chunk of house had been missing until recently, you might not notice anything wrong.

"Wonder if there's anyone in Columbia who doesn't know what happened here?" I mused.

"What?" Charlotte had started walking toward the house, and now she turned around to look at me.

I shook my head. I already knew the answer: nobody. Everyone in town probably knew that our house had been blown up. "Nothing. Don't worry about it."

She gave me a look, but didn't pursue the subject. "Paul told me about the murder victim," she said instead, as she headed across the grass toward the front door.

Paul? "When did you talk to Detective Jarvis between last night and this morning?"

Or had he spent the night?

I didn't think they'd taken the relationship to that level—I hadn't been sure there was a relationship there at all—but maybe I was wrong.

"He called," Charlotte said, with a betraying blush in her cheeks. "He's the one who told me about the video."

"And the body?"

She nodded. "What's going on?"

"Well…" Until Grimaldi's personal connection to case was public knowledge, I should probably stick to the basics. "I don't know that I know a whole lot more than Paul Jarvis. Someone found the body of a woman at the truck stop up by the interstate, and the sheriff's office got called in. Because there's some indication that she's the victim of a serial killer who's been operating up and down I-65 for fifteen or twenty years, Rafe got called in. Now they're talking about maybe having to call in the FBI."

Charlotte nodded, and looked sorry she'd asked. I put the baby carrier down on the concrete stoop (that not even a box full of Tannerite had been able to budge) and nudged her out of the way so I could insert the key in the lock of the brand new front door we'd had to install after the previous door had been blown to pieces.

"Don't worry about it," I told her over my shoulder. "It has nothing to do with you. Or with us."

She nodded, but didn't look convinced. I twisted the knob and pushed the door open. And stuck my head through the opening. "Well, hell."

Three

"What?" Charlotte wanted to know, pushing against my shoulder. Her voice hit somewhere between frantic and resigned.

She's a few inches shorter than me, so I stepped aside to give her access to the doorway. She peered past me. "Oh, no."

"It's no big deal," I said, even though my heart had dropped when I'd first seen it. "Just a broken window." And some glass on the floor. "We can replace it."

Charlotte gave me a look. I avoided her eyes. "Looks like a baseball."

It was in a corner of the living room, up against the wall. I continued brightly, "It's not a brick or a rock. Breaking the window was probably not deliberate. And whoever did it doesn't seem to have entered the house."

The broken window was still in place. No one seemed to have reached in, undone the lock, and pushed the sash up so they could crawl across the sill and inside.

"Probably just kids," I said.

Charlotte looked unconvinced, and when she crossed the threshold, her shoulders hunched, like she was waiting for that proverbial other shoe to literally fall out of the ceiling onto her head.

It didn't. We took Carrie inside and locked the door behind us, and then we made a reconnaissance of the rest of house to see whether anything else had gone wrong since we'd been here yesterday.

Nothing had. Everything else was in place, and looked the way it should. "See?" I told Charlotte. "Nothing to worry about. Just an accident."

She looked reluctantly convinced. "So we're ready to go on the market again?"

"Once we fix the window," I said. "Shouldn't take too long. I'll start breaking out what's left of the pane if you'll go buy a new piece of glass."

Charlotte nodded. We both remembered the dimensions, since this wasn't the first broken window pane we'd had to replace.

By the time she came back, thirty or forty minutes later, I had the rest of the glass swept up and removed, and it was a matter of a few minutes to pop the new window into the old frame, push in the little points that held it in place, and then run a new bead of putty along the edges.

We both stepped back and contemplated it.

"Looks good," Charlotte said.

I nodded. "I'll call the photographer and have her come back out."

Charlotte glanced at me. "Do we need new pictures?"

"I guess we could put up the old ones. The finishes are all the same." Paint color and tile and all the rest. "But the place was staged the first time we put it on the market." And Michelle the stager absolutely refused to rent us furniture a second time, since several of her pieces had been damaged in the vandalism. "It would probably be best if we got some pictures of the house the way it looks now."

Charlotte sighed. "More money."

"Yes. But we don't want to market a house full of lovely furniture and then have people show up and be disappointed when they see empty rooms."

We were headed out when Charlotte's phone emitted a little chirp, different from the usual ringtone or message sound. She dug it out of her pocket and peered at it, brows arching. "There's another video of Rafe."

I leaned in. "How do you know?"

"I set an alert," Charlotte said.

"On videos of my husband?"

She shrugged. "I figured you'd want to know. And you might not think to set one yourself."

She was right. I hadn't.

"I have an alert on Richard's name, too. Just in case something happens and he gets out. Someone loses their mind and gives him the chance to post bail, or he arranges a prison break, or something."

I glanced at her. "You aren't really afraid of that, are you?"

"Not really," Charlotte said. "Not when I'm sane. I know he's probably safe where he is. And I hope if he does get out, he won't come for me. Or the kids. But if something changes and nobody tells me, I want to know about it."

Hard to blame her for that, when this was the guy who had put her and their children into a car at gunpoint, and tried to drive them back to North Carolina. "How do you know to do this, anyway?"

"Paul showed me," Charlotte said.

I gave her a closer look. "Something going on with you and Jarvis I should know about?"

"No," Charlotte said, but she flushed again. "Worry about your own husband. Look at the video."

"It's just twenty seconds of Rafe walking from his car into the police station." And while he looked just as good as he always does, he wasn't doing anything that could get him, or anyone else, in trouble.

"Somebody stood outside the police station and waited for him to show up so she could film him getting out of the car and walking up the stairs and through the door," Charlotte said. "She called out to him so he'd turn and smile at her, too. And then she posted it online. And several hundred other women piled on with hearts and comments. You don't find that a little creepy?"

The first part, maybe. The second I was used to. Women always make googly-eyes at Rafe. In person, most commonly, but I wasn't surprised that he was a hit on social media, too. "How do you know she stood there and waited?"

"Either that or she was following him," Charlotte said tartly. "Which do you prefer?"

Now that I thought about it, I decided I preferred neither. "Couldn't it just be a coincidence? She happened to be there, and…"

I trailed off, because it didn't make much sense. People don't tend to loiter outside the Columbia PD unless they have business there. And anyone who had legitimate business there wasn't likely to be filming my husband get out of his car and walk into the building.

Plus, she'd known his name. She'd used it when she called out to him.

If she'd had a gun, she could have shot him.

I dropped Charlotte's phone and dug for my own. It rang once, twice, then—

"Darlin'," my husband's voice said in my ear. "This ain't a great time for chit-chat."

"Are you OK?"

His voice changed, went crisp and lost the Southern drawl. "What's wrong?"

"Nothing," I said. "It can wait."

"Hang on a sec." I heard him excuse himself to whoever he was with, and the sounds of him, probably, exiting whatever room he was in. I pictured him leaning a shoulder against the wall in the hallway, phone to his ear. "What's going on, darlin'?"

"I panicked," I admitted, now that I'd had a few seconds to think about it. "There's another video of you on social media. Some woman stood outside the police station and waited for you to show up this morning, so she could film you."

He sounded more amused than bothered. "More hearts and kisses?"

"Yes. Lots of them. But that's not the point. Some woman is stalking you. She stood there and waited for you to show up, and when you did, she called out so you'd turn around. Do you remember?"

There was a pause. "Yeah. Maybe."

"So you know what she looks like."

"No," Rafe said. "Some woman called my name when I was walking up to the door. I turned around, but I didn't see nobody, so I kept walking."

Another pause. "I don't like it," I said. "I mean, we don't want a repeat of Elspeth, do we?"

Elspeth, who had done her best to kill me, so she could have him to herself...

"No, darlin'. But that was a different situation. I knew Elspeth. I slept with Elspeth. Hell, I knocked her up..." Even if he hadn't known about it at the time. And that was Elspeth's fault, for not telling him.

"I know it's not the same," I said. "This is someone you don't know—"

Or so I assumed. I gestured to Charlotte, who had picked her phone up when I dropped it, and was examining it, maybe for damage. Now she dutifully handed it over. I peered at the screen. "Do you know someone named Jessica Rabbit?"

"No," Rafe said, his voice amused.

Yeah, I hadn't thought so. "It doesn't sound like a real name."

"No," Rafe agreed, while next to me, Charlotte wiggled her

fingers. I handed the phone back while I kept talking to Rafe.

"The point is, this woman took the time to stand outside the police station this morning until you got there, just so she could film you walking from your car through the door. She might have been the one filming last night, too. Or one of the ones..."

Charlotte was shaking her head.

"No?" I said.

"Not as far as I can tell. Those videos were posted by other people. She might have been there, but without filming, or she might be someone who saw the video last night and decided to show up today and get a video of her own."

"What's that?" Rafe wanted to know in my ear. I repeated what Charlotte had said. "Could be," he agreed. "I'll keep an eye out."

"Thank you." I resisted the temptation to suggest that he should put on a flak vest and keep it on. "What's going on where you are?"

"The victim's been identified," Rafe said. "Her name was Ramona Mitchell. She had a record for solicitation in Nashville."

"So he picked up a prostitute." Probably at a truck stop not unlike the one he'd dropped her off at.

Had he picked up another one here in Columbia and taken her south with him?

But no, probably not. Most of these guys—serial killers—don't kill several people a day. So far, the eighteen victims we knew about had been spread out over almost as many years. It might be months before he took someone else. Maybe years.

"Will you have to go to Nashville to investigate?"

"No," Rafe said. "Tammy's called in a favor from a friend."

"Not Goins, I hope?"

Detective Goins with the MNPD was a former colleague of Grimaldi's, and a particular thorn in my side. A few months ago, he had pulled a gun on Rafe while my husband was holding my daughter. I didn't think I'd get over that anytime soon.

"No," Rafe said, sounding amused. "And not Jaime Mendoza, either, before you can ask. You don't waste a homicide detective on this."

"Why not?" It was a homicide, wasn't it?

"They have cases of their own to investigate," Rafe said. "Tammy asked Spicer and Truman to ask questions. They're driving around the neighborhood all day anyway."

Our Nashville neighborhood, I assumed. Spicer and Truman were the two patrol officers who had responded to my 911 call the day we—Rafe and I—discovered Brenda Puckett dead in Mrs. Jenkins's house on Potsdam Street.

"I guess we're talking about the truck stop on Trinity Lane?"

"No idea," Rafe said. "There are several of'em along the interstate in that part of town. When Miz Mitchell was picked up last time, she was walking up and down Dickerson Road."

Of course she was. "So Spicer and Truman are going there?"

"They're going everywhere," Rafe said. "To Dickerson Road, to the truck stop on Trinity Lane and the one next to the bridge on James Robertson. It's a long shot, but if we—if they—can figure out where she worked these days, maybe they can find someone who saw her leave with this guy."

"And you're sure you don't need to be there?"

"Spicer and Truman can handle it," Rafe said. "I'm better off trying to find someone who saw what happened here."

"Didn't Bob do that last night?"

"Yes," Rafe said, "but it gotta be done again this morning. Different people at different times of day."

That made sense. "So you'll be careful? In case this nutcase follows you around?"

"If all she's gonna do is shoot pictures," Rafe said, "I ain't that worried."

Well, no. Seeing as he'd been shot by something other than a camera last month, I could understand that a cell phone didn't worry him much. But— "Elspeth ended up with a gun."

"She didn't try to shoot *me*," Rafe pointed out.

No. "She did try to shoot me, though. And came pretty close to taking you out at the same time."

"I'll be careful." Something rustled on his end of the line and he added, "I gotta go."

"I love you," I said quickly.

"Love you too, darlin'. Take care of my baby."

He hung up before I could respond. Charlotte was still watching her own phone, and I asked her, "Any way to figure out who this person is?"

"From the Facebook profile?" Charlotte shook her head. "I've been looking at it. It's brand new. Created yesterday. The name is obviously fake. Nobody's really named Jessica Rabbit."

No. Or at least it seemed unlikely.

"Does she have a profile photo? Can we try some kind of facial recognition software?"

"A picture of Jessica Rabbit for the profile," Charlotte said. "No headline picture. Nothing on the timeline except the video from this morning."

"Not even the video from last night?"

She shook her head.

"I don't like it," I said.

Charlotte nodded. "I get that. I don't like it, either."

"Maybe we should check the other video. The one from last night. If she saw that, and that's how she focused in on Rafe, maybe she dropped a heart emoji or a comment."

Charlotte didn't answer, and I added, "As herself, I mean. Maybe we could track her down that way."

"There are at least a thousand comments on that thread,"

Charlotte said. "And probably five thousand heart emojis. It would take months to track them all down."

"Probably not months. Maybe days. But chances are only a few are local. If we can isolate them…"

Charlotte thought about it, and shrugged. "We're not doing anything else."

"Come on back to the mansion," I said, "and I'll fix you lunch. Then, when Carrie's napping, we can make a list."

"And start snooping?"

"I'm game if you are," I told her. "And if that doesn't work, we can always follow Rafe around, and see if we can find her that way."

Charlotte tagged along behind as I headed for the front door. "What was that you were saying about Elspeth Caulfield?"

"That she tried to kill me? " I glanced at her over my shoulder as I bent to scoop up the baby. "Did I never tell you about that?"

"I don't think so," Charlotte said, sounding doubtful.

"Then remind me to do that over lunch. It's quite the story."

"I can't wait," Charlotte said, and followed me across the threshold and onto the porch.

Four

Back in Sweetwater, I let Carrie nurse herself to sleep while I told Charlotte about Elspeth Caulfield, and how she had ended up trying to kill me. "You know that Elspeth talked her way into Rafe's bed in high school, right? Or invited him into hers, or just pulled him off into a field somewhere?"

Charlotte nodded.

"He graduated and was arrested for fighting with Billy Scruggs. She got pregnant and didn't tell him about it, because he was in prison. She had the baby and her father made her give it up for adoption."

"And that's David," Charlotte said.

"That's David." Who was living in Nashville with his adoptive parents, very happily. "Twelve years went by. Rafe got out of prison and started working for the TBI. LaDonna died, and he figured out who his father was, and that his grandmother was still alive. He showed up in Nashville, and ended up calling me to show him the house on Potsdam Street."

Charlotte nodded.

"Rafe and I danced around each other for a few months, and during that time, I ended up talking to Elspeth about him. She decided she wanted him back. I think she had a plan for getting David away from the Flannerys, too, and she had some sort of idea that the three of them were going to be a family…"

"But you were in the way," Charlotte said, "because he was getting involved with you."

I nodded. "First she killed Marquita Johnson—you know, Cletus's wife—because Rafe hired Marquita to take care of Mrs. Jenkins. Marquita was living in the house with Mrs. Jenkins, and with Rafe when he was in town, and Elspeth thought Marquita might be poaching, so she killed her. And then she came after me."

"And Rafe killed her."

"Jorge Pena killed her," I corrected. "Rafe killed him. And I owe her for that. She planted herself in front of Rafe and refused to move even though Jorge said he'd shoot her. If she hadn't, Rafe might be dead."

Or not. He might still have gotten the drop on Jorge. But the chances of him surviving that encounter would have been much fewer.

"Anyway," I said, as I lifted Carrie to my shoulder and patted her back. She was already asleep, her head lolling. "The last thing I want, is another experience like that."

"No kidding," Charlotte said.

I got to my feet. "I'm going to put her to bed. I'll be right back."

Charlotte nodded and reached for her phone. I carried the baby up the stairs to her crib and headed back down. "Let's go in the kitchen. I'll make some lunch. Anything new?"

Charlotte shook her head. "More hearts and comments on the video she put up two hours ago, but nothing else."

"Do you think I'm overreacting?" I glanced at her over my shoulder as we traversed the hallway down to the kitchen in the back of the house. Pearl had already greeted Charlotte when we first came home, and had spent the time while I was feeding Carrie curled up on a pillow in the corner of the parlor. Now she lead the procession, her stub of a tail jauntily raised.

"Go outside?" I asked her, and her tail gave a wag. I

headed for the back door and pulled it open while Charlotte answered my question.

"Hard to say. You said it yourself, most women are attracted to Rafe."

And then some. It's a curse.

"She might just be some lonely woman who thinks he's hot, and after spending a couple of days following him around, she'll stop."

Yes, she might be. "He pointed me out last night, though. Both me and Carrie. *That's my wife and my baby in the car.* Isn't it weird that anyone would go that gaga over a married man?"

"Most women lust over married celebrities," Charlotte said with a shrug. "It might be something like that."

It might. I peered out the window to where Pearl was squatting in the grass. "So you think I shouldn't worry?"

She hesitated. "I think it's probably going to be fine. But I understand why you're concerned."

"Maybe I should just give it a day or two before I start freaking out?"

Pearl was up again, and on her way back toward the house. I opened the door for her.

"It can't hurt to do a little investigating," Charlotte said, and got comfortable on one of the stools in front of the island. "We may not be able to discover who she is. But it can't hurt to look."

Pearl bounded up the couple of steps into the kitchen and stopped to look at me, tongue hanging out of her mouth.

"Good girl," I told her. "Sit, and I'll give you a cookie."

She thumped her haunches down on the floor and brushed the little bit of her tail that was left back and forth. I fished a dog treat out of the jar on the counter and held it out to her. She took it daintily from my fingers and proceeded to chomp it into bits.

"Good girl," I said again, as she trotted over to her water

bowl for a couple slurps of water. "Go on and lie down on your pillow. We're going to be in here for a while."

Pearl headed for the pillow, and Charlotte arched her brows. "She understood that?"

"I'm not sure she understood anything more than 'good girl' and 'pillow.' But it got the point across."

Pearl circled twice and settled down with a sigh, and I turned back to Charlotte. "Let me throw some sandwiches together, and then we can get to work."

"I'll just get started while you cook." She hunched over the phone. I started dragging containers of cheese and lunchmeat out of the fridge.

Two hours later, by the time Carrie woke up, we had eliminated several hundred of the commenters on the original video. Some because they were male—Jessica Rabbit didn't sound like a guy—but most because they listed their location as somewhere other than Middle Tennessee.

"I'll keep going at home," Charlotte told me, as we both got up from the loveseat in the parlor (it was a lot more comfortable than the stools in the kitchen, so we had moved in there after the sandwiches were devoured). "After I relieve my mother of babysitting duty and spend some time with my kids."

I nodded, as I headed for the stairs to rescue my squalling daughter. "Let me know if you find anything. I'm going to arrange to get the house photographed and back on the market in the meantime." Since we'd forgotten all about that in the excitement of a possible stalker.

"Deal," Charlotte said. She let herself out the front door, and I twisted the lock behind her. We live in the country, outside a small town, and random crime is pretty non-existent, but it never hurts to be careful. Especially since we both, Rafe and I, seem to attract trouble.

That done, I headed up the stairs to take care of Carrie and give her tummy time on the floor while I focused on real estate for a while.

When Rafe came through the back door and into the kitchen, it was after seven, and dinner had been pushed back to accommodate a late arrival. He hadn't let me know why he'd be late, just that I shouldn't expect him until after his usual time, but the black cargo pants tucked into black boots, and the black T-shirt that molded his chest and shoulders, told me all I needed to know. "I didn't realize you guys were still doing SWAT practice," I told him, as I turned up the heat under the pot of water on the stove to bring it to a quick boil for the angel hair spaghetti.

"Prob'ly gonna keep doing that for as long as I'm here, darlin'." He gave Pearl a scratch between her furled ears, and dropped a kiss on top of Carrie's curly head—she was kicking her feet in her bouncy seat— before he came over to me. And backed me up against the counter before he framed my face with his hands and leaned in for a kiss. By the time he lifted his head, those fingers had migrated into my hair, and the water in the pot was bubbling.

"Nice to see you, too," I said breathlessly and reached for the box of angel hair. "Dinner in five minutes."

"Guess I'll shower later." He moved a few feet so he could tickle Carrie's feet and make her giggle.

"The threat's over, though," I said, as I nestled the pasta into the pot. "Isn't it? You caught the guy who lead the neo-Nazi group, and put him away. along with his second-in-command. The third guy gets off because he didn't do anything except shoot at paper targets."

"He's a nasty little tick," Rafe said, "but yeah. He gets off."

"So what's the SWAT practice for? They already gave it their best shot at the dedication of the bauta in The Bottoms. It didn't come off, or at least not the way they'd hoped." Way fewer casualties than they'd hoped for, I was sure. "Isn't it over?"

"Mostly we think it is. Clay's still working at the body shop in case someone shows up looking for Lance or Rodney, but so far it's been quiet."

"I didn't realize Clayton was still here," I said. Clayton Norris was a young associate of Rafe's from the TBI, who had been brought to Columbia to infiltrate the neo-Nazi gang and report back. "I haven't seen him."

Nor, as far as I knew, had Rafe.

My husband smiled. "You're not supposed to see him, darlin'. That's what undercover work's all about. You can't be seen in public with the people you're reporting to, or your cover's blown."

Well, yes. I guess that made sense.

"So you haven't seen him, either."

He shook his head. "He's a neo-Nazi skin-head. He has a reputation to uphold. Can't be seen with the likes of me."

No, I guess he couldn't. "So who is he reporting to?"

He eyed me.

"You can tell me," I said. "Who am I going to tell?"

"You know a lotta people. But I don't imagine any of'em would be putting Clay in danger."

Not likely. "So…?"

"Yvonne," Rafe said.

My eyes widened. "You conscripted Yvonne?"

He chuckled. "Not really. He goes in there and has breakfast every couple of days."

I grinned. "Let me guess. He has an expense account?"

Rafe grinned back, but didn't confirm or deny the existence of any such thing. "She asks him how he is. He says he's fine. If he ever says anything else, she's supposed to contact me."

"And you run to the rescue?"

"Not hardly," Rafe said, leaning his posterior against the island and folding his arms across his chest. The viper tattooed around his bicep flexed. "Yvonne calls me, I call someone else, and somebody shows up at the body shop with a rattle in the engine of their car. While Clay takes a look, he passes on the message. Then that message comes back to me the same way, and I determine what needs to be done."

Fascinating. "But that hasn't happened yet."

He shook his head. "So far, everything's been fine. No need for interference."

Hopefully that would continue to be the case. I fished a strand of angel hair out of the pot, bit into it, and caught the dangling ends. "This is done."

"I'll get the plates," Rafe said and headed for the cabinet while I took the pot to the stove and drained the pasta into the colander that was waiting there.

"So what's going on with the serial killer case?" I asked three minutes later, when we'd gotten the food onto plates and were sitting side by side at the kitchen island digging in. "Any news?"

"Not on the serial killer." He put a forkful of pasta in his mouth and tucked the dangling ends tidily in at the end. When he'd finished chewing, he added, "The ME said the COD was manual strangulation."

"He wrapped his hands around her throat and squeezed," I translated.

Rafe nodded. "Face to face and with his bare hands."

So a fairly intimate way to commit murder. Except— "There's no reason to think he knew these women, right?"

Rafe shook his head. "He mighta known one or two. Most likely the first. They often start with someone they know."

'They' being serial killers, I assumed. "Have you looked into the first victim this guy killed?"

"Today I've been looking into the last," Rafe said and

tucked another forkful of angel hair into his mouth.

"Did you find out anything you didn't know this morning?"

"Spicer and Truman tracked her down to the truck stop down the street from your old apartment, down there by the bridge. A waitress in the restaurant said she was there in the early part of the day, but she don't know what happened to her after that."

"Cameras?" I twirled my fork around in the angel hair and conveyed it to my mouth.

He shook his head. "Nothing on'em that we can use. Spicer and Truman checked. If this is a route he's been driving for two decades, he knows how to avoid the cameras."

Clearly. "I don't suppose they keep track of the trucks that come through?"

"No," Rafe said. "It's just like any other gas station and market along the interstate, only for bigger vehicles. The truckers don't have to check in or nothing."

Of course not. That would be too easy.

"So pretty much all we know is that sometime between the early part of the day, when the waitress saw her, and whenever the body was discovered at the truck stop here in Maury County, she got into somebody's vehicle."

"That's it," Rafe nodded.

"It's only about an hour's drive, maybe a little less, so where were they during the five or six or however many hours they were together?"

"Coulda been parked in a corner of the lot in Nashville," Rafe said. "Coulda been parked in a corner of the lot here. Coulda been parked somewhere along the way."

"Wouldn't somebody have heard..." I hesitated, "something?"

He arched a brow. "Screaming? Not sure anybody'd notice. A lot of the truckers pick up women, and when they park outta the way, the other truckers generally assume it's for privacy. Besides, it's easy to soundproof the cab of a truck. A lot of truckers do it just 'cause the engine's loud."

And whatever they did to keep the sound of the engine out would work equally well to keep any sounds from within the cab in. Right.

"So nobody saw or heard anything."

"Nobody I've talked to so far," Rafe said.

"What's next?"

He shrugged. "Talk to more people. And I oughta find out if somebody like the FBI has some sort of a task force going. If they do, they're gonna want in. And they ain't gonna be happy if they find out we kept it from them."

I shook my head. "Probably best to stay on the right side of the FBI."

Rafe nodded, and pushed his plate away. "I'm gonna go grab a shower if you don't mind. Rinse some of the sweat and frustration off."

"Go ahead," I told him. "I'll clean up."

"Thanks for dinner, darlin'." He dropped a kiss on top of my head on his way out of the kitchen. I finished eating while I listened to the rushing of water in the pipes. Pearl was snuffling on her pillow, and Carrie was cooing in her seat, trying to get a foot up to her face so she could gnaw on it.

When the phone chirped, I pulled it closer with one hand while I kept feeding myself pasta with the other. And saw Charlotte's name and *New iMessage* on the screen.

"Uh-oh."

New video, Charlotte told me.

I followed the link to Jessica Rabbit's page, and saw that she—probably she—had uploaded another snippet of film of my husband, in his SWAT clothes and boots this time, leaving the police station and getting into his car. There were the usual heart-eyed emoji and verbal sighs, but less than last night's and this morning's video. Hopefully the rest of the public at large was starting to lose interest. And if that happened, maybe Jessica would lose interest, too. There was just the chance that she—probably she—was doing this for attention and not because she had any particular interest in my husband.

That wasn't my biggest concern at the moment, though.

The pasta started to taste like sawdust in my mouth, so I stopped eating and started clearing the island, and putting the dishes into the dishwasher. When the kitchen was neat and tidy again, I stuck the phone in my pocket and picked up Carrie and her seat. "We're moving to the parlor," I told Pearl. "You can stay here if you want, or come with us."

She contemplated me for a second, but when I headed across the floor and into the hallway, she got up and stretched and padded after me, her nails clicking on the hardwood floors.

Rafe joined us a couple of minutes later, dressed in faded jeans and a soft T-shirt, with his feet bare and his hair—what little he has—still wet.

"Come and look at this," I told him. "Jessica Rabbit posted another video of you."

He watched it in silence. It wasn't long.

"Did you notice her this time?"

He glanced over at me. "Can't say as I did, darlin'."

"She didn't call your name?"

He shook his head.

"If she'd had a gun," I said, like I'd said earlier, "you'd be dead."

He nodded. "Looks like I'm gonna have to be more careful tomorrow."

"I wish you would. I'd also like to know whether you noticed anybody following you home tonight."

"No," Rafe said.

"No, you didn't notice? Or no, nobody—"

His voice was clipped, but I don't think he was upset with me. "Nobody followed me home. It takes training and experience to shadow somebody. And I've been trained to look for a tail. She'd have to be really good for me to miss her, and I don't imagine she is."

Most likely not. Most people aren't good enough for that. And very few people have been trained.

"So she doesn't know where we live."

"I don't imagine so," Rafe said, and his voice slowed into more of his usual drawl when he continued. "Sorry, darlin'."

"Goodness," I told him, "you don't have to apologize. I know you don't want this."

"No. Bringing something like this home's the last thing I want." He glanced over at Pearl, who had curled up on her pillow with her snout on her back legs. "Good thing you have protection."

She might look placid now, but we both knew that if someone threatened me, Pearl would be all up in their business in no time, and it wouldn't end well.

I nodded. "She's healed well from the gunshot last month. I'd hate for something else to happen to her, but I'm glad to have her."

We sat in silence a moment and watched the baby kicking her feet on the blanket and Pearl supervising.

"Looks like she's trying to turn over," Rafe said.

It did. "It's about time for that. According to the books. She's over four months."

We watched for a little longer. Down on the floor, Carrie was rocking back and forth from side to side.

"After that," I added, "she'll start crawling."

Rafe gave me a look. "Not sure I'm ready for that."

I nodded. "I know. Me either. Once she starts moving around, she can run into things, and fall down the stairs, and get hurt…"

Rafe shuddered. Visibly. Down on the floor, as if to prove the point, Carrie rocked far enough onto her side that she tipped over on her stomach. Her little squeak of surprise made Pearl lift her head to make sure that everything was all right. Seeing that it was, she put her head back down again.

"She did it," Rafe said. His voice was flat.

I nodded. "No going back now."

He leaned his head against the back of the sofa and groaned. Over on the pillow, Pearl raised her head and gave him an inquiring look.

"It's OK," I told her. "He's just being dramatic."

Rafe rolled his head in my direction and grinned. "No stopping time, I guess."

I shook my head. "I'm afraid not. We brought her into the world. Now we've got to deal with bringing her up."

"I suppose there are worse things," Rafe said.

"Much worse. Besides, we both made it to adulthood." Him at considerable odds. "She'll be all right."

"She ain't the one I'm worried about," Rafe said.

Five

He was up bright and early the next morning. That was usual. What wasn't, was that I was right behind him. When he got out of the shower, I got in, and by the time I dripped my way out of the bathroom, he was dressed and on his way down the stairs.

"Don't leave without me," I told him.

He glanced at me—wet hair wound up in a towel, a second towel wrapped around my dripping body—and grinned. "Is it Bring Your Wife to Work Day?"

"Not as far as I know. Just don't leave." I dashed into the bedroom and started throwing on clothes. Five minutes later—and any woman out there will appreciate what a sacrifice this was—I was dressed and had picked up the baby, changed her diaper, and carried her downstairs. My hair was still wet, now bundled into a messy topknot, and I had no makeup on.

"Good." I dropped onto one of the stools. "You're still here."

My husband, who was making himself toast on the other side of the island, arched a brow. "What's going on, darlin'?"

"I just don't want you to leave before I've had time to feed the baby," I said.

"'Cause?"

"I'm following you to work."

"Some reason you think I can't get there on my own?" He

leaned against the counter and folded his arms.

"Of course not," I said, hitching my shirt up for the baby.

"Thinking I'm stopping off somewhere on the way?"

"Don't be ridiculous." I glanced up at him and saw that his lips were curved. "You're not serious. Good."

"Why'd I wanna stop off anywhere when I got you at home?" He wandered over and dropped a kiss on my mouth, and then wandered back to catch the toast as it popped out of the toaster.

"No reason at all," I told him. "I'm not driving in with you. I'm taking my own car."

"I figured. You wanna see Tammy or something?" He reached for a butter knife to smear some of the yellow stuff across the piece of bread.

"Not today. I mean… I'm always happy to see Grimaldi. But today I'd rather see the person who's skulking around filming videos of you."

"Ah." He bit into the toast. It crunched, and crumbs dropped. He caught them in his hand and flung them into the sink. "You think you're gonna catch somebody in the act."

"Somebody's doing it," I said, "and probably not from the building across the street. Most likely whoever it is, is in plain sight, outside or maybe in a car. And if so, I should be able to see him or her."

Most likely her, but you never know. Rafe's been known to set the pulses fluttering on gay guys from time to time, too.

"This something you're worried about, darlin'?"

"Enough to look into it," I said. "Neither of us wants a repeat of Elspeth Caulfield."

He shook his head. "No."

"Better if Grimaldi could give you a bodyguard, I suppose—"

He looked deeply offended at the idea that he couldn't take care of himself, or that anyone else could take care of him better than he could, "—but she probably doesn't have anyone to spare. Not if all this person is using to shoot, is a camera. A gun would be worse."

"No kidding," Rafe said. "No reason to worry about that, though."

No more reason than usual, anyway. He'd been shot just a few weeks ago. Or grazed, at least. And while it didn't seem to bother him much, I remembered every time I got him naked and noticed the—still pink, still healing—scar.

Not the first one on his body, either. He had plenty. And I'd like it a lot if he could refrain from getting any more. Although there's a big difference between getting injured in the line of duty, when you're someone who has signed on for a job where you run toward trouble when everyone else runs away, and getting shot by some fruitcake who has seen you on social media and decided you look good.

"Just let me finish with Carrie, and we can go. I'll just follow you there, and hang back a little. Park around the corner or something, and take a look around."

"Better if you head out first," Rafe said, "so you can park and get into position before I get out of the car."

Good idea. And nice of him to enter into the plotting with so much gusto, especially when he probably figured it was nothing to worry about, and mostly a big joke.

"I'll do that," I said, as I moved Carrie from one arm to the other. "What's going on with you today?"

"Just more digging. Tammy's determined to find this guy."

"How does she plan to do that? He's probably not even from around here."

He didn't answer, and I added, "Right?"

He shook his head. "Prob'ly not. No."

"He could be from anywhere between Mobile and… where?"

"Gary, Indiana," Rafe said. "And there's no saying he's

from somewhere along the I-65 corridor. He could be from somewhere else and just drive up and down the interstate."

"Why would he do that?"

He shrugged. "Job?"

"Sure. But doesn't it make more sense that he's from somewhere not too far from I-65, or he wouldn't have taken a job driving up and down I-65? I mean, if he lives in Memphis, say, it would make more sense to drive I-40, and kill women there instead."

"Or he's like Samuel Little," Rafe said, "just driving around for his own pleasure, getting rid of people he comes across."

Maybe so. "You think he's a trucker, though. Don't you?"

"It makes the most sense. Anybody who ain't a trucker stands out at a truck stop. Several of the women were picked up from, or dumped at, truck stops. It's most likely he's someone who fits in there."

Carrie indicated that she'd had enough to eat for the time being, and I lifted her up to my shoulder and patted her back. She emitted an unladylike belch, and Rafe grinned.

"So that's what we're doing," he added. "Starting with companies that run trucks up and down the interstate."

"How many of them are there?" I handed him Carrie so I could get my clothing in order before going out.

He put her up against his own shoulder, with one hand on her tiny, ruffled butt. "Too many to count. Bob's got a wet-behind-the-ears deputy sitting over at the sheriff's office making cold calls. I'm not sure anything's gonna come of it, but I guess it's gotta be done."

"Unless you can find something else to narrow it down. Someone who saw him, or something."

"That's my job," Rafe said, swaying gently back and forth with the baby. "And now I guess I oughta get to it. You ready?"

I was ready. Or as ready as I ever am, without makeup. I

got to my feet, still adjusting my blouse. "Let's go."

"After you," Rafe said, and nodded toward the door.

The trip into Columbia was short and uneventful. I went first, and found myself a parking spot near the police station, where I could see the door and the parking spaces up front. Rafe doesn't park in the lot behind the building, since he's in and out all day, and gone more than he's inside. When he pulled up, I started scanning the surrounding area.

Last night's video had been taken from the vantage point of where I was sitting, more or less. This side of the building, anyway. I'd seen the outline of City Hall in the background when Rafe got into his car. So I'd parked myself down here, in the same vicinity, thinking Jessica Rabbit might choose to do her filming from the same spot this morning.

The engine of the Chevy shut off, and the door opened. I kept my eyes peeled as Rafe got out.

And I'll admit I held my breath, too. I wasn't really worried that anyone was going to take a potshot at him—there was no reason to think Jessica Rabbit was out for blood—but it's a habit that's hard to break, especially when I know someone's watching.

Rafe stood for a second, looking around, before he shut the car door. I knew he'd seen me—he doesn't miss much, and besides, he knew I'd be nearby—but he didn't acknowledge the car in any way. Nor would I expect him to. He knows better than that.

When nobody called out, and nothing else happened, he headed up the steps to the front door. Two seconds later he was inside. If anyone had been filming, they'd been doing it from somewhere they weren't immediately visible.

I stayed where I was, scanning the surrounding area. Wondering whether Rafe was doing the same, inside the building, behind the tinted windows.

Nothing happened. The seconds ticked by in silence, and turned into minutes. I started thinking about leaving.

A car engine started up nearby. I looked around, and saw a light-colored compact roll out of a parking spot farther up the street.

It had been parked rear in and was coming toward me, so I couldn't see the license plate. And speaking of tinted windows, I couldn't get a good look at the driver through the windshield, either. I got the impression of a pale oval surrounded by darkness, but that was all. I couldn't even, honestly, swear to whether it was a male or a female.

And then it—or he or she—was past me, and on its way down the street. I wrestled the Volvo out of the parking space I was in—not a compact, my Volvo—and got it turned around, in time to see the tail end of the car I was chasing zip around a corner a couple of blocks down the road.

I leaned over the steering wheel and lowered my foot on the gas pedal. The last few blocks of Columbia went by in a blur. But even so, by the time I got to the corner and around it, there was no sign of the compact. The street was open and empty, with not a car in sight.

I looked, of course. Left and right as I navigated slowly down the street. Up and down the cross streets. Into the driveways along the road. There was no sign of the tan car. After a couple of minutes I gave up, and went around the block and back to the police station.

This time I parked legitimately out front, because I wasn't trying to hide. And I grabbed Carrie from the backseat, and hung my bag over my shoulder, and headed up the stairs and through the doors into the lobby.

Up until a few weeks ago, the front desk at the police station had been manned by a young officer named Felicia Robinson. She'd had something of a crush on Rafe, and as a result, she hadn't always been polite to me. It had been an annoyance every time I'd walked through the doors into the police station, looking for him.

Then, a few weeks back, Felicia had gotten shot by the neo-Nazis. Now, still, it always came as a shock every time I walked through the door and she wasn't there.

This morning, that feeling was mitigated by the scene that took place in front of me.

The front desk was occupied by an officer in a spotless uniform, so young he probably didn't have to shave yet. He sat behind the desk, his eyes focused on whatever was in front of him—a screen, a TV monitor, maybe a lurid novel—but they didn't move as if anything was actually going on behind the eyes. Instead, his ears practically vibrated as he tried not to miss anything of the low-voiced conversation going on in the middle of the lobby.

It involved three people, and Rafe was one of them. Grimaldi was another. She stood, dressed in one of her usual no-nonsense pantsuits, confronting a third woman, someone I hadn't seen before.

Like Grimaldi, she had black hair and dark eyes. Like Grimaldi, she was dressed in a dark suit. They were around the same age. And there the similarities ended. Where Grimaldi's short heels and cropped curls spoke to her preference for low maintenance and easy movement, the other woman had paired her black pants and jacket with three inch heels, and her hair hung like a straight curtain most of the way to her waist. The pants clung to a nice posterior and flared out at the bottom, while the jacket was cut to nip in around a tiny waist. The crisp white blouse set off a perfectly made-up face with almond-shaped eyes and flawless skin.

"What's going on?" I asked, and it might have come out a little sharper and louder than I'd intended. But I'd just come smack up against my prejudices for the kind of woman I've always imagined being Rafe's type.

I know he married me, a not-skinny blue-eyed blonde, but I've never quite gotten over the idea that he's supposed to be with some exotic beauty as dark and gorgeous as he is.

Here I was looking at her. And she was looking at me, with calculation in those black eyes.

"Darlin'," Rafe said. And said no more.

Grimaldi didn't, either. "Savannah." She nodded a greeting before turning back to her adversary. Her nostrils flared.

No one seemed inclined to do the polite thing, so I took matters into my own hands, and stuck one out. "Savannah Martin. Collier."

The woman took it. Her palm was surprisingly rough for such a delicate-looking creature. "Really?"

"Yes," I said, and squeezed. She had a firm handshake, too.

She turned back to Rafe. "Your wife?"

He gave a curt nod. *Uh-oh,* I thought, looking from one to the other of them. An old girlfriend, or maybe more accurately, someone he'd shared his bed with at some point between high school and when he met me again? Sometime during the undercover years?

That had the potential to get ugly, if so.

She turned back to me, her smile blandly polite and her eyes flat black. "I'm Agent Leslie Yung with the Federal Bureau of Investigations."

The FBI? Rafe had slept with an FBI agent?

"Nice to meet you," I said pleasantly. "How do you know Rafe?"

She glanced at him. "We met in Memphis."

During the undercover years. Check.

"Agent Yung hauled me in for questioning a couple times," Rafe added. The flash of white that accompanied the statement was more a baring of teeth than an actual smile. "Always bothered her when she couldn't hang nothing on me."

Yung gave him a scathing look. "And now I see why. You

might have let me know that you were working undercover for another agency. I wouldn't have wasted my time on you."

Ouch, I thought, while Rafe said, blandly, "That'd defeat the purpose, don't you think? Not much point in being undercover if everybody knows you're undercover."

"The FBI—!" Yung began, and then seemed to think better of it. We stood in silence for a moment while she breathed heavily through her nose.

"Welcome to Columbia," I told her when I figured she'd gotten herself under control again and wasn't going to blow up. "What's the FBI doing in our neck of the woods?"

As if I couldn't guess.

"We were just discussing that," Grimaldi said tightly. And added, with a switch of subject that made it clear that the discussion wouldn't be continuing while I was present, "What are you doing here, Savannah?"

"Oh." I switched gears. "I just came to let Rafe know that I saw a car pull away and leave just after he went inside. It was coming toward me, though, so I didn't see the license plate, and the windows were tinted, so I couldn't see the driver. And by the time I'd gotten the Volvo turned around so I could follow it, it was gone."

There was a second's silence. "What kind of car?" Rafe wanted to know.

"Tan compact. Nothing unusual about it in any way. Not that I could see."

He nodded. "I'll keep an eye out."

It was painfully obvious that they all wanted to get rid of me, so I figured I'd oblige. "I'll head home. Walk me out?"

Rafe nodded. "Back in a minute," he told Grimaldi, who turned to Agent Yung with rather heavy courtesy.

"Why don't you come on back to my office, Agent Yung. We'll continue the discussion when Agent Collier comes back."

The two of them headed for the door at the far end of the

lobby while Rafe took Carrie's car seat off my hands and put one of his own at the small of my back to guide me outside.

I managed to keep my mouth shut until we were beyond the doors, where the young cop behind the desk couldn't hear us. And then I couldn't hold it in any longer. "Old girlfriend?"

He gave me a surprised look. "Yung? Hell, no. She's much too straight-laced to get involved with the likes of me."

"Then what was all that tension about?" We continued down the shallow steps toward street level.

"What tension?" Rafe wanted to know, and chuckled when I slid him a look. "She had some preconceived notions I had to disabuse her of."

"She thought you were a criminal," I translated.

He nodded. "We went to some lengths to make it look that way back then, yeah."

'We' being him and his handler, and the rest of the TBI.

"I guess she didn't like being fooled," I said.

"Seems that way." He waited for me to unlock the car and then he opened the back door and put Carrie's seat on the base for the ride home. "Nothing ever happened aside from her wanting to arrest me. Nothing you need to worry about."

"She's gorgeous," I said. "And I'm standing here with no makeup on and my hair undone. And at least ten pounds of excess baby-weight I haven't managed to lose in the past four months…"

While Leslie Yung was a perfect size four in her clingy pants. I haven't been a size four since middle school, and I don't expect I'll ever be one again.

"You'll get there, darlin'." He put an arm around my waist, while the other hand crept up into my hair. His fingers started undoing the messy bun. "And if you don't, it was well worth it."

I suppose Carrie was worth an extra ten pounds of weight, if he wanted to look at it that way. "I love you," I said.

He grinned. "I love you too, darlin'. Now go on home and let me deal with Yung."

"She's here for the murder investigation?"

He nodded.

"Is she going to try to take it away from you?"

"I imagine she's gonna try," Rafe said. "I better get in there, darlin'."

I nodded. "Let me know what happens."

He said he would. And then he leaned down and gave me the kind of kiss that's more suited for the bedroom than the sidewalk outside the police station. It ended with me hanging from his arm, as limp as a noodle, and it resulted in catcalls and whooping from a couple of cops who were walking by, and wolf whistles from up the street.

Rafe chuckled and set me upright. "You OK to drive?"

"I'll sit a minute and catch my breath before I attempt to navigate," I promised him. "Go on inside and make sure Grimaldi doesn't murder Agent Yung. I'll see you later."

"I'll be in touch." He jogged back up the stairs and let himself into the police station while I folded myself behind the wheel of the Volvo and, as promised, sat there until my legs stopped shaking before I turned the key in the ignition and headed home.

Six

I was halfway there when the phone rang. The display showed Charlotte's name, so I picked up with a cheery, "Good morning."

"That was quite the kiss your husband laid on you," my old friend informed me, with a ripe chuckle.

"How did you—? Oh, my God." I fought an instinctive inclination to turn the car around. "Someone filmed that?"

"And uploaded it to Facebook," Charlotte confirmed. "It just came on two minutes ago. I have an alert set."

So she'd told me. I was starting to think I might have to set my own alert.

"I followed Rafe to work this morning," I told her, "to see if I could spot whoever's doing this. And I thought I had."

I told her about the tan compact that had gotten away from me. "It didn't even occur to me that someone might still be there. I was so sure whoever it was had escaped me…"

"So you went back?" Charlotte prompted when I fell silent.

I nodded. "Yes. To tell him I'd lost whoever it was, but to keep an eye out for the car. And when I walked into the lobby, I found him and Grimaldi in a face-off with Agent Leslie Yung from the FBI."

"What's an FBI agent doing here in Maury County?"

I hadn't gotten around to asking, but I could guess. "Probably because of the murder. Rafe said he might have to contact the FBI and see if they have a task force put together for this guy. He's killed a lot of women in a lot of states, so it makes sense that they would."

I just hadn't realized he'd done it yet. Rafe, I mean. Called the FBI. Judging from his expression inside the lobby earlier, he hadn't expected to see Agent Yung. He certainly hadn't prepared Grimaldi for her. The scene I'd witnessed bore every evidence of being adversarial, the way it would be if Yung had shown up and tried to take over.

"Tell me about it when you get here," Charlotte instructed.

"Here?" Did we have an appointment I'd forgotten?

"You want to see the video, don't you?"

I did. But I could look it up myself. Or she could send it to me.

I deduced, cleverly, that she wanted to show it to me in person, though. So—

"Sure, I'll come over. Are you at your mom's house?"

She said she was, and I dropped the phone in the console and navigated my way past the mansion, into Sweetwater proper, and down Green Street.

Charlotte was in the front parlor when I pulled up, and opened the door before I'd even latched the picket-fence gate behind me. "It must be quite the video," I told her as I trudged up the walk to the front porch.

She smirked. "Wait until you see the comments. X-rated, some of them."

"Jesus. I mean… sheesh. Don't people have better things to do?"

"Apparently not," Charlotte said, and closed the door behind me. "Put the baby down. Here."

She handed me her phone, already cued up, and bent over Carrie. My daughter gurgled and cooed as she was lifted out of the carrier and snuggled in Charlotte's arms. Her youngest, Richard Junior, or JR, was going on three now, so maybe she missed holding babies.

I turned my attention to the video.

It was taken from the same angle as the others, from the area down the street where I'd been parked and waiting this morning. And it started with Rafe and me coming out of the police station. He kept his hand on the small of my back on the way down the steps, and then we stopped next to the car. I watched as he pulled open the back door and put Carrie inside before turning to me. We exchanged a few words, and then he put his arm around my waist. I watched myself lean back to look up at him, and reflected that I didn't recall doing that when I'd been standing there. It was very evident on the video, though.

A few more words were exchanged—I remembered them, but whoever had been holding the camera; probably a phone— hadn't been close enough to catch what we said. Then I smiled up at him, and he nodded, and then he—as Charlotte had put it—laid a kiss on me that had certainly curled my toes at the time, and did it again now.

"Sheesh," I said, my cheeks burning.

Charlotte chuckled. She was bouncing Carrie up and down, and my daughter was giggling. "Pretty hot, isn't it?"

"It was. I just never realized what it might look like from the outside."

"Now you know," Charlotte said as, on the screen, I came up for air. My expression was part dazed, part aroused, and wholly embarrassing.

"Oh, my God." I closed my eyes in mortification, as another wave of heat flooded my cheeks.

"At least you know what Rafe sees when he looks at you," Charlotte told me, and I guess she had a point. It explained that amused chuckle he usually gave me at times like that, too.

On the screen, he waited until I was steady on my feet, and then he tucked me into the car with another quick kiss. He bounded up the stairs and through the door, and the camera stayed on me while I reversed out of the parking space and rolled off down the street. The video ended with me passing the car where the videographer had been sitting.

"Should I read the comments," I asked Charlotte, "or is that just going to embarrass me further?"

She pursed her lips. "Hard to say. Most of them don't mention you, other than to say things like *'Lucky girl'* and *'Wish I were in her shoes.'* The rest of it is all about *'he can kiss me like that anytime,'* and stuff like that."

"Any comments from Jessica herself?" I started scrolling as I asked, down through the comments and heart-eyed emoji Charlotte had quoted.

"I didn't notice any." She bounced Carrie again, and the baby gurgled. "She's precious, Savannah."

"Looks like her daddy," I said.

"She has your eyes."

She did. Bright blue, against Rafe's dusky skin and curly, almost-black hair. "Oh, great. Someone's calling me a fat cow and wondering how someone like me ended up with someone like him."

Not like that thought hadn't crossed my mind too, a few times. That didn't mean I appreciated anyone else asking the question.

"And here someone else who says he should be with a black girl."

"I think he'd disagree," Charlotte said calmly. "Besides, they're just jealous."

Maybe so. "It doesn't matter, anyway. I married him, he's mine, and it doesn't matter what someone else thinks."

"You go, Savannah," Charlotte said, grinning.

"Well, it doesn't. I spent too much of my life thinking I knew who he should be with, and it wasn't me. It happened this morning, too. I took one look at Leslie Yung—she's stunning—and I immediately thought she was an old girlfriend, because that's the kind of woman I feel like he should be with. Not someone boring and fish-belly white like me."

"I think he'd disagree," Charlotte said again.

"I know he'd disagree. He told me he disagreed. Just before he laid that kiss on me."

"Ah!" Charlotte said, as if that proved something.

"So I don't care that some woman thinks I shouldn't be with him, and she should. He's *my* husband and I'm keeping him."

"Maybe you want to leave a message on the thread saying that?"

"No," I said. "I don't think so."

She smirked. "Afraid they'll cancel you?"

The thought had crossed my mind. I'm in a profession where public opinion of me matters. "If I just ignore it, maybe it'll go away."

"Maybe," Charlotte agreed. "This can't be comfortable, though. And next thing you know, she might be following you home. Or him."

She had a point. "Surely this is illegal? It's stalking, isn't it?"

"That's something you should be asking Rafe," Charlotte said. "Or your friend, the police chief. Or Sheriff Satterfield. Or Todd. Or Dix or Catherine."

Plenty of people I could ask, it seemed. My life was full of law enforcement and lawyers.

"Not much we can do about it until we figure out who she is, though. You can't arrest someone, or serve papers on someone, if you don't know who they are."

"No," Charlotte said. "I guess you didn't notice anyone filming you earlier."

"After that kiss? I wouldn't have noticed a full crew with a dolly and a boom mike."

"That's what I figured," Charlotte said.

We spent some time rewatching the video—it made me squirm with embarrassment each time, although I suppose the squirming might have lessened a little by the third time through—but it turned out to be for naught, since rewatching didn't show us any clues we hadn't noticed before.

"The interior of her car looks messy," I said. "And not new."

"A lot of cars are messy and not new. My minivan was."

"I don't think this is a station wagon," I said. "The camera's too close to the ground."

Charlotte squinted at it. "Maybe."

I lowered the phone to my lap, where it kept going through the same video again. "I'm not sure what to do, other than follow Rafe around all day. And now that she's seen—and filmed—my car, I can't really do that."

"We can borrow Mom's car," Charlotte said. "She won't mind, if we leave her yours."

Really? "You'd spend your whole day following my husband around?"

"It beats sitting here," Charlotte said.

I shrugged. "I guess it does. I have to be over at the house on Fulton by eleven to let the photographer in. But before and after that, I guess we could follow Rafe around and see what he gets up to."

He'd notice us, of course. Maybe not at first, if we used Charlotte's mother's car, one he wasn't conditioned to look for. But it wouldn't take him long to pick up on any car that was shadowing him. He's had a lot of practice.

"Let me talk to Mom," Charlotte said and breezed out of the room, still holding my daughter. I turned my attention back to the phone in my hand.

By the time she came back, with the news that her mother would be happy to let us borrow the little hybrid in exchange for my gas-guzzling Volvo, I had watched the video one more time, and had noticed something.

"See this shadow here, across the top of the dashboard? She's got something hanging in her front window." Looped around the mirror, maybe. "Looks like a scarf, or maybe a thick chain of something..."

"Mardi Gras beads," Charlotte said, in the process of dumping Carrie back into her car seat. "A handful of Mardi Gras beads. I've seen people do that."

I had too, now that she mentioned it. I examined the shadow again. "Could be. It gives us something to look for, anyway. A car with a bunch of beads, or something that casts the same shadow as a bunch of beads, around the rearview mirror. Can't be too many of those around."

"More than you'd think," Charlotte said, straightening, "but at least it narrows it down from every car on the road."

It did. "Unless she takes them down."

"No reason for her to do that. She doesn't know we noticed them." Charlotte looked around for her purse. "She doesn't know we're looking for her. Not yet."

Maybe not. "What about your kids?"

"Mom's staying with them," Charlotte said, heading for the door. "Come on."

I grabbed Carrie and the car seat and followed.

Fifteen minutes later, we were back outside the Columbia PD again. Rafe's loaner was still parked at the foot of the stairs, so he was either inside, or had left by other means. Since we didn't know which was the case, we decided to go with the assumption that he was still there, and that his stalker might be, too.

"She doesn't know what I look like." Charlotte said, surveying the street outside the police station with shining eyes. "I should be the one getting out and looking around."

"Be my guest." She was really getting into this, so who was I to deprive her of any of the fun? "I'll just stay here with Carrie."

"I'll be back in a few minutes," Charlotte said, and swung the hybrid's door open. I watched her walk away, up the street toward the police station, while she peered intently into every car she passed. Once she'd reached the top of the street, I saw her cross over to the other side, and come back down, doing the same thing to the cars parked on the other side. She was about as circumspect as that proverbial bull in the china shop, but since nobody peeled out of their parking spot and took off on her approach, I figured nobody had a guilty conscience or anything to hide.

"Nothing?" I asked politely when she opened the door again, and fit herself behind the wheel.

She shook her head. "Not in this section. Not now."

"What do you want to do?"

I glanced at the dashboard clock. With everything that had already happened today, it was still only nine-fifteen. "We have about an hour and a half until we have to head over to Fulton Street for the photographer."

"I guess we wait and see if Rafe comes out," Charlotte said, moving her seat back and getting comfortable, "and if he does, we follow him. And in the meantime, we check any new cars that come along."

Fine by me. If we didn't know where Rafe was going, it wasn't likely that Jessica Rabbit knew, either—she'd have to be here to follow him, too, and if she was here, Charlotte would have seen her—but I didn't have anything else to do for the next hour and a half, so I figured I might as well stay here and enjoy the company.

As it happened, we got lucky. We hadn't been sitting there more than ten minutes when the door to the police station opened and Leslie Yung stepped out. A second later, Rafe followed. He gestured to the tan Chevy, and Agent Yung headed down the stairs.

"Who's that?" Charlotte wanted to know, her nose so close to the windshield her breath was fogging up the window.

"That's the FBI agent I was telling you about."

She shot me a look. "I can see why you thought she might have been an old girlfriend."

I nodded, as I watched my husband open the door of the Chevy for Agent Yung and hold it while she arranged herself in the passenger seat. Then he closed the door behind her and walked around the car. He stopped for just a second to run his gaze over the street—for a second I could have sworn he looked straight at me—before he opened his own door and slid behind the wheel.

"Better get ready," I told Charlotte. "He takes off like a bat out of hell."

She nodded. "Where do you think they're going? Left or right?"

My money was on right—toward the interstate and the road to Sweetwater, but— "I guess we'll find out."

The Chevy reversed out of the parking space and took off. I sincerely hoped—with only a little malice—that Agent Yung was hanging onto the door handle and barely avoiding peeing her pants.

"Don't let them get too far ahead," I told Charlotte as the Chevy headed past us and down the street. "The way he drives, we'll lose them."

Charlotte nodded. She was already moving backward out of the space while I watched the Chevy in the mirror.

By the time we'd gotten turned around, they were out of sight down the road. "Step on it," I told Charlotte, "and let's see if we can catch them."

She obliged, and the little hybrid took off like a shot down the street.

I had kept watching until I couldn't watch anymore, and hadn't seen them turn off the main drag, so I kept Charlotte going straight. And every time she slowed down a little—because neither one of us is used to speeding through residential areas—I exhorted her to go faster. As a result, we caught sight of the Chevy after a couple of minutes, up ahead of us and halfway to the interstate.

"Probably taking her to see the crime scene," I said. "That had to be why she's here. The serial killer case."

Unless she, too, had seen the video of Rafe. And—still believing he was a criminal—had rushed to Columbia to tell Tamara Grimaldi that she was employing an imposter.

That would have been an interesting conversation to sit in on, if so.

But more likely she was here to consult on the serial killer case, and hadn't known Rafe was here until he walked in.

I wished I could have seen her face when that happened, too.

"What serial killer case?" Charlotte wanted to know. "You didn't say anything about a serial killer."

"I didn't? Must have been an oversight on my part. The body that was dumped yesterday is the last, or the latest, in a series of eighteen victims this guy has claimed."

"God," Charlotte said, and shuddered. The little hybrid did, too. Compared to my sturdy Volvo, and Rafe's even sturdier SUV, I felt like I was riding in a tin can.

She shot me a look. "You said 'claimed.' How does he claim them?"

"Oh." Not sure I wanted to go into the details of that, because it was unpleasant and because Charlotte, like me, was a gently-bred Southern girl, who was supposed to be ladylike and squeamish. "He numbers them."

"How?"

"I'm not entirely sure," I admitted. "I haven't seen the body, or looked it up." The information was probably online. Unless this was one of those pieces of info the police hoarded, to use against the bad guy when they caught him. Although if that were the case, surely Grimaldi wouldn't have told me about it. "The word Grimaldi used was 'carved.'"

"God." Charlotte turned a shade paler.

"I know. It's icky."

She didn't say anything else, and I added, "They're signaling. Better slow down."

We watched the Chevy zip out of sight on the right. The hybrid came to a crawl as we approached the spot where the Chevy had vanished.

And yes, it was as I'd thought. We were near the interstate, and the SUV had taken a turn into the parking lot of the truck stop. As we crept closer, we saw it come to a stop toward the back of the lot, near an overflowing dumpster.

"Go over there," I told Charlotte, waving my hand in the opposite direction. "Find somewhere to stop where we can still see what they're doing."

She rolled off in that direction, obediently. I kept my eyes on the Chevy, and saw both doors open. Rafe and Agent Yung got out, and headed for the dumpster.

And then disappeared behind the dumpster.

My eyes narrowed. Not—I swear—because I thought they were doing anything untoward behind it. If Rafe wanted to make out with Agent Yung he wouldn't do it behind a smelly dumpster. Nor would he make out with anyone but me.

But I couldn't see them, and that was annoying.

Still, there wasn't much question about what they were doing. He was showing her the crime scene, or more accurately, the dump site. The place where the body had been found. Most likely not the place where she'd been murdered. I didn't they had any idea where that had happened.

A few minutes later, they came out and got back in the car. The Chevy swung around and came back toward us.

"Duck!" I told Charlotte, and tucked up into a ball in my seat. Next to me Charlotte did the same. We watched the Chevy cruise by through strands of hair, kind of like an ostrich believes that if it can't see anyone, no one can see it, either.

The Chevy hit the road and turned back toward Columbia, and I shook my hair out of my face and nudged Charlotte. "They're out of sight. Let's go."

She took her foot off the brake and rolled toward the exit. But a truck was coming in just as we were going out, and so we had to hang back until it had made its wide turn into the lot. I stared hard at it, wondering whether a truck like this was the last thing Ramona Mitchell had seen before she died, and whether there was a dead woman, or a bound and gagged woman, inside this one. Not that there was any reason to suspect this truck in particular; it was just there at a time when I was thinking about it.

And then it was past us, and the hybrid leapt out of the lot and onto the road, and took up the chase after the Chevy, which was nowhere in sight.

We'd driven maybe a minute when my phone rang. I pulled it out of my purse and looked at it. "It's Rafe," I told Charlotte, before I put it to my ear. "Hi."

"Darlin'."

It was all he said. The silence stretched out.

"What do you want?" I ventured. He didn't sound upset, so there was that, at least.

"Don't you think that oughta be my question?"

I sighed. "Where are you?"

"About twenty feet behind you."

I glanced in the side mirror. Yes, there he was. Or there the Chevy was, at any rate. I could make out the pale oval of Leslie

Yung's face through the windshield.

"How did you get back there?" He'd been in front of us when we left the lot. Or so I'd assumed. "No, never mind. We were just looking out for you."

"How d'you figure that?"

"There's a new video out on social media. Of you and me kissing. Outside the police station earlier."

That got a chuckle. "No kidding."

"I'll send it to you. Some of the comments are saying I shouldn't be married to you."

"Whoever says that is wrong," Rafe said, while in the background I heard Leslie Yung's voice mumble something. "What's it gotta do with you and your sidekick following me around?"

"We figured, if someone else was following you around, we'd see them."

"Ain't nobody but you two following me around right now," Rafe said, without pointing out that if we hadn't noticed him circling around to end up behind us, we weren't likely to notice anyone else, either.

"Are you sure?"

"I caught you, didn't I?"

He didn't wait for me to answer, just added, "Go home, darlin'. If this person turns out to be a problem, I'll deal with it. But I don't want you and Carrie mixed up in this business. Or Charlotte. Tell her to take you home."

"She can hear you," I said, while next to me, Charlotte rolled her eyes. "Where are you going?"

"I guess if I don't tell you, you're gonna tail me over there?"

Again, he didn't wait for my response. "I'm taking Agent Yung to the sheriff's office in Sweetwater. Feel free to follow us there if you don't believe me."

"Don't mind if we do," I said, since my car was in

Sweetwater anyway. "You want to pull around, since right now you're the one following us?"

"No," Rafe said. "Just keep going until you hit Sweetwater. We'll be right here."

Fine. "Promise you'll be careful?"

"Always." He hung up before I could point out that he always said that, and never was.

"What do you want me to do?" Charlotte asked.

I sighed. "Drive to Sweetwater. There's nothing else we can do."

She nodded. "At least we know he's keeping an eye out."

Yes. At least we knew that. And I guess it was better than nothing.

Seven

When we turned down Green Street, the Chevy with Rafe and Agent Yung continued straight ahead into Sweetwater. I left Charlotte and the hybrid in front of the Albertsons' Victorian and transferred myself and Carrie back into the Volvo. When I swung by the sheriff's office on my way out of town, I saw that Rafe's Chevy was indeed parked there. And although I drove slowly and took a good look around, I didn't spot anyone lying in wait with a camera on a tripod, waiting for him to come back out. I gave up and headed home. And realized, halfway there, that I still needed to go back to Columbia and unlock the door of the house on Fulton for the photographer, so we could get it back on the market sooner rather than later.

So off I went, back to Columbia yet again. By the time I had let him in and explained what I wanted, and told him how to lock up and dispose of the key after he was done, and I had driven back to Sweetwater yet again, Carrie was ready for a nap, and so was I. I fed her and changed her and put her in her crib, and then I mixed up some tuna and capers and curled up on the loveseat in the parlor, to watch an hour of mindless TV to relax.

Only to have to get back up ten minutes later, when I heard the crunch of tires outside.

I figured it would be Rafe. That he had ditched Leslie Yung at the sheriff's office, pawned her off on Bob Satterfield, and had decided to stop by for lunch on his way back to Columbia and the police station.

It wasn't. It was Grimaldi's official vehicle that had come to a stop at the bottom of the stairs, and the detective—chief of police—herself climbing the couple of steps toward the porch floor.

"De… um… Tamara."

Her eyes glinted with amusement. It had taken both of us quite some time to get over the *Detective/Ms. Martin* bits.

Now that she wasn't a detective anymore, and I wasn't Ms. Martin, old habits still died hard.

"What can I do for you?" I added. "Want some lunch?"

"No, thank you. I grabbed a sandwich on the way."

She moved past me and into the foyer. I shut the door behind her. She greeted Pearl, and gave a compreshensive look around. "Baby asleep?"

I nodded. "I put her down fifteen, twenty minutes ago. She'll stay there for another hour, at least. Something you need to talk about? Something wrong?"

She shook her head, and then shrugged.

"Let me get you a drink, at least. It's getting warmer out there." I pushed past her and headed down the center hall toward the kitchen. "Come on."

I didn't look back, but I heard the noise of her heels on the old plank floors as she followed: less the clicking of high heels than the clomp of low ones.

In the kitchen, I gave Pearl a treat for being such a good guard dog, and filled two glasses with iced tea from the fridge—Grimaldi was on duty, so there was no point in bringing out the bottle of white wine I had cooling in the same place—and put them both on the island. "Chips and salsa? Cheese and crackers? Hummus and crudités?"

Her lips twitched as she sat down on one of the bar stools. "No. Thank you."

"I can't help it," I said. "I went to finishing school. Making people comfortable is part of the job."

"I'm comfortable." She reached for one of the glasses and took a sip. "See?"

"Sure." I took the other and did the same. "So what can I do for you?"

"I came to talk," Grimaldi said.

My brows rose. "Really?"

"I talk."

"I suppose." I mean, yes. She did. "You just don't usually talk to me." Or not about anything important.

She shrugged and took another swig of tea. And turned the glass over in her hands.

After a few seconds I decided to make it easier on her, since she obviously didn't know how to start. "Rafe took Agent Yung around to the crime scene and to see Bob."

Grimaldi's lips curved. "Yes."

"Did you call her in, or did Bob? Or did she just show up on her own?"

"She saw the video," Grimaldi said, with an amused look at me.

"The video of Rafe?"

She nodded. "She'd heard about the new victim of the Classicist, of course."

The Classicist? "Is that what you're calling him?"

"It's what she's calling him," Grimaldi said. "We reported the murder to VICAP, of course."

I must have looked blank, because she added, "The Violent Criminal Apprehension Program. It's an FBI database that keeps records of violent crimes across state lines. Like this one."

"And Leslie Yung works for them?"

"Leslie Yung works for the Memphis office of the FBI," Grimaldi said. "She ran across your husband a few years ago, in his undercover persona."

I nodded. "I got that much from the scene this morning."

"Well, after she found out about the new victim, she did some internet searching. And in the process, stumbled across the video of Rafe doing his macho thing with Tucker and the kid."

"Curtis."

Grimaldi nodded. "She recognized him—your husband—and, believing him to be a dangerous criminal, came down here to warn me."

Huh. "I'm surprised the Memphis FBI office didn't catch on before now," I said. "I thought Rafe's cover blew so spectacularly that everyone in law enforcement knew."

"I guess Memphis was too far away."

Maybe. Although— "He worked there a lot. For a long time. I'm surprised they didn't keep up."

"I don't know," Grimaldi said. "The scene got pretty heated."

So I'd seen. "They seemed to be getting on OK when I saw them earlier."

She squinted at me across the island. "When did you see them earlier?"

"I was following him around to see if I could get a bead on this person who's been uploading the videos," I said. "There's another one now. Taken this morning." I pulled my phone closer and cued up the video. "Here."

Grimaldi watched the clip, and watched it again. "Quite the movie kiss," she said blandly when she handed the phone back.

I flushed. "I know. If I'd known that someone was filming…"

But honestly, if I'd known that someone was filming, I wouldn't have done anything differently. I was kissing my husband, as I had every right to do. I just considered myself lucky that Mother hadn't noticed.

And no sooner had the thought crossed my mind that somehow, like magic, her name flashed on the screen. I made a face and turned the ringer down.

Grimaldi smirked, but didn't comment. "So you were following him around…"

"Charlotte and I. Thinking maybe we'd see whoever's doing the filming. That's why I was there this morning, too. At the police station."

She nodded.

"We followed him and Agent Yung to the truck stop out by I-65, and then we followed them back to Sweetwater, to the sheriff's office. Rafe noticed us right away, of course."

"Of course," Grimaldi said, grinning. "Well, I'm glad he and Yung are getting along. He's going to have to work with her, it looks like."

"I figured he'd be working with you," I said, and watched her shake her head.

"Conflict of interest. One of the victims was my mother. Besides, it isn't my case. Bob called in the TBI, and now the FBI's gotten involved, but it's still not the Columbia PD's case."

I guess it wasn't. "So what do you want from me? Rafe will tell you everything directly if you ask him." Or Bob would. Nobody would keep any secrets from her.

"I want to run my own investigation," Grimaldi said, and I opened my eyes wide to stare at her. "Unofficially."

"Do you think Bob and Rafe and Agent Yung won't do a good job?"

"I think they'll do a fine job." After a second she added, "I don't know Yung. But both Bob and your husband will."

"So why get in their way?"

"I don't want to get in their way," Grimaldi said. "But this is personal. I can't just sit on the sidelines and let them do the work. Not when it was my mother who was killed."

"That's why you're supposed to sit on the sidelines, though. It's personal to you. And that's why you're not supposed to investigate it." And I had no idea why I was telling her this, when I knew she knew it.

"I can't," Grimaldi said. "When your sister-in-law died, you knew I was investigating. You trusted me to do a good job, because you knew me."

I nodded. I'd known her, and liked her, and had believed she'd give the case everything she had to get justice for Sheila.

"You still looked into things on your own."

Yes. I had. "It wasn't because I didn't trust you. But she was my brother's wife, and…"

"It was personal," Grimaldi finished. "It's not that I don't trust them. I do. There's nobody I'd rather have investigating this than your husband and Sheriff Satterfield. But she was my mother. I can't sit here and do nothing now that another case has landed practically in my lap."

No, of course she couldn't. When Rafe had disappeared—been taken—the night before our wedding, Grimaldi and Wendell Craig had both been looking into it, and looking hard. There are no two people I'd trust more to figure out what was going on than the two of them. But I'd still looked into it on my own, too. It was better than sitting at home doing nothing.

"What do you want me to do?" I asked. "This isn't something I'm going to have to hide from Rafe, is it?"

"No," Grimaldi said. "Of course not. We'll share anything we discover with them."

Good. I don't like to keep things from my husband. Not only isn't it fair—I don't want him to keep things from me, so the least I can do is return the favor—but I'm the world's worst liar, so he always knows when I'm being less than truthful.

"What do you want help doing?"

"Just looking around," Grimaldi said. "Following up on anything they're not following up on. Or anything we think is interesting that they don't. Whatever we decide to do."

"I can do that." I'm naturally nosy anyway. Poking into things is what I do. "When do you want to start?"

"ASAP," Grimaldi said.

"It'll have to wait an hour or two. Carrie's asleep."

She grimaced. "Then we might as well sit here and talk things over. See where we are."

"Fine by me. Let's go into the parlor. It's more comfortable."

And my tuna and crackers were there.

"Here's what we know," Grimaldi said, when we were situated in comfort in the parlor and I was nibbling on my interrupted lunch. "Over the past dozen and a half years, someone has killed eighteen women in Alabama, Tennessee, Kentucky, and Indiana, and dumped the bodies along Interstate 65 in one of those states. Sometimes the victim was picked up in the same state she was dumped, sometimes she wasn't."

I nodded, chewing.

"A lot of them—the majority—have been prostitutes, but not all."

"Like your mother."

She nodded. "She was working the night shift at a motel near the interstate. The police said she was picked up walking home from work one morning."

"And there's no reason to doubt that."

It wasn't a question, but she answered it anyway. "None at all. I've seen the police report. The hotel staff saw her leave. She didn't make it home. And because of the number—numeral III—we know it was this same unsub."

"I've been meaning to ask that," I said, and lowered the cracker I had just lifted, since it suddenly seemed unpalatable.

Grimaldi looked from my face to the cracker and back. "About the numbers?"

"You said he carves them into the victims."

She nodded.

"Before or after death?"

"After," Grimaldi said. "He doesn't seem to be into torture. Whoever he is, he picks them up, rapes them, strangles them, and dumps them, in pretty short order. Like in this case. We didn't know Ramona Mitchell was missing when we found her. It had only been a few hours between the time we think she left Nashville and the time she was found here."

"A lot longer than it would take to drive here from Nashville, though."

Grimaldi nodded. "But not long enough for anyone to notice she was gone. If he were the type to enjoy dragging things out, to play with his victims, he could have held on to her a lot longer. Days. Maybe weeks."

"Unless he couldn't," I said. "Truckers try to make good time, don't they? They don't get paid until the load is delivered, or something?"

Grimaldi shrugged, and I added, "Or maybe he was close to home, and he couldn't bring her there, or there's nowhere at home he can keep her. Maybe he lives with someone, or has an apartment or something like that. Somewhere where other people would have heard her, or would know she was there."

"He could have kept her in the truck," Grimaldi said.

Maybe. "I guess we don't actually know for sure that he's a trucker, but if he is... do they own their trucks, or are they just drivers, and the company owns the trucks?"

"It depends," Grimaldi said. "Some long-distance drivers own their own rigs, some drive for a company."

"So maybe he doesn't have his own, and had to deliver the truck when he got to the end of the line. So he couldn't keep her in it, and he couldn't take her home..."

"That's something to consider," Grimaldi said. "It would probably mean that the end of the line—where he works or lives—is close to here."

Close being relative, I assumed. "I suppose it might. Although there's that old adage about fouling ones own yard. He probably wouldn't have left her on his own doorstep, so to speak. He could have gotten back on the interstate and driven another couple hours after dumping her."

Grimaldi shrugged.

We sat in silence a minute before I dragged the conversation back to where it had been before we'd gone off on this tangent about locations. "So he numbers them after they're dead. Not because he likes to inflict pain, but because they're... numbers?"

"A series," Grimaldi said. "There could be others, that he hasn't numbered."

"Why would he number some and not others?"

"Don't know," Grimaldi said. "For some serial killers, not every victim measures up to the ideal, for one reason or another. Or there could be something special about this group."

"Like what?" I risked another cracker. It turned to sawdust in my mouth, so I gave up and pushed the plate away. Over on the pillow in the corner, Pearl looked hopeful, and I heaped the rest of the tuna onto one of the last crackers and handed it to her. She took it daintily from my hand and then wolfed it down.

"That's all," I told her, and curled back up on the loveseat next to Grimaldi. "What do they have in common other than that they all died somewhere close to I-65, presumably by being strangled by the same guy?"

She shook her head. "They're all around the same age. Late twenties to mid-thirties. They're almost all white, but not exclusively. There's been a couple of Latinas, and a couple of black women."

I nodded.

"The black women were both light skinned, so his type seems to be female, thirty to thirty-five—give or take a year or two in either direction. Dark hair. Medium skin."

"Like you," I said. Grimaldi's Italian, with black hair and olive skin, so her mother had probably looked similar.

She nodded. "Most of them have had dark eyes, but not all. It seems like the overall look is more important than the specifics."

"And since he's probably had access to blondes, and has chosen to forego them, he must have a preference for brunettes."

"So it seems," Grimaldi agreed. "Unless he's killed blondes, but they aren't part of this series."

Maybe so. Maybe that's what 'didn't measure up' meant to this guy. Brunettes were preferable, but he'd kill a blonde if he couldn't find a suitable brunette. He wouldn't make her part of the same series, though.

"Do you think he has another series? One for blondes?"

"If he has, we haven't connected them," Grimaldi said. And continued with her profile of the killer, "The assumption is he's white, since most of the victims have been white. Age range…" She hesitated. "Forty to seventy, on the outside."

I counted on my fingers. "That would make him around twenty-five when the first victim was killed. Surely that's too young?"

"Some serial killers have developed that early," Grimaldi said. "Some have developed earlier."

"I'll take your word for it. If all the victims have been between thirty and thirty-five, isn't it more likely that he was that age when he started? Putting him in the—" I counted quickly, "fifty to sixty range now?"

"More likely," Grimaldi agreed. "But not impossible."

Fine. "So a white man, maybe as young as forty, but more likely older. And… isn't seventy too old? Would a seventy-year-old have the muscle to subdue a much younger woman, and then carry her dead body to where he left her?"

Grimaldi didn't answer, so I went on. "A white man, maybe as young as forty and maybe as old as seventy, but more likely in the middle of the range, who has been driving a truck—most likely a truck—up and down Interstate 65 for almost twenty years."

Grimaldi nodded.

"How do we go about finding a guy like that?" Especially since we had four states to search? "Rafe and I talked about investigating trucking companies along the I-65 corridor..."

"That's something the FBI can do much better than you and me," Grimaldi said. "Where I want to start, is Victim One."

"His first?"

"The first in this series. She might not be his first overall. But if she were his first..."

She sat in silence for a second, maybe trying to determine how much to tell me. "The first victim of a serial killer is called an origin kill. Often, that murder is the prototype, in a way, for the others. Some killers continually try to recreate that crime, to kill that person again and again. For others, it's just the trigger that made them start killing, not necessarily something they're trying to recreate, specifically. Often, the first victim wasn't planned, the way the rest were. The first happened, and he started following the pattern after that. Either way, a serial killer's first victim can give important information about him."

Ugh. "Who was this guy's first?"

"The first in this series was Laura Lee Matlock. Thirty-three. Born in Damascus. Wound up dead beside the road near Bowling Green, Kentucky."

"Damascus?" I repeated. "The town a few miles from here? Where Yvonne lives? And Elspeth Caulfield grew up?"

She nodded. "Mrs. Matlock hit hard times around thirty. Her husband went to prison for a while. They had two kids, and it was hard for her to keep things together alone, so she started picking up extra money working the night shift at the truck stop down by the interstate."

"The same place where the most recent victim was dumped?"

"Yes," Grimaldi said. "She was waiting tables, but sometimes she'd go off with a trucker for an hour for some extra cash, too. The assumption was that that's what happened, although nobody knows for sure."

"But she disappeared from the truck stop?"

"She finished her shift," Grimaldi said, "but never made it home. Her mother, who babysat the kids overnight, reported her missing halfway through the day. By then, Kentucky State Police had already found her, and it was just a matter of putting the two together."

The missing woman and the dead one, I assumed. The same victim.

"So she got into a truck with somebody, and he drove north from here and pushed her out of the truck an hour and a half to two hours later, in Kentucky."

"Longer than that," Grimaldi said. "It would have taken some time to do what he did to her, too."

Right. So maybe three to four hours later.

"And she was Number One. Numeral I."

"Yes," Grimaldi said. "Although at the time, she was just a dead women with a slash on the inside of her arm."

Right. "How long did it take to figure out that they weren't just slashes?"

"By Victim Three there was a pattern," Grimaldi said evenly, not betraying by so much as an eyelash flicker that Victim Three was her mother. "By Victim Four, they became numerals. IV instead of IIII. When Number Five was a capital V instead of four vertical lines with a diagonal line across them, it became a certainty."

I nodded. "I wasn't thinking about the straight lines with the diagonal lines across them. That's the simplest way to keep track of numbers, isn't it? All straight lines. I was thinking he might have gone with the numerals because they would be easier to carve than the curves in numbers like 2 and 3."

"But straight lines with diagonal lines would have been easier still," Grimaldi said.

I nodded. "So the numerals must mean something. Beyond just keeping a tally of victims."

"They might," Grimaldi nodded. "It's too soon to say that they must."

Maybe. "Who would chose to keep track of things with Roman numerals? What kind of person, I mean? Most of us would either think in normal numbers, 1 and 2 and so forth, or the single line tally marks with the diagonal line. Score marks, or whatever they're called. What kind of person goes to Roman numerals first?"

"Not necessarily first," Grimaldi admonished. And continued, before I could argue with her, "Someone who studied Latin? Someone with a parochial school education?"

"Catholic, you mean? Did you go to Catholic school?" She was Italian; it seemed a logical question.

"No," Grimaldi said. "We couldn't afford private school. Tony and Francesca and I all went to the local public school."

"So did I." And sometimes I wondered why, since Mother and Dad had certainly had the money to send Dix, Catherine, and me to private, or even boarding school. But instead they'd kept us home and let us duke it out with the unwashed masses in general education. "It's been a few years, but I think Latin was an elective at Columbia High."

"You didn't take it?"

I shook my head. "French. The Martins come from France originally. Besides, Paris."

Grimaldi nodded. "But the local high school offered it.

Maybe our unsub went to Columbia High."

Maybe. Although— "I'm sure it isn't the only school along the I-65 corridor that offers Latin."

"No," Grimaldi said, "but it's where Victim One went, most likely."

"Did she grow up in Damascus?"

Grimaldi nodded.

"Then yes," I said. "Unless her family paid for private school—" And that wasn't likely, if she'd fallen on hard enough times later to have to sell her body to make ends meet, "—or home-schooled her, she would have ended up at Columbia High. All the rest of us did. And Damascus is closer to Columbia than Sweetwater."

"Somewhere to start."

I looked at her, and she added. "Damascus, and Columbia High. And whoever took Latin class with Laura Lee Matlock thirty-three years ago."

"When the baby wakes up," I said.

Grimaldi sank back against the sofa and sighed.

Eight

I tried to talk Grimaldi into taking the Volvo, since the base for the car seat was in it, but the idea of having someone else drive her around must have been too much, because she insisted we move Carrie's car seat into the official Columbia PD SUV, where she could take the wheel. She did, however, and reasonably graciously at that, agree to stop by the house on Fulton so I could make sure everything was locked up nice and tight after the photographer had left. Everything looked fine, so I hiked my posterior back into the SUV and nodded. "All good. We can go do what you want now."

"Much obliged," Grimaldi grumbled, and rolled away from the curb. "Any reason to think things would not be fine here?"

I made myself comfortable against the gray leather. "When we got here yesterday morning, someone had tossed a baseball through the living room window."

She shot me an alarmed look—like me, she remembered only too well the many mishaps we'd had last month, including the final one, when half the house blew off—and I added, "I figure it was just kids. But I'm a little more jumpy than usual, after everything that happened before."

She nodded.

"Richelle and her son are still walking around, right?" They were the two people who had vandalized the house the first time. The second time it had been someone else, and I knew where they were: safely behind lock and key.

"Yes," Grimaldi said. "The Tremaynes paid their fines and walked away. And I don't think they're going to bother you again. Both your husband and the DA's office made it clear that they wouldn't get off as lightly a second time."

"That was nice of Todd." Todd Satterfield, Bob's son—my old boyfriend—is the assistant DA for Maury County. And he didn't owe me anything, especially since I'd thrown him over for Rafe.

"He's a nice man," Grimaldi said, and kept the SUV zooming down the street.

"He and Marley are getting married this summer, I guess."

She nodded. "Your brother is best man. He has all the details if you want to know."

"I'm sure I'll find out when it's time. And if Todd doesn't want me there, watching him marry someone else, that's his prerogative."

"I think he's over you," Grimaldi said dryly. "It all worked out the way it was supposed to."

Good. And even if it hadn't, I would have still chosen Rafe, so there was that.

"What happened with Sergeant Tucker after the other night?" I wanted to know, as we zoomed down the road toward the little town of Damascus, to the south and west of Columbia.

Grimaldi's hands tightened on the wheel for a second. I looked for anything ahead of the car that might have caused the reaction—a squirrel, an oncoming car—and saw nothing. Her voice was even, anyway, when she answered. "He's back at work. Showed up yesterday morning as usual. When I called him into my office and asked him about it, he said he hadn't done anything wrong."

"I'm not sure he did," I said. A little reluctantly, since I wasn't a huge fan of Sergeant Tucker. "The store owner called the police. The shoplifters got away, but Curtis was still there, so it wasn't surprising that Tucker grabbed him. And I don't know what happened before we got there, but it's not impossible that Curtis tried to fight his way out once he realized he was about to be arrested for something he didn't do."

"Or said he didn't do," Grimaldi said.

I glanced at her, but she was staring straight out the windshield, keeping her eyes firmly on the road.

"Yes. Something he said he didn't do. It sounded like he was telling the truth, but what do I know?"

She didn't answer, so I continued. "It wouldn't surprise me if Curtis might have had a moment of panic and tried to get away from Tucker. I guess, to Tucker, it could look like resisting arrest. And he wasn't doing anything to him, other than keeping him in place. Curtis wasn't hurt."

Grimaldi nodded. "Happily for Tucker."

"He wasn't very happy about Rafe coming in and ordering him to leave."

She grimaced. "No. And I heard plenty about that."

No doubt. "The optics—that's what Rafe called them—were bad. But for what it's worth, I don't think Tucker really did anything wrong. It's hard to know what else he could have done under the circumstances."

"He could have kept the kid upright," Grimaldi said. "That would have helped."

Well, yes. But not having been there when it went down, determining whether Tucker had been out of line or not was above my pay grade. "There was no harm done, though. Curtis isn't suing, right? And the only thing that seems to have come from the video, is that Rafe has picked up a stalker. It could have been worse." Riots. Looting. Murder...

"You said there was another video this morning."

I nodded. "The first one was that night. The next day,

someone filmed Rafe outside the police station. So this morning, I went in with him, to see if whoever was still there. I followed a car out of town after he went inside, and that's when I came back and the two of you were dealing with Leslie Yung."

Grimaldi nodded.

"But it wasn't until after that, that the new video was posted. Someone filmed Rafe kissing me when he walked me out."

"So the car you followed wasn't the stalker."

"Unless she realized I was following her, and she decided to follow me back. I never did catch up to her, or see the car again after it turned off the main drag, so it could have happened that way."

Grimaldi nodded. "There are cameras on the corners of the police station. I'll have someone take a look. See if we can catch a glimpse of the car."

"I would appreciate that," I said sincerely. "Let me know if you discover anything."

The tiny flyspeck on the map that is Damascus appeared on the horizon, and a minute later we were in the thick of town. A minute after that, we pulled up in front of a small rambler set on a postage sized lot. I looked around. "This is where Laura Lee Matlock lived?"

Grimaldi nodded.

"Yvonne's house is over there." I pointed across the street and half a block down. "And there is Millie Ruth Durbin's house."

"Who's Millie Ruth Durbin? Another classmate?"

I shook my head. "Teacher. Science or something like that. Rafe had her, I didn't. I think she retired in the couple of years between. She taught Dix and Catherine, I think, but not me."

"But all this was much later than Laura Lee."

"Oh, definitely. Rafe graduated almost fourteen years ago. I graduated almost eleven years ago. Laura Lee was thirty-three, you said, when she died? She would have graduated fifteen years before that, and that was sixteen or seventeen years ago…"

"She might know something," Grimaldi said. "Which house?"

"Ms. Durbin? The little white one with all the flowers. She gardens. And has cats, I think."

Grimaldi gave me a dubious look, but legged it down the street. I grabbed the baby and followed. On the other side of the white pickets, a broad figure started the process of getting from her knees and up to standing.

Millie Ruth Durbin is a dumpling. Short, round, cute, with swaying skirts and a demeanor much younger than her years. When she got upright, she put her grubby gloves on her ample hips and contemplated us.

It took a moment, then… "I know you."

"Savannah Martin," I told her. "Collier now. I married Rafe."

She nodded. "I remember. And this is…?"

I made the introductions. "Tamara Grimaldi's been the chief of police for Columbia since January."

"Sad business about Carter," Millie Ruth said, and stripped the dirty gloves from her chubby little hands. She slapped them against her thigh a couple of times while she contemplated us from under the brim of a ratty sunhat, her eyes bright in the shadows. "We're outside Columbia here, though. Sheriff Satterfield takes care of us."

"We're just doing some legwork," Grimaldi said easily. "Savannah's husband is working with the sheriff of behalf of the TBI, and we're just tying up some loose ends."

Millie Ruth nodded. "Loose ends pertaining to what, exactly?"

"There was a body found at the truck stop down by the

interstate a couple of days ago, and we thought—"

Millie Ruth nodded. "You thought of Laura Lee. Of course."

"Did you know her?"

"From school," Millie Ruth said. "And then later, she moved into the house down the street with Frankie."

"Her husband."

Millie Ruth nodded. "Always in trouble, that boy. I had him in school, too, and he spent more time in the principal's office than in class."

"What happened to him?" I asked. Grimaldi probably had this information already—Laura Lee's husband would have been a viable suspect, I assumed, before the authorities realized she'd been the victim of a serial killer—but if she knew, Grimaldi hadn't mentioned it.

"After Laura Lee died, you mean?" Millie Ruth turned to me. "The kids moved in with her mama. When Frankie got out of prison, he came back into the house for a bit, but it didn't stick, and within a year, he was back in trouble."

"Would you happen to know where I could find him now?" Grimaldi wanted to know.

"I'm sure I don't know," Millie Ruth told her. "He sold the house eventually, took the money and left. Her folks live over in Sunnyside, if that helps."

Grimaldi allowed as to how that helped a lot, and took down the names of Laura Lee's parents. "Savannah tells me you were a teacher at Columbia High."

"I told you that," Millie Ruth said tartly. "Almost forty years I taught. I retired the year before she started." She glanced at me. "Had her sister and brother and her husband in class, though."

"I don't suppose you taught Latin?"

"You suppose right," Millie Ruth said.

"Who did?"

Millie Ruth thought back. "When I first started, Mr. Wilkins was the Latin teacher. Older than God, he retired five or six years after I came on. Dead now, rest his soul." She thought for a moment. "Then we got Mr. Hanson, or maybe Mr. Olson, for a year. But something happened there, something to do with a student, as I recall, and he left under something of a cloud. And now there's Miss Stevens."

"I remember Miss Stevens," I said. "She was there when I attended Columbia High." Not that I'd studied Latin. But I'd known who the Latin teacher was. "Did Laura Lee take Latin? Or Frankie?"

Millie Ruth giggled. "I doubt that very much. Not really scholars, the two of them."

I had assumed as much. Scholars, from what I know about them, don't usually end up in prison or working at truck stops.

We bid Millie Ruth a polite goodbye, and went back to the SUV.

"About Frankie's prison record…" I said, when the car was rolling down the street.

Grimaldi nodded. "I'll pull the records. But I know for a fact that he was locked up when his wife was killed. He was cleared as a suspect because of it."

"He might have killed the others, though. You said the origin kill may have tipped the serial killer over the edge, right? Maybe the murder of his wife, by someone else, tipped Frankie over the edge. He wasn't there to protect her, and she got murdered. That would be enough to tip anyone over the edge."

Not into serial murder, of course, but into depression and self-flagellation and guilt.

"Possible," Grimaldi admitted. "If he's been in and out of prison for the past sixteen years, there might have been enough time between sentences to commit the murders."

Her eyes were distant, looking beyond the road and into

her own head. Behind us, Damascus faded into the background. Grimaldi added, "It would explain the long cooling-off period between murders. There are usually only two things that'll keep a serial killer from killing, and those are…"

"Death and incarceration," I said, since I've watched my share of *Dateline* and *48 Hours*.

Grimaldi nodded. "I'll get the records, and we'll see whether there's any overlap between Frankie's periods of freedom and the murders. That would make it simple."

It would. "Are you certain the Roman numeral I on Laura Lee's arm was actually a Roman numeral I and not just a scratch? Because if it is Frankie, and he thought it was a numeral I, he could have started marking his own victims from that."

"If he didn't study Latin," Grimaldi said, "he'd be more likely to go with the usual tally method, most likely. They're not Serif letters. They're Sans Serif."

I blinked at her, and she added, "The I doesn't have the little line at the top and the bottom. It's just a single stroke with the knife. Like a tally."

"Oh." It had been a while since I'd worked on my magnum opus, *Bedded by the Bedouin*, but I knew what she was talking about. "Arial instead of Times New Roman."

"Yes," Grimaldi said. "I'll check the crime scene photos from back then, and see if the line on Laura Lee's arm looked like it might have been an accidental slash. Maybe he uses a knife to threaten them. Maybe she resisted and it's a defensive wound."

"It's worth checking out. And if it looks like it might be, then Frankie might be a viable suspect." If he'd had time between his various prison sentences to kill seventeen other women. And his prison record, once Grimaldi pulled it, would tell us that.

"Where to now?" I added.

"I figured we'd hit the high school before they close for the day, see if we can get contact information, or any other information, for Mr. Hanson or Olson, or Ms. Stevens. Mr. Wilkins is dead, so it can't be him."

No. Not if one person had committed all the murders. If one person had started and another person had picked up where that person left off, then it was possible that Wilkins was involved.

"An apprentice situation?" Grimaldi tilted her head in thought. "That's a possibility. Serial killers do sometimes have them."

"And copycats," I said. Again, because I've watched *Dateline* and *48 Hours*.

She nodded. "The numerals are information we haven't released. It's known that the bodies are marked, and that's how we know they're part of the same series, but the specific marking is a closely guarded secret. We need that kind of information for when we catch the killer."

"I guess maybe it would have been better not to ask Millie Ruth about the Latin. So as not to give her any ideas."

"I'm not worried about Millie Ruth," Grimaldi said and steered the SUV back toward Columbia High.

Walking up the steps to the front doors of the school was like stepping back in time. "I don't think I've been back here since I graduated. The reunion last year was somewhere else."

And the less said about that, the better. It had been a bloody mess, and I mean that literally.

Grimaldi nodded. "I haven't been back to mine since I graduated, either. For a reunion or anything else."

She was a few years older than me, I knew. "How long since you finished high school?"

She shot me a look. "Fifteen years."

She was a year older than Rafe, then. Two older than Dix.

Not that that mattered. If the two of them didn't care, why should I?

And since their relationship, whatever it was, was none of my business either, I didn't say anything about it. Instead I looked around at the long hallway that ran through the middle of the building. "It smells just like I remember." Of pencils and cafeteria food and sweaty gym socks and teenage angst.

Grimaldi smirked. "You couldn't pay me to go back to high school."

Me, either. Although it had had its moments. I dredged up the memory of a teenage Rafe, in a basketball jersey and with his hair in cornrows, swaggering down the hallway while everyone—me included—gave him a wide berth.

He'd told me once he'd liked me back then, but beyond a flirtatious wink and a cheeky "Looking good, sugar!"—to which I had responded with an upturned nose—he hadn't done anything about it. I was, as he'd said, jail bait, and I came with an older brother and that older brother's best friend, who wouldn't have thought twice about ganging up on him.

With a sigh, I popped the memory bubble and followed Grimaldi through the door into the main office, and from there, into the lair of the principal, Mrs. Halliburton.

She'd been around when I was here, too, but as assistant principal then, if memory served. She looked about the same: maybe a little grayer in the hair and a little bigger around the middle, but otherwise the same. "Yes?" she said briskly, eying Grimaldi's badge, "what can I do for the Columbia PD?"

Grimaldi explained that she was gathering information on a local cold case that had come across her desk recently. "The murder of Laura Lee Matlock. I understand she went to school here?"

"Yes," Mrs. Halliburton said, "but she graduated at least a decade before she died. She was in her thirties then."

Grimaldi nodded pleasantly. "I'm aware. We're just

checking on a couple of loose threads. I don't suppose I could have access to the yearbooks for the years she attended school here? It would only take a few minutes."

Mrs. Halliburton sighed, like it was putting her out considerably, but she got up from her desk and went to the door and told the dragon at the front desk to pull the yearbooks. The receptionist got to work, and Grimaldi slid out the door with a glance at me. I took it to mean that it was my task to keep Mrs. Halliburton busy for the couple of minutes this was going to take.

I gave her a winning smile. "I don't know whether you remember me, but I used to attend school here. Savannah Martin."

She looked me up and down. "Of course I remember."

It didn't look like the memory brought her any pleasure whatsoever, either.

I looked around. "I don't think I spent any time in the principal's office back then."

She smiled. Tightly. "Of course not. You were a well-behaved family, as I recall."

We had been, overall. Catherine had had her short phase of rebellion in high school—dating Darrell Skinner, of all things!—but she'd kept it so quiet I hadn't known about it until last fall, when Darrell and all the other Skinners got themselves killed. And as for me, I hadn't started acting out until a long time past high school.

I switched Carrie's car seat from one arm to the other—it's heavy when you have to stand around holding it—and the baby cooed. Mrs. Halliburton zeroed in on her.

"Yours?" she asked after a second.

I nodded. "She takes after my husband."

There was a moment's silence when we both contemplated Carrie. In case I've neglected to mention it, she's a very pretty baby, with Rafe's skin and dark curls, but my eyes, surrounded by long, curving lashes.

"You married the Collier boy," Mrs. Halliburton said eventually.

I nodded. "Yes. I did." And she clearly remembered him, too. But probably not because he'd been so well-behaved.

"How is that working out?"

"Just fine," I said. What did she expect me to say?

Oh, wait. I knew what she expected. For Rafe to be the same screw-up everyone thought he was in high school—with some cause, I'll admit. She probably thought he'd have left us already.

"It's the best decision I've ever made," I added, just in case she was in doubt.

Between you and me, it might not have been. Divorcing Bradley might have been better. If I hadn't done that, I wouldn't have gotten my real estate license, and if I hadn't gotten my real estate license, I wouldn't have been in the office the morning Brenda Puckett died, and I wouldn't have gotten the call to go out and meet Rafe outside Mrs. Jenkins's house, and if I hadn't done that, we might not have met again, and then someone else might be standing here right now, holding Rafe's baby.

But either way, it came to the same thing. Rafe was still the best thing that had ever happened to me.

"How's your family doing?" Mrs. Halliburton changed the subject. Or maybe it wasn't so much a change of subject as a question as to whether my family approved of my husband.

"They're fine," I told her. "Catherine and Jonathan are still married, with three kids. Dix is slowly getting over losing Sheila, and Mother is living in sin with Sheriff Satterfield. She adores Rafe. Like, seriously adores him. Couldn't love him any more if she'd given birth to him."

Mrs. Halliburton didn't respond. I'm not sure whether she just didn't know what to say, or she didn't want to say whatever came to mind. Either way, we stood in silence for the minute or two until Grimaldi stuck her head back into the room. "Thank you, Principal Halliburton. I have what I came for."

She caught my eye and motioned with her head toward the entrance. I gave the principal a pleasant smile. "Nice to see you again, Mrs. Halliburton. I'll tell Rafe you said hi. I'm sure he spent a lot more time in this office than I did."

Mrs. Halliburton nodded weakly. I turned my back on her and followed Grimaldi through the outer office, down the hallway, and outside.

"Problem?" she asked when we'd reached the SUV and I was putting Carrie's seat onto the base.

I glanced over. "Just someone else who remembers all the worst things about Rafe. It gets old."

She nodded and opened her car door. "Her loss."

I guess it was. I scooted into the passenger seat next to her and put Halliburton and high school in the past, where it belonged.

Nine

"Did you find out anything interesting?"

"Nineteen boys took Latin during the years Laura Lee Matlock—Drimmel, back then—went to Columbia High," Grimaldi said, turning the key in the ignition. "Three of them matriculated after her freshman year."

So they were three years older. The same as Rafe is to me.

"In addition to the three boys who graduated after her freshman year, four more graduated after her sophomore year. Three after her junior year, and two after her senior year. Those two, she went to school with all four years of high school. Then there were four the following year, four the year after that, and then a single male student whose first year of high school was Laura Lee's last."

"Latin didn't draw a big crowd, did it?" Thinking back on my own high school days, I couldn't recall many students studying it then, either.

"No," Grimaldi said. "Most of the kids took living languages. In addition to the nineteen boys over that seven year period, there were also twelve girls who took Latin. But since our unsub is male, there's no sense in focusing on them."

No. I couldn't think of any reason why we should. "I assume you've got everyone's names?"

"I took pictures of the pages," Grimaldi said, patting her pocket. "And the assistant principal looked up Ms. Stevens's address. She didn't know where to find Mr. Jurgensson."

"That was his name? The guy who only lasted a year?" Not Hanson or Olson?

"Jurgensson," Grimaldi confirmed, spelling it for good measure. "That, I did write down, because I wanted to make sure I had it right."

"I don't suppose the receptionist told you why Jurgensson lost his job?"

"Sexual misconduct," Grimaldi said, "like Ms. Durbin said."

"He slept with a student?"

"I'm not sure what he did. The woman in reception didn't work there then, and doesn't know the details. I'll have to check the files and see whether an official complaint was filed. Statutory rape is a crime. If not, we'll have to find someone who was around then, who's willing to give us the details."

"Millie Ruth might," I said.

"If she didn't tell us already, I don't know how much she knows or is willing to say. It would be better to find someone else. Someone who knows and doesn't mind talking."

"Ms. Stevens might know." She hadn't been around until the next year, but she might have been told the details.

"I'll check," Grimaldi said. "Are you ready to go home?"

Hard to say whether that was an attempt to get rid of me or not. "Not necessarily," I said. "Is there somewhere else you'd like to go? To Sunnyside to see Laura Lee's parents, maybe?"

"I'd rather do some checking before I do that," Grimaldi answered. "When I talk to them, I already want to know Frankie's arrest record, and whether he could be involved or not. He's their son-in-law, and depending on how they feel about him, then and now, it would be good to know the score."

"Maybe they can tell you what was going on with Laura Lee during the period when Frankie was locked up. Something they weren't comfortable telling the police back then. Maybe she had another boyfriend or had hooked up with an old one, or something."

"Maybe," Grimaldi said pessimistically, "but I'm not sure what good it'll do if she did. This guy doesn't stalk his victims. Not as far as we know."

"She was the first, though. The origin kill. You said the methodology might be different."

Grimaldi didn't answer, and I added, "That's why we're here, looking into this, right? Because she was the first victim and the killer might have known her better than the others?"

"Yes," Grimaldi admitted. "But I still want to check Frankie's periods of incarceration before I talk to Laura Lee's parents."

No problem. "Back to the police station, then?"

"Might as well," Grimaldi said. "Do you want me to take you home first? Or do you want to come with me?"

I checked the dashboard clock. "It's almost quitting time, isn't it? Rafe doesn't have SWAT practice or anything like that tonight, does he?"

"That was yesterday," Grimaldi said.

"Maybe I'll just come with you, then, and wait around for an hour—maybe you'd let me look at the surveillance footage from this morning while I wait?—and then I can drive home with him."

"And stake your claim in front of Agent Yung again?" She sounded amused.

"I'm not worried," I said sturdily. And then, when the look she gave me was amused as well, I added, "She didn't sound like she was interested in him that way. And I don't think he'd cheat. But I'll admit that women like her make me feel dumpy and like I don't deserve what I have."

"I've seen the two of you together," Grimaldi said. "And I've seen you separately. You have nothing to worry about."

Good to know. "I just feel like a slug, you know? Big and

blobby and slow. And she's so tiny and trim and perfect, and she can probably kick ass while mine's twice the size it used to be, because I still can't fit into my pre-pregnancy clothes…"

"You're fine," Grimaldi said, her lips twitching. "You're not a slug. You're not big or blobby. You have a husband who loves you, and a beautiful baby. But you're right: she probably can kick your ass. So can I, if it comes to that."

"I don't mind you," I said. "You're not after my husband."

"She's not, either. If she were interested on a personal level, that kiss would have told her how unlikely it is that he'd be interested in her. And I disabused her of the notion that he's a criminal. She didn't like it much, but she believed me."

"Then I guess she's going to have to settle for arresting the killer," I said, "when we find him."

Grimaldi nodded. "Although I hope to slap those handcuffs on myself. I don't mind if she's there, though. Just as long as she's not getting in my way."

"Sounds like a plan," I told her, as we swung into the parking lot behind the police station, into the prominent slot reserved for the chief of police, and she cut the engine.

Inside the front doors, she sat Carrie and me down behind the front desk with the young man on duty.

"Officer Rehman." She gave him a nod.

"Ma'am." He blushed, and reminded me rather forcibly of my buddy Officer Truman in Nashville, who did the same thing whenever someone female spoke to him.

The resemblance ended there, though. They were both young, but George Truman was a peach-fuzzed blond, while Rehman was as black-haired and dark-eyed as Truman was fair.

"This is Mrs. Collier and her little girl." Grimaldi nodded to me and Carrie, awake and cooing in her car seat. "I want you to show her the camera footage from outside the building this morning."

"Ma'am?" Rehman reddened further.

"Someone filmed my husband and me outside the front door earlier," I said, before Grimaldi could yell at Rehman and make him feel worse. "The video appeared on social media. We're trying to figure out who it was."

"Oh." Rehman turned to one of the computers and began to manipulate buttons. Grimaldi withdrew, but not without an annoyed shake of her head. I waved her off before I looked at the eight little screens that each showed a small part of the police station.

"This one." From the angle, it looked like it was placed in the corner above the front door. "This one and that one." One on each side of the building, turned toward the middle, filming the street and the cars going by. "Are any of the others overlooking the front?"

Rehman shook his head. "Just those three. What was the angle of the video?"

"I'll show it to you," I said, and dug my phone out of the bag I'd dropped on the floor. It was already cued up on the video, from watching it before, and I started it playing and handed it to Rehman. And watched him blush a bright, painful red as he watched.

He handed it back without meeting my eyes. "Looks like whoever filmed it was parked down on the other end. If he—"

"She," I said.

Rehman nodded. "—if she didn't cross in front of the police station before parking, it isn't likely we have her on camera."

No, it wasn't. It was most likely she'd come from outside downtown up to the police station, rather than going around City Hall and down the street past the police station before parking. Most people tend to avoid driving straight through the town square if they can avoid it.

"Just see if there's anything helpful," I told Rehman. "Anything would help. We have no idea who this person is, other than that she keeps hanging around and filming my husband. And since he has a habit of attracting nutcases, it's concerning."

"He's the one who got shot last month," Rehman said, eyes on the screen, "right?"

I nodded. "It wasn't bad. The bullet lodged in his vest and only broke a couple of ribs, so it could have been worse. But it isn't the first time it's happened, and it probably won't be the last. And I don't like psychos after my husband."

"Here's something." Rehman stopped the video that was scrolling and rewound it. "This is the two of you... um..."

Kissing. I nodded.

"This is the camera above the front door."

He switched screens. "This is the one on the left corner of the building. Right hand from where we're sitting now."

I nodded. The angle of the picture was different. Rafe and I were much farther away, off on the edge of the screen, and the rest of the shot was taken up by the street in front of the police station, the sidewalk across the street, the bottom halves of the buildings over there, and some parked cars.

"This car—" Rehman pointed to one of them, "pulled up during the minute or two you were inside. Here you are—"

He scrolled farther back, and showed me myself chugging up the hill and parking in front of the police station, then grabbing Carrie from the backseat and hauling her and her carrier up the steps to the front door and through. No sooner had I disappeared inside—the door hadn't completely closed behind me yet—before a small, light-colored compact came into view on the other side of the screen. It zipped into a parking space on the other side of the street, and stopped. I kept watching, but nothing happened. Nobody opened the door and got out. Whoever was inside stayed in their seat—or perhaps moved around the interior of the car—but didn't leave the vehicle.

My eyes narrowed. "That's suspicious."

Rehman didn't answer, just kept watching.

The next thing that happened, other than that a car or two passed by, slowly, was that the front door of the police station opened again. I came through, followed by Rafe. He walked me to the Volvo and put the car seat with Carrie into the rear of the car. Then he kissed me.

"Keep your eye on the other car," Rehman said softly. This time he didn't blush. I guess repeated exposure to the clip had boosted his immunity, or maybe he was just too focused on what he was doing. He rewound again, to where Rafe was coming out the door. "Look." He pointed to the other car. "The window's going down."

It was. Lowering smoothly. I could see the outline of a phone appearing in the gap.

"Can you zoom in on that?"

"I can try," Rehman said, "but it's going to pixelate badly."

He tried, and it pixelated badly, the image going more and more grainy the closer he got to it. "I can play with it," he said, dark eyes fastened on the screen. "See if I can clean it up a little. But it's dark in there."

It *was* dark inside the car. The windows were tinted—I was pretty sure this was the same car I had followed out of downtown earlier; the driver must have circled around, back to the police station. Very cunning behavior. Quick thinking, too.

And it had certainly resulted in a memorable video.

At any rate, even if Rehman could sharpen the image enough, there were no guarantees that we'd be able to see whoever was inside the car. Not with the dark windows, and the way they kept the light from penetrating the interior.

"Keep the video running, please. The car has to pull out eventually. When that happens, maybe we can see the license plate."

Rehman hit the button and let the video scroll. On the tiny

screen, Rafe finished kissing me, and bounded up the steps to the police station again. The Volvo stayed still while I gathered myself. So did the little compact. The Volvo pulled out, presenting a nice, clear view of the rear license plate to the camera, and rolled off down the hill, past the compact. The car window was closed again now, I saw.

The Volvo disappeared out of the frame. The compact stayed for another minute—the seconds ticked by as Rehman and I both stared at it, unblinking—before it also moved. But instead of following me, it came toward the camera.

"I'm pretty sure that's the same car I followed this morning," I said, as it rolled past the police station. "If you switch to the camera on the other side, we might get lucky and see the license plate."

Rehman manipulated the buttons. As the compact disappeared out of sight on one side of the screen, it jumped back, disconcertingly, on the other. The license plate was visible, but hard to read. It was some sort of specialty plate, with a landscape of colored sky and dark hills, and the black silhouette of some kind of animal on one side. The black numbers of the plate were difficult to make out against the darkness of the bottom half of the plate.

"That's a three," I said, "or an eight, or a nine..."

"Maybe an O."

Could be an O. Or a Q. Or anything else with a round top. Like an S or even a C or G.

"I'll play with it," Rehman said again, as the compact zoomed out of sight around the corner.

I sat back. "I'd appreciate that. This woman—this person— makes me nervous."

Rehman nodded. "We don't want another situation like the one last month."

No, we didn't. "Thank you," I told him, and gathered up my bag and my baby. "I should go find Grimaldi."

"Straight back to the end of the hall." He gestured to the door.

I told him thanks, and headed out, leaving him to pore over the video footage.

At the end of the hallway, Grimaldi was sitting behind her desk peering at the computer. I put Carrie's seat on the floor and made myself comfortable in one of the visitor's chairs. "Anything?"

"A few details." She dragged her eyes from the monitor and leaned back. "You?"

"We found footage of someone filming," I said. "But the license plate was hard to make out. Officer Rehman said he'd play with it and see if he could make it any sharper."

Grimaldi nodded. "What kind of car?"

"Some sort of light-colored small one." I hadn't been paying enough attention, to be honest. Too intent on making out the plate to focus on the insignia. "Pretty sure it was the same one I followed down the hill this morning. She must have doubled back and come in the other way."

Grimaldi nodded.

"I think it was a Japanese import. But whether it was a Toyota or Honda or Nissan or Mazda, I couldn't tell you. They all look very much the same to me."

"Rehman'll figure it out," Grimaldi said.

I hoped so. "What about you? What did you discover?"

"Not much," Grimaldi said. "I'm still waiting for Frankie Matlock's incarceration record. I need it to be pretty detailed—if he had twenty-four hours furlough at any point in the past sixteen years to go to his grandmother's funeral, I need to know about it—so it won't be immediate."

Understood. "Anything else?"

"Still tracking down Jurgensson," Grimaldi said, "but I have narrowed it down to the single year he spent here."

"Did that coincide with any of Laura Lee's years at

Columbia High?"

"As a matter of fact," Grimaldi said, "he was there her junior year."

"When she was sixteen."

Grimaldi nodded. "No reason to think she was the student he misbehaved with any more than anyone else, though. Whoever it was didn't file a police report, so there's no official record one way or the other."

"But it could have been Laura Lee."

"Could have," Grimaldi said. "She was a student there, so that would have given him opportunity. That doesn't mean it was her. There were a lot of other kids at Columbia High that year, too. I'll have to find someone who remembers, who's willing to talk."

It made a nice, little syllogism, though. If syllogism was the word I was looking for. If Mr. Jurgensson had had an affair with a student and lost his job over it, it had probably destroyed his career. No other school was likely to hire him after that. And if he'd lost not only that particular job, but his ability to find another, he might have held a grudge. And over the next decade and a half, that grudge could have turned to obsession. Lacking the means to make a living in his chosen profession, he might have taken a job driving trucks. And sixteen years later, if he came across Laura Lee again, slinging hash and selling her body at the truck stop in Columbia, things might have boiled over. And then, after he killed her in a fit of lunacy, he went on to recreate that murder again and again, marking each victim with a Latin numeral.

It sounded like something that belonged on *Dateline* or *48 Hours*, all right.

I shook myself, since the thought was creepy. "Do you know where he is now?"

"I'm still looking," Grimaldi said. "There's no sign of him. His social security number hasn't paid taxes since he taught at

Columbia High, but there's also no death certificate on file anywhere. Or not one I've found so far."

"So he's either in a shallow grave somewhere, and hasn't been found—or identified—or he's living and working under someone else's name."

"Or under the table," Grimaldi said. "Or he's made it across the border to Mexico, and is living the high life, drinking tequila on the beach and teaching people to surf."

I suppose. "Any idea which scenario is more likely?"

"No," Grimaldi said. "But once I figure out who the girl was—or boy—I'll hopefully be able to eliminate at least the possibility that he's rotting in a shallow grave somewhere."

Because if he was dead, it was likely related to the statutory rape he'd committed here in Columbia, and if so, the girl's—or boy's—family hit the top of the suspect list.

I tilted my head to look at her. "Do you feel like we're getting anywhere? Or just turning over rocks, looking for slimy things to crawl out?"

"A lot of police work is turning over rocks and looking for slimy things," Grimaldi said. "But these are two reasonably strong strings to pull. All in all, I think we're making progress."

Good to know. "Any idea when Rafe is expected back?"

"I imagine it won't be long," Grimaldi said, with a glance at the clock. "He's been gone all afternoon."

She glanced at the door. "In fact…"

Yes, I heard him, too. And so did Carrie, it seemed. She started gurgling louder and kicking her feet harder. When the half-open door opened further, with a knock that was perfunctory at best, my daughter squealed at the sight of her daddy.

"Hi there, pretty girl." He bent and tickled her feet before turning to me. "Didn't expect to see you here."

"Grimaldi and I have been hanging out," I said, and tilted my head back for the quick kiss he dropped on my upturned mouth.

Not until all that was done, did Rafe greet his boss. And not in a very subservient manner, either. "What are you getting up to with my wife?"

"We've been to Damascus and Columbia High." Grimaldi nodded him into the second chair in front of the desk. "This guy's first victim was local. A Damascus woman who was picked up at the same truck stop where the latest victim was dumped. We—" She glanced at me, "thought we'd do some digging into the cold case."

Rafe leaned back on the uncomfortable chair. I guess Grimaldi had picked them so people wouldn't linger long. "Any luck?"

Grimaldi updated him on Frankie Matlock and Mr. Jurgensson. "Laura Lee didn't take Latin, and there's nothing to indicate she was the student he misbehaved with. But there's no reason she couldn't be, either. They were there the same year."

Rafe nodded. "Even if she was, that don't mean nothing. She could have, like you said, misbehaved with a teacher when she was sixteen, and gotten killed when she was thirty-three, and there's no connection."

"Of course," Grimaldi said. "What's new on your end?"

"Yung's a pain in the—" He glanced at me and changed what he'd been about to say to, "butt."

"It was probably disappointing to her when you turned out to be a hero and not a criminal," I said.

He grinned in my direction. "Not so much a hero. But I'm sure she was looking forward to catching me red-handed. Too bad."

"Did she give you a hard time?" Grimaldi wanted to know, not that there was much she could do about it if Agent Yung was. Yung didn't work for Grimaldi and wouldn't be open to taking orders or suggestions from that quarter.

"Nothing I couldn't handle. She tried to get something going with Bob—him being a good old Southern boy and all—but he wasn't having it."

I hid a smile. No, acting the hotshot FBI agent with the sheriff wouldn't have won her many points. He isn't a Southern bumpkin and wouldn't have agreed to play one for her. He is a gentleman, though, so I imagined he'd probably been more pleasant than perhaps she deserved.

"Once we got that straightened out," Rafe added, "she consented to give us all a presentation of the case as a whole, from Victim One down through the line. She presented the FBI profile—"

Grimaldi arched her brows, and he shook his head. "Nothing we didn't expect. Most likely male, most likely white, most likely between fifty and fifty-five, but could be younger or older by a decade or more. Most likely a long haul trucker, but don't disregard other folks who move up and down the interstate—"

"Who else moves up and down the interstate?" I injected, and they both glanced at me. Down in the car seat, Carrie kept gurgling and trying to chew on her toes. I deduced she'd probably start asking for food soon. She was getting pretty close to the age when we could start feeding her solids—or semi-solids—and that would help her stay full longer, and would keep me from having to nurse every couple hours around the clock.

"Bus drivers," Rafe said, and Grimaldi added, "But it's hard to find the time to murder women when you've got a schedule and a bus full of passengers to get somewhere on time."

Rafe nodded. "Could just be somebody who lives in Mobile but has family in Ann Arbor, and a couple times a year he makes the trek to see his grandma."

Could be. The murders were infrequent enough that that

wasn't a bad idea. "How do we find him if that's the case?"

Grimaldi made a face. "It's harder. But if that's the case, he's someone who'd stand out at a truck stop, so someone might have noticed him."

Maybe.

She turned to Rafe. "Any luck on the surveillance videos?"

"Nothing out of the ordinary," Rafe told her. "One of Bob's guys has been over every second of the video, for several hours before the body was discovered, and there's nothing to see. Just the usual trucks coming and going. No passenger cars going past the camera. But if this guy routinely drives this route, he'd most likely know where the cameras are located, and be able to avoid them."

Grimaldi sighed.

"We're trying to trace as many of the trucks as we can," Rafe added. "Most are marked with a company name on the cab or the cargo. Bob's got a couple deputies on it, and Yung offered some FBI grunts if we need more help."

Grimaldi nodded. "But if this guy is a truck driver, and he's familiar with the truck stop, he'd make sure he wasn't caught on camera."

"The camera's hard to avoid if you're driving an eighteen-wheeler," Rafe answered. "A small passenger car, you can maybe skim underneath. But not a full size truck. If he was there—and he was—we most likely have footage of him."

"So now all we—" Grimaldi caught herself, "all *you* have to do, is identify all the trucks and all the drivers, and then determine which of them had the opportunity—over the past sixteen years—to commit eighteen murders."

"If it was easy," Rafe said, "everybody'd be doing it."

That got a smile, at any rate. But I got the impression that Grimaldi was feeling overwhelmed with the task she had set herself.

"Where do we start tomorrow morning?" I asked, to take

her mind off the enormity of the job and put it back on the individual steps we, and Rafe, and Agent Yung and Sheriff Satterfield, would have to take, to figure out who the killer was, and catch him.

She shook herself, more of a mental shake than a physical one. "You want to come with me?"

"I thought we were a team," I said. "You, me, and Carrie."

She smiled. It was faint, but there. "I'll come pick you up. Nine?"

Nine would be fine. It was a Saturday, but with the current case, and Agent Yung in town snapping the whip, I was sure Rafe would have to work. Without Grimaldi, I'd just be sitting there by myself all day.

"Anything you need me to do overnight? Anyone I need to talk to?"

She hesitated. "I can do it myself..."

"But?"

"If Laura Lee was thirty-three sixteen years ago, and left high school fifteen years before that, she'd be around fifty now. A little too young for your mother—"

"My mother grew up in Georgia, anyway," I said. "She's one of the Georgia Calverts."

Grimaldi gave me a sardonic look, and Rafe chuckled. I blushed. "Yes, that's too young for my mother. She's almost sixty. Audrey's sixty-one. So was my dad. And my aunt Regina is a few years older. But she works for the local paper. She might have taken an interest in the case back when it happened. I can check with her whether she remembers anything."

"I'd appreciate it," Grimaldi said formally.

"Don't mention it." I grabbed the diaper bag, Rafe grabbed the baby, and we headed out.

Ten

My aunt and uncle live in a small, pink Victorian cottage in the center of Sweetwater, just a block or two from the Albertsons, and about the same from the love nest Mother shares with the sheriff.

Aunt Regina is my father's sister, a couple of years older, and she's the gossip columnist for the local paper, the *Sweetwater Reporter*. It's more make-work than anything else, I guess, or at least it doesn't pay her a living wage, but Uncle Sid had a good job until he retired at sixty-two, so they don't need, and never did need, Aunt Regina's salary. Now, Uncle Sid spends his time golfing, while Aunt Regina does what she's always done, and sticks her nose into other people's business, for pay.

She was in the yard when we pulled up outside the fence, kneeling on some sort of little foam board—easier on aging knees than the hard ground, I figured—and she was pulling weeds from one of the flower beds. In addition to gossip, gardening is one of Aunt Regina's passions.

She turned when she heard the car pull up and stop, and shaded her eyes from the late afternoon sun still hanging above the rooftops across the street. "Oh," she said after a second, "it's you two."

"Three." I pulled Carrie's seat out of Rafe's—or the police department's—Chevy and headed for the gate. Rafe was there before me, and swung it open, gallantly, before he sauntered across the grass—his saunter can cover ground about as quickly as I can run—and extended a hand to Aunt Regina.

She contemplated it, contemplated her gardening glove, and decided to hell with it. She put her hands in his, both of them, and let him haul her to her feet. "Thank you."

"The pleasure was all mine," my husband assured her, with a wink. "Savannah has a couple questions."

"You want to come inside?" Aunt Regina trotted toward the steps to the porch, pulling her gardening gloves off as she went. "I have some lemonade, or I can make tea or coffee."

"It won't take long," I said, "and it's nice out here."

"Then have a seat." Aunt Regina gestured to the porch swing. "You two sit there. I'll take this precious bundle." She fell on the car seat and extricated Carrie while Rafe and I made ourselves comfortable in the swing. He pushed off with his foot, and while the swing squeaked ominously, it didn't creak like it was about to give way.

"Uncle Sid golfing?" I asked, while Aunt Regina held Carrie on her lap and cooed at her.

She nodded, and spared me a single glance before turning her attention back to Carrie. Aunt Regina and Uncle Sid married late, and never had kids of their own, so they've more or less adopted us and ours. Between Catherine and Jonathan, Rafe and me, and Dix, there are now six grandchildren. Plus David, but he's rarely in Sweetwater.

Catherine and Jonathan are probably done. Dix may not be. He's only thirty, and if he gets remarried, his new wife might want kids of her own. And Darcy has no children at all so far. If she and Nolan figure out their relationship, Aunt Regina might end up with a few more.

But all of that was beside the point at the moment. I cleared my throat. "I wanted to ask you something."

"Go ahead," Aunt Regina said.

"I guess you heard about the dead woman found down by the interstate?"

She made a face. "Terrible doings. But she was from Nashville, wasn't she?" And no problem of ours, in other words.

I nodded. "Rafe's investigating."

Aunt Regina arched her brows at him. "I thought it was the sheriff's case."

"It's everybody's case," Rafe said. "Just this morning, we had an FBI agent drive in."

"Goodness gracious." Aunt Regina turned Carrie around and cradled her, the better to pay attention to what we were saying. "That's a lot of manpower for a dead prostitute."

"It's a serial killer case," I told her, and watched her eyes widen while Rafe's brows lowered.

"Darlin'—"

"We have to tell her," I said. "Otherwise, how is she going to understand why we want to know?"

He didn't say anything, but he shook his head. "You can't publish nothing," he told Aunt Regina sternly. "Some of this is information we don't want to get around. Right now, nobody's made the connection between this murder and any of the others, and the longer we can sit on that, the better."

Aunt Regina nodded, as innocently as if butter didn't melt in her mouth. "Of course, Rafe."

He gave her a narrow-eyed stare—I didn't blame him—but she added, "You can trust me. I won't betray a confidence from a family member. I promise."

"Then go ahead," he told me, "ask her."

I turned to Aunt Regina, but she was already talking. "Serial killer?"

"Eighteen women," I said, "that we know of—"

Her eyes widened.

"I'm serious, Aunt Regina. This is a huge case. A really big deal. You can't leak it."

"I promised I wouldn't, Savannah." She bounced Carrie up and down as the baby started to fret. "Just tell me what I can do for you."

"She wants food." I reached for her. "Do you mind…?"

Aunt Regina shook her head and handed the baby over. "So eighteen dead. What is it you want from me? I didn't know this woman. And to the best of my knowledge, I don't know any serial killers."

"The first victim," I said, while I hoisted up my blouse and got Carrie situated, "was local. Laura Lee Matlock."

She leaned back, a sort of instinctual recoil. "Laura Lee."

"You remember her."

She glanced from me to Rafe and back. "Yes, of course. We don't have that many murders around here. I went to the funeral. But there was no talk about a serial killer back then."

"She was the first," Rafe said. "It took a couple more victims for anyone to see the pattern."

"Was there any talk at the time?" I wanted to know. "Anything anyone was saying that might pertain?"

Aunt Regina didn't answer immediately, and I added, "The sheriff is pulling the old records, of course, and sharing them with the TBI and FBI and Chief Grimaldi. But I was wondering whether you remembered anything that wouldn't be in the official reports."

Aunt Regina leaned back, and her eyes—dark like Catherine's and Dad's—grew unfocused. "She was working at the truck stop down by the interstate. Picking up extra cash because her husband was in prison. Can't remember what he did to land himself there… got drunk and in a fight, maybe."

I exchanged a glance with Rafe, who'd landed himself in prison after getting in a fight, too. His lips twitched, but he didn't say anything, just nodded to Aunt Regina. *Pay attention, Savannah.*

"Her kids were with her mama," Aunt Regina said. "She had two, I think. An older girl and a baby boy. They'd be in their teens or early twenties now."

They would, and I didn't know why I hadn't thought about them.

But they were too young to be involved in this, and probably wouldn't be able to remember much about what had happened. Nor would anyone have shared many of the details, I imagined, with the victim's young children.

"Frankie got out of prison, but the kids stayed with the Drimmels. He hung around for a while, and then disappeared. Not sure whether he moved away, or something happened to him. I know he went to prison at least a couple more times."

I nodded. There was nothing there that Grimaldi and Millie Ruth Durbin hadn't already told me. "Can you remember a Latin teacher at Columbia High whose name was Jurgensson? That would have been a decade and a half earlier, probably."

"A Latin teacher?" She thought about it. "Can't say that I do. Why?"

"He lost his job for sexual misconduct," Rafe said, and Aunt Regina's eyes widened.

"Of course. Why didn't you say so?"

I had my mouth open to tell her that I had said so, but she barreled right over me. "It was a very big deal when it happened. That kind of thing was less common twenty-five or thirty years ago, or maybe we just didn't hear about it as much."

Maybe not. "But you remember it?"

"Of course," Aunt Regina said. "I just didn't remember the man's name. But everyone knew that a teacher from the high school had been let go for improper attentions toward a student."

Improper attentions... "Do you know which student?"

"Not Laura Lee Drimmel," Aunt Regina said, "if that's

what you're thinking."

No? "Are you sure?"

"As sure as I can be," Aunt Regina said.

"So you know who it was?"

She shook her head. "But I know it wasn't Laura Lee."

"How?" If she didn't know who the student was, how could she know definitively that it hadn't been Laura Lee?

"Because it was one of the boys," Aunt Regina said. And added, when I just sat there with my mouth open, "This was about a decade into the AIDS epidemic. Gay relationships weren't as accepted as they are now."

No. And it's not like they're always accepted now, either. Legally, yes. Legally, a gay couple can get married as easily as a straight couple these days. But there are plenty of people who still aren't OK with it in practice.

Besides, statutory rape is still statutory rape, whether the victim is male or female.

"One of the boys," I said.

Aunt Regina nodded. "There was a lot of talk, and a lot of concern about a lot of things. Whether the teacher had AIDS and had given it to the boy. Whether the teacher would be arrested. Whether the teacher had turned the boy gay. Whether anyone could turn someone else gay."

"I don't think that's possible," I said. Next to me, Rafe made a soft sound of amusement.

"I know, Savannah," Aunt Regina said. "I'm just telling you what was being said. And why I'm sure this was a boy, and not Laura Lee Drimmel."

Yes, it sounded like we could be reasonably sure about that. "But you don't know who it was."

She shook her head. "I don't think I ever knew. Some of the kids might have known, and whispered about it, but nobody told me. And it wasn't someone local. He was from elsewhere in the county, not Sweetwater."

"Who would know?"

"Someone who went to school with him," Aunt Regina said. "Although I don't understand why this matters, Savannah."

I didn't, either, when I thought about it. "If it had been Laura Lee..."

"But it wasn't," my aunt said.

I nodded. "Any idea where Jurgensson ended up?"

"Not a clue. He wasn't local, either. I guess he went back to where he came from."

That made sense. Although he hadn't. Grimaldi had told me that Jurgensson's social security number hadn't filed taxes since he worked at Columbia High. "Anything else you can think of?"

"Nothing pertaining to this," Aunt Regina said. "I'm interested in the videos, though."

"The... oh. The ones of Rafe?"

She nodded. My husband smirked.

"We don't know who's behind those," I said. "I've been trying to find out, but with no luck so far."

"Could be anybody, I imagine," my aunt said.

"Oh, sure." I nodded. "Anyone with two X chromosomes—or an X and Y, if it comes to that—with access to a cell phone and social media. There isn't a woman—or gay man—in existence who doesn't think my husband's hot."

Rafe chuckled. "Thank you, darlin'."

"I was being sarcastic," I said, although there was a certain amount—a rather large amount—of truth to it. "I think it's probably a woman, and not just because she calls herself Jessica Rabbit. It doesn't sound like a moniker a man would choose. But there's a female feel to the whole thing."

"Could just be 'cause you remember Elspeth," Rafe said.

I nodded. "It could. But I'm going to be very surprised if it turns out to be anything but a woman. Or girl. I wonder whether Agent Yung would give me a profile of your stalker if I asked nicely?"

"Couldn't hurt to ask," Rafe said. "You prob'ly wanna be prepared for Yung turning her nose up, though."

"At me? At you? At the idea that this person could have a profile?"

"Oh, I'm sure there's a profile. I'm just not sure Yung's gonna wanna share it."

I narrowed my eyes. "You don't think it's her, do you?"

He laughed. "No, darlin'. She was in Memphis yesterday, and inside the police station when I was kissing you. She couldn't have taken that video."

Right. "I forgot," I said. "Besides, if she had any kind of obsession with you—"

"It'd be for dragging me off to jail." He shook his head. "Don't worry about it, darlin'. But ask her for a profile, by all means. I wanna be there to see her face when you do."

I turned back to my aunt, who'd been following this exchange with interest. "Agent Yung?"

"The FBI agent who showed up this morning. She recognized Rafe from the first video, and from when he was doing undercover work in Memphis. Except she didn't know he was undercover..."

"Good grief," Aunt Regina said. "So she came haring out here hoping to arrest him?"

I nodded. "Grimaldi set her straight. But it looked pretty tense when I walked in on them this morning. Face to face and yelling at each other."

Aunt Regina shook her head, and then looked past me to the street. "Here's Sid."

Yes, indeed. There he was, pulling up to the curb and hoisting his golf clubs out of the trunk of his car. "What are you two planning to do tonight?" I wanted to know. "It's a Friday. Do you have a big night planned?"

"I'm cooking chicken," Aunt Regina said, "and then I imagine we'll watch some TV."

She looked at my face and laughed. "What are your plans, Savannah?"

"I imagine I'll be cooking chicken, too," I said, since that's often what I do, "and we'll end up watching TV…"

"I like TV," Rafe informed us both. "None of the guns are pointed at me, and none of the bullets are lethal."

He had a point. "What kind of chicken?" I asked my aunt.

She smiled. "Enough for four, if you want to stay."

But— "Rain-check," Rafe told her, and made it to his feet just as Uncle Sid reached the front porch and noticed us. "Sid."

"Rafe." Uncle Sid waved him back into the chair and turned to me. "Savannah."

I waved. "Hi, Uncle Sid. I'd get up and give you a hug, but as you can see…"

He nodded, looking from one to the other of us. "Family meeting? Something going on that I need to know about?"

We all hastened to assure him that nothing whatsoever was going on, or nothing he needed to worry about. "A name came up in one of Rafe's cases that we thought Aunt Regina might know something about."

Uncle Sid fitted himself in next to his wife, with a grin at her. "And did she?"

"Not much," Aunt Regina admitted, her tone disgruntled. "It was about that teacher at the high school in Columbia who had sex with the student…"

Uncle Sid was nodding long before she finished the sentence. "I remember that."

"Do you know who it was?"

Rafe and I asked at the same time, and exchanged a look.

"The kid?" Uncle Sid shook his head. "I don't think that was ever revealed. I remember the teacher, though."

"Jurgensson?"

"Kent," Uncle Sid said. "Nice guy. Played golf."

"Do you have any idea what became of him?"

But Uncle Sid didn't. "Haven't seen him since it happened. Poor bastard lost his job, of course, and had a hard time finding another. Last I heard, he was working some menial job in Tupelo or Tucson or someplace like that."

"Who told you that?" Rafe wanted to know.

Uncle Sid turned to him. "He made up part of a golf foursome. One of the other players stayed in touch with him for a bit."

"Name?"

"Art Mullinax," Uncle Sid said. "I just played a round with him this afternoon. But if he's heard anything from Kent in the past ten years, he hasn't said anything about it."

"It's worth checking," Rafe said easily. "Where can I find Art Mullinax?"

Uncle Sid sighed. "He lives on the other side of Columbia, not too far from that house you blew up." He glanced at me. I wanted to protest that I hadn't blown up the house; other people did that, but I decided it was better not to derail him. "Big spread called Daffodil Hill Farm. Him and his wife and about fifty acres."

"I'll have a look," Rafe said. "Don't worry, Sid. I'm not looking to rake up old scandals. And I won't mention your name."

"It won't matter," Uncle Sid said. "Everyone knows who you are, and that you married my niece. When you show up, he'll know who you talked to."

Maybe someone else could go talk to Art, then. Someone other than Rafe. Someone like… oh… Leslie Yung, for instance.

Before I could open my mouth to say so, Rafe had gone on. "I'm just trying to track down the teacher, Sid. Nothing to do with your friends at all."

I lifted Carrie to my shoulder and patted her back while

Uncle Sid looked unhappy. "What's the use of dragging it all back out after all this time?" he wanted to know. "Just let bygones be bygones, is what I say."

"I wish it was that easy," Rafe told him, "but if there's a connection to my murder case, I need to know about it."

"What kind of connection?" Uncle Sid threw both hands up. "He wasn't a murderer, for God's sake. He was a gentle scholarly guy who taught Latin and played golf. Not the type who would have forced himself on anyone."

I opened my mouth to mention that force doesn't have to enter into a statutory rape charge, but before I could, Uncle Sid went on, a little more calmly. "Yes, he got off easier than he should have. No question. There should have been charges files and he should have gone to jail, or at least had his name added to the sexual offender registry. Instead, he vamoosed before any of that could happen. But he wasn't a murderer!"

"Nobody's thinking he is," Rafe said. "It's just a loose end I have to tie off. His name came up, and I've gotta check it off the list. That's all."

Uncle Sid nodded. Reluctantly.

"We appreciate it," Rafe said. He glanced at me. I nodded, too. I was ready to go. My clothes were back together and Carrie had been burped.

I lowered her into the car seat. "Enjoy your evening. Maybe we can do dinner together some other time. At the Wayside Inn or Beulah's or somewhere, so no one has to cook."

"I'd like that," Aunt Regina said and got to her feet to buss my cheek. Then she bussed Rafe's. "Take care of your girls."

He nodded. "I intend to. Sid."

He gave my uncle a polite nod. Uncle Sid nodded back, but he looked unhappy. Since there wasn't anything we could do about it, or anything we could say that hadn't already been said, we wandered down the garden path and through the gate in the picket fence while Aunt Regina and Uncle Sid took themselves into their little pink cottage for chicken and whatever else Aunt Regina had planned.

"A boy," I said, when Carrie was strapped into the back seat and we were strapped into the front, and Rafe was behind the wheel and navigating the Chevy back in the direction of the mansion.

He nodded. "I didn't see that coming."

I hadn't either, although I saw no reason to admit it. "That takes Laura Lee out, if not Frankie."

"Plus a whole lotta other boys," Rafe said. "Frankie wasn't gay, though. Not if he married Laura Lee."

No. But— "He might have experimented. Some boys do." Some girls, too, at least from what I hear. I've never had a single romantic or sexual feeling toward anyone of my own gender, ever, but some people are more fluid.

I knew Rafe wasn't. We'd discussed Big Ned before—the cell mate he hadn't had at Riverbend Penitentiary—and he'd assured me that Big Ned didn't exist and nothing like that had happened to him.

"And some boys get raped," I added. "That doesn't just happen to girls."

My husband nodded. "It woulda been statutory rape either way, if the boy was underage. But if Jurgensson assaulted him, he wouldn't need to be gay."

"And might be struggling with some issues because of it."

Rafe nodded again. "Hard to see the progression from that to killing a bunch of women, though."

Yes, it was. If he'd gone on to kill a bunch of middle-aged, gay men, that would make more sense.

"This is confusing," I said.

"Tell me about it," Rafe answered, and zoomed past the entrance to the mansion.

I looked at it over my shoulder. "What's going on?"

He glanced at me. "Did you have something planned for dinner?"

Well, no. I was here, with him. If I'd had something planned, I'd be home, cooking.

"You mentioned Beulah's," Rafe said. "I got hungry."

"And you want to ask Yvonne if she knows anything about Jurgensson."

"Yvonne's younger than me," Rafe said. "It happened years before she went to Columbia High."

"She's from Damascus, though. She might know something about Frankie and Laura Lee."

"Can't hurt to ask," Rafe said, and headed for the small cinderblock building.

Eleven

Yvonne McCoy is my brother Dix's age—a year younger than Rafe, two older than me—and in high school, the two of them had a brief fling.

Yvonne and Rafe, I mean. She isn't Dix's type, although she'd like to be. I think Yvonne would like to be everyone's type. She likes men, has been married more than once, and going on a year ago now, she inherited Beulah's Meat'n Three after Beulah Odom passed on. There's still some question as to whether that passing was natural or not, but Yvonne isn't a suspect, and Todd doesn't seem inclined to get busy indicting the wife and daughter of Otis Odom, who'd be the guilty parties if Beulah was killed…

Anyway, we walked through the door, and Yvonne was standing there at the hostess station with her hair—flaming red—piled on top of her head and a big grin on her face.

"Saw you coming," she told us. "Evening, princess."

That's her nickname for me, so I answered politely. "Hi, Yvonne."

"Hi, precious." She tickled Carrie's feet. Carrie gurgled and Yvonne laughed. She doesn't have any children of her own, and I sometimes wonder if she wishes she did. Or whether she just wishes she had Rafe's baby.

She turned to him. "Evening, handsome. Saw a friend of yours earlier."

Rafe arched a brow. "Yeah? Everything OK?"

"Fine," Yvonne said. "You two here for dinner?"

Why else would we be here?

And then the import of that 'friend of yours' statement sank in. Clayton Norris had been by, and had reported to Yvonne that all was well, and now she was passing on the message.

"Yeah," Rafe said. "I need me some meatloaf and peach cobbler."

"Let's get you to a table, then." She grabbed two menus and preceded us down the aisle between the booths by the window and the breakfast counter. Her hips were swaying underneath a tight, black skirt, and Rafe grinned at me when I caught him looking.

"Been there, done that," he told me, *sotto voce*.

"Just as long as you don't plan to go there again," I answered, as I slid into the booth Yvonne indicated.

She tilted her head. "Go where?"

"Nowhere," Rafe told her. He maneuvered onto the seat across from me, and Yvonne distributed the two menus.

"What can I get you to drink?"

I ordered a sweet tea and Rafe a Coke, since Beulah's doesn't run to fine wine or beer. Yvonne nodded and reached for the car seat. "I'll just take this little bundle off your hands for a few minutes. You can pretend you're on a date."

We had family we could drop Carrie off with if we wanted a proper date, but there was no need to point that out. It was a kind gesture. "Thank you," I said.

"No problem, princess." She whisked Carrie off toward the kitchen.

I turned to Rafe, who reached across the table and twined his fingers with mine. "Just the two of us."

"For the couple of minutes it'll take her to show off the baby and come back."

"We better make the most of it." He lifted my hand and kissed my fingertips and then the inside of the wrist.

"That's getting a little personal for Beulah's," I told him, and retrieved my hand. He chuckled, but didn't try to hold on to it. "So this is one of the places where your friend checks in."

Rafe nodded. "He has a couple ways of communicating if he needs to. But so far everything seems slow on that front."

"Maybe there just aren't any others to be rounded up. Maybe once Lance ended up in prison—" And his name hadn't actually been Lance, but I still thought of him that way, "anyone else who was out there just decided to fade away quietly."

"Might could be," Rafe nodded and glanced at the menu. "You know what you wanna eat?"

I didn't, so I spent a minute perusing the specials. We'd been at Beulah's enough that I knew the standard fare well enough not to have to check that. "Cobb salad."

"That don't sound like it's gonna be enough fuel for what I have in mind for later," Rafe said, "but you do what you want."

"If you're looking at other women's rear ends, don't you think I should take better care of my own?"

"Ain't nothing wrong with your rear end, darlin'," my husband informed me, "and if you'd been walking in front of me, I woulda been looking at it. Eat what you want."

Fine. "What do you have in mind for later?"

"Nothing we can discuss in public," Rafe said, and glanced around the interior of the restaurant. He's adept at hiding his reactions, but I've known him long enough now—and have watched him intently enough—that I caught the slight check when he saw someone he knew.

"Who's back there?" I made to turn, and he shook his head.

"Don't. It's Tucker."

"Sergeant Tucker? From the police department?"

He nodded.

"Uh-oh." This could get ugly. Or so I assumed. Tucker hadn't been real happy when he slammed away from Green Street and Broad two nights ago, and he hadn't liked Rafe much before then. "Have you seen him since?"

"In passing," Rafe said, keeping his eyes on a packet of sugar he was turning over in his hands. "We haven't talked."

"Grimaldi talked to him, right?"

He nodded. "Yeah. I wasn't there, though."

Probably a good thing. "Did he have to go on administrative leave or anything?"

"No," Rafe said, still contemplating the sugar packet. "He didn't do nothing wrong. That's why he's gonna be even more angry about me picking him off of Curtis."

"Has he seen you?"

"Not yet. He's talking to Mo."

Mo—Maureen Boyd—is one of the waitresses. A woman into her middle years, with an impressive beehive hairdo, she's worked for Beulah's practically as long as I've been alive.

"I've seen him here before," I said. "With Felicia Robinson. A few days before… you know."

Before Felicia had been shot and killed in the line of duty, by the same guys who had shot—and failed to kill—Rafe.

He nodded. "They were friendly. Tucker knows Felicia's mama."

"Well, just pretend you haven't noticed him. If he wants to acknowledge you, he can. Otherwise, let him be."

"Hard for him to get past me without some kind of acknowledgement from either of us," Rafe said dryly, and of course that was true. There was only the one aisle, and it wasn't wide. But at least there was no point in calling Tucker out prematurely. If he wanted to cause a scene, he could do it when he left.

Maureen made her way over to our table and cocked a hip.

"Yvonne getting your drinks?"

I nodded. "She took the drink orders and the baby. I'm not sure where she got to."

"Showing her off in the kitchen," Maureen said, with a glance that way. "I'll go check on the drinks. You folks know what you wanna eat?"

Rafe ordered the meatloaf. I went against my better judgment and asked for fried chicken with mashed potatoes and carrots. Salad would have been better for me, but if Rafe had plans for later, and he thought I needed to keep my strength up, I figured I'd better be ready for whatever he had planned.

Maureen wandered off again, and Rafe lowered his eyes back to the sugar packet. It was unusually coy of him—he doesn't normally mind confrontation. When I commented on it, he told me, "Tucker didn't like me to begin with. To him, I'm still that eighteen-year-old punk he arrested for trying to beat the crap outta Billy Scruggs, but now he has to be polite to me. And not just that, but I got Felicia killed—"

"You did not!"

If anyone had gotten her killed, other than the man who shot her, it was me. I was the one who had suggested that she could volunteer for the job of keeping surveillance on him.

He put a finger across his lips. "From where he's sitting, I did. If it hadn't been for me, Felicia would still be alive. He ain't wrong."

Perhaps not. But that didn't make it Rafe's fault.

"Don't make no difference," he told me. "He don't like me. What happened the other night didn't help. And one of these days, Tucker might be the only thing standing between me and another bullet. When that happens, I don't want him to step outta the way because he'd rather see me dead."

No. I didn't want that, either.

"I'm trying my best to stay on good terms with him. Life

ain't making it easy."

No, it wasn't. "Just focus on dinner," I told him. "If Tucker wants to talk to you, he can initiate a conversation. Hopefully it'll be a polite one. If he just walks by without acknowledging you, then we'll just be grateful he didn't cause a scene."

"Sounds like a plan." He looked up when Maureen stopped by the table again, and deposited our drinks. "Food's coming up in a few minutes."

Rafe nodded. "What happened to the baby?" I asked, since she—and Yvonne as well—were still MIA.

Maureen nodded toward the kitchen. "Still back there. Can I get you anything else while you wait?"

I had my mouth halfway open to say we were fine when Rafe got in ahead of me. "How old are you, Mo?"

"What kind of question is that to ask a lady?" I wanted to know, but Maureen just chuckled.

"Too old for you, sugar."

When he just grinned, she added, "I just celebrated the big five-oh back in February. Why?"

"Just wondering whether you went to Columbia High the year Kent Jurgensson taught Latin there."

Maureen's face closed. "I didn't take Latin."

"But you were there that year?"

She tossed her neck, so the beehive swayed. "What if I were?"

"Just wondering whether you remember what happened."

"We all remember what happened," Maureen said. "Old Mr. Wilkins left, we got a new teacher, and he only lasted a year because he and one of the students got up to something they shouldn't have after hours."

"Do you know which student?" Rafe asked. If Maureen's delivery had bothered him, he didn't let it show.

"How would I know that?"

"It was a pretty big deal. Jurgensson lost his job. I imagine people were talking."

She didn't answer, and he added, "There was no police report filed, though."

"Why d'you wanna know?" Maureen demanded. "It's old news. Ancient history. Why drag it out again now?"

Rafe's tone was as calm as Maureen's was agitated. "It might pertain to a case I'm working on. A murder case."

He let that sink in for a second before he added, "I just want to have a conversation with whoever it was. I'm trying to track down Jurgensson. Depending on the relationship, his…" He hesitated, "victim might have some idea where Mr. Jurgensson ended up after he left here."

"It was a long time ago," Maureen said again, but she sounded less confrontational now. Maybe it was the mention of the murder case, maybe the fact that Rafe was doing his best to be reassuring. "But I guess it can't hurt to tell you. The boy's name was Trent. Noah Trent. He's dead."

"Dead?" I echoed.

Maureen nodded. "Dead. Buried at Oak Street cemetery, if you want to check."

"That likely won't be necessary," Rafe said. "Recently?"

"Ten years ago or so. Suicide."

I winced. So did Rafe, if very faintly. "Thanks, Mo."

"Don't mention it," Maureen said and walked away.

I made a face at her retreating back. "Ouch."

Rafe nodded. "This job don't usually make you popular."

No, I could see that. "So Jurgensson's victim isn't your serial killer. If he's been dead for ten years, he couldn't have killed the woman this week. Or the one last year, or the year before that."

Rafe shook his head.

"That's a dead end, then."

"There's still Jurgensson," Rafe said. "And Trent's family."

"His father would be too old, don't you think? And why

would one of Noah Trent's family start killing women because Noah was molested by his teacher? His male teacher?"

"No idea," Rafe said. "They prob'ly didn't. But I still need to track down Jurgensson. Who'd prob'ly be too old, too…"

I nodded. "And if he's gay, he wouldn't really have a reason to go around killing women. He certainly wouldn't be raping them. The incident with Noah wasn't the trigger, because that happened fifteen years before the first murder, and Noah's death wasn't, because that happened almost a decade after…"

Rafe nodded. "Chances are this don't have nothing to do with the case. But I still gotta tie it off."

Because loose ends in a murder investigation made it hard to get a verdict later. Right.

"So if Jurgensson and what happened back then doesn't have anything to do with the case, what about the…" I hesitated, since the Roman numerals weren't public knowledge, "Latin connection?"

He shook his head. "No idea. Who else knows Latin?"

I thought about it. "Doctors, I guess. But a doctor isn't likely to be cruising I-65 killing women."

"No less likely than anybody else if he goes around the bend," Rafe said, "but he wouldn't be a truck driver."

Probably not. "Doctors have other ways of killing patients, anyway. A doctor would probably be more likely to poison them."

Rafe didn't say anything to that, and I added, "Archaeologists know Latin. They're always finding those old Roman temples and things…"

"Not in Tennessee," Rafe said. "And an archaeologist probably wouldn't be driving a truck up and down I-65 either."

No. "Maybe it's a way to confuse the issue. I mean, we both know certain Latin letters and numbers, and we aren't doctors or archaeologists. Everyone who watches movies knows that the year the movie is made is written in Latin at the end of the credits. Most of us try to make it out. And a lot of clocks have Roman numerals instead of regular numbers. I think the courthouse clock on the square in Columbia does."

Rafe's eyes went a little distant as he thought about it. "Pretty sure you're right."

"So Roman numerals aren't hard to come by. Maybe it's just a regular guy trying to be fancy. No connection to anything Latin at all."

"Maybe." He looked up as someone approached our table, and his eyes went cool, even as he nodded politely. "Sergeant."

Tucker didn't bother to slow down on his way toward the front of the restaurant and the door, but he did dredge up a sneer. "Collier."

I waited for Rafe to say something else, or for Tucker to, but neither did. Tucker moved past, and Rafe kept his eyes on mine as the sergeant stopped at the register to pay his bill before heading out into the gathering darkness.

"He's gone," I said.

Rafe nodded. "Sorry."

"What for?" I went on without waiting for a response. "You aren't afraid he's going to shoot you in the back or anything, are you?"

"Not in here, at any rate. No, darlin'. I think he'd like to be rid of me. He don't like me. He's never gonna get past arresting me. And lately I've been doing some things that haven't made him like me any more. But I don't think he'd do anything to hurt or kill me. Nothing active, at any rate."

"But if he was standing between you and a bullet," I said, repeating the same words he'd used earlier, "he might step out of the way."

He didn't answer, just shrugged. Although it was answer enough. "Have you talked to Grimaldi about it?" I asked.

"What am I, twelve years old?" He shook his head. "No. I'll deal with it. I'm prob'ly wrong, anyway. He's been a cop a long time. It's in his bones by now. He wouldn't let a fellow officer down just because he didn't like him personally."

Hopefully not. But since there was no point in talking about it, I changed the subject. "Yvonne's been gone a long time."

"Just showing off the baby," Rafe said, and nodded behind me. "Here she is now. Safe and sound."

She was, cooing in her car seat and looking just as beautiful as always. Yvonne slid the carrier onto the seat next to me, and the two plates with our food in front of us.

"You make beautiful babies," she told Rafe. "Your daughter was a hit with everyone who saw her. You're going to have to beat the boys off with a stick when she gets older."

"If anyone can do it," I said, "he can."

Rafe grinned. "She ain't going on a date till she's twenty-five. And she's only dating boys with pickup trucks."

Pickup trucks? Because…?

It hit me. "No back seat?"

Yvonne was already chortling appreciatively.

"Yes, darlin'," Rafe said, with a wink at her. "I married a lady."

"So you did." Yvonne grinned at me. "Enjoy your food, princess."

"Thank you," I said demurely, as I picked up my fork. "I will."

We were on our way home, replete with food and the cobbler Rafe had insisted on having to finish off the meal, when my phone made a noise. I fished it out of my purse and peered at it while Rafe kept the Chevy going in the direction of home.

"It's Charlotte. She says there's another video up."

He glanced at me. "Of us?"

"Maybe. Probably." I had clicked the link and was waiting

for the video to start playing. "Yes. You and me. Inside… that's you and me inside Beulah's."

Where he was kissing my fingertips and the inside of my wrist, before I had taken my hand away. The heart-eyed emoji were already mounting up.

"She was there," I said. "Inside the restaurant."

Rafe nodded, looking faintly amused as the camera zeroed in on his face and stayed there as the video ended. "Looks that way."

"You don't suppose Yvonne…?"

"She's too busy to spend her time following me around to take pictures of me," Rafe said. "She's got a business to run."

After a second, he added, "And she wouldn't do that to you."

Good to know. "I'm sure it isn't Mo. And she—this woman, Jessica Rabbit—was behind me, where she could zoom in your face. You don't think Tucker…?"

Rafe started laughing. "No, darlin'. I don't think Sergeant Tucker is stalking me and posting videos of me on social media."

"It could be some kind of underhanded way of getting you in trouble. You know, make you enough of a public spectacle that Grimaldi won't want you around because you're a liability. Because you make the Columbia police department look like a bunch of TV cops, or something."

"I'm a real cop," Rafe said. And added, "Or at least I work like a real cop."

But he looked good enough to play one on TV. I didn't bother saying it. I had already offended him, it seemed.

The phone dinged again, with another message from Charlotte. I opened it, expecting a comment on the video or a question about what I was planning to get up to with my oh-so-hot husband tonight.

It wasn't either of those things.

"She says there's another picture that was just uploaded. Did we do anything else?" I clicked the link. "God, I hope whoever it is, wasn't close enough to record our conversation."

We'd been discussing serial murder and confidential information, and Grimaldi would kill me—and probably Rafe—if that conversation was made public. I could see that the idea worried Rafe, too.

And then that concern, and all the others, vanished as I got a look at the still picture that had been uploaded after the video.

A close-up of my daughter, with her glossy curls and big blue eyes and pink rosebud lips, and Yvonne's hand wrapped around the handle of the baby carrier.

#beautifulbaby, the caption read. *Looks just like her daddy!*

Twelve

I was flung against the seatbelt and then side to side as Rafe whipped the car around from one direction to the other and floored the gas pedal on his way back to Beulah's.

"Take it easy," I told him breathlessly. "I don't want to die on the way back there."

He gave me a dark look, but didn't respond.

I pushed myself upright. "She probably isn't even there anymore. She would make sure she was long gone before the video posted."

"She can't be that long gone," my husband growled. "It's only been a couple minutes since we left."

"Yes. But she probably left before we did."

"Don't care," Rafe said. "I wanna see if anybody knows who she is. I wanna get there before anybody else leaves, so I can talk to them."

That wasn't a bad idea, actually. Beulah's is a small place, and a lot of the customers are regulars. There was a good chance that somebody would know who we were looking for. Yvonne, if no one else. She'd been holding the baby carrier when that picture had been taken.

"I'm glad you're taking this seriously, anyway," I told Rafe. And I thought I sounded pretty placid, and not at all accusatory, but he shot me a look.

"If somebody's acting foolish over me, that's their business, darlin'. Nothing you or I need to worry about."

His voice was deathly calm, the tone so chill that it sent a shiver down my spine.

Some of the heat came out, though, when he added, "But when it comes to Carrie, that's a different story. Nobody threatens my family and walks away."

"Are you sure it's a threat?" It felt like one, but I was trying—hard—not to freak out, and to keep an open mind, just in case I was overreacting. It didn't feel like I was overreacting, but I was doing my best to stay calm. "I mean, there isn't anything particularly threatening about it. Carrie *does* look like you."

"Someone I don't know gets close enough to our baby to take a picture of her, that's threat enough."

He took the turn into the parking lot outside Beulah's on two wheels and slammed to a stop just at the bottom of the stairs. The car quivered. I did, too.

He pushed his door open. "Stay here."

Normally, I would have told him that I'm not a dog and he can't order me to sit and stay, but under the circumstances, I figured he'd get more done on his own, and besides, I didn't want to remove Carrie from the car. I wanted her safe, cocooned, where I knew no one could get at her. I waited for him to slam the door and then I locked the car from the inside, and watched him take the steps up to Beulah's front door two at a time. When he wrenched the door open and strode in, like the wrath of God in human form, the look on his face and the tension in his body ought to have been enough to have any evildoers scurrying for cover.

No one did. Or at least nobody came out of the restaurant after he went in, so if our unknown photographer was still in there, she was sticking it out.

I was pretty sure she was gone, though. I wouldn't have been. And not only that: from where I was sitting, I had a view of the entire parking lot, to the left in front of the building, to the right, beside the building, and the area next to the entrance. There was no small, light-colored compact anywhere.

Unless our unknown stalker had access to more than one car, and if so, all bets were off.

The phone rang, and I took my eyes off the parking lot, and the front door, to see who it was. It came as no surprise that it was Charlotte. "Are you OK?" she wanted to know.

I told her where I was and what I was doing. "Rafe's inside, putting the fear of God into whoever is left in there. I don't think the person who took the picture is still inside, but if anyone knows who she is, he'll get it out of them."

Charlotte made an agreeing sort of noise. She knows how scary Rafe can be when he puts his mind to it, and besides, Yvonne probably wouldn't be OK with this either, and would put her own weight behind his to get whoever knew something to spill.

"Are you OK, though?" Charlotte asked again.

"I'm…" I hesitated. "I'm not sure what I am. It was frustrating and a little funny when it was Rafe getting the attention. I only got worried because of Elspeth, and I didn't worry much, because I know he can take care of himself. I figured, if this person went around the bend and came after me, I'd deal with it. But Carrie…"

"She's a baby," Charlotte said, stating the obvious.

Yes. She was. And she was *my* baby. I wasn't any more inclined than Rafe to sit back and let anyone threaten her. My first instinct hadn't been to go on the warpath and flex my muscles and yell at anyone, though. What I did first, was to lock all the doors and hunker down, where I could keep my eye on her.

Some sort of ancestral memory thing, probably. The man goes out and beats his chest, killing the mammoth and dragging it home, and the woman tends the home fires and the babies, and beats off any predators that happen by with a stick.

The door to Beulah's opened, and Rafe came out, with Yvonne right behind. For a second it looked like she was escorting him out, sort of forcibly. But as he stepped down to the ground and turned to talk to her, I could see that she looked distraught, not angry. And while Rafe was still tense, his body had lost that '*touch me and I'll flick you into next year*' brittleness it had had when he bounded up the steps.

"He's coming," I told Charlotte. "I'll call you tomorrow."

"I'll pick you up at seven-thirty," Charlotte corrected. "We'll get to the police station early and keep watch. And we won't use your car, since she's seen it."

Good idea. "Are you sure you have time?"

"I have nothing but time," Charlotte said expansively. "When are we putting the house back on the market?"

Oh. That had totally slipped my mind in everything else that had gone on this afternoon and evening. "As soon as I get the photographs. Maybe tomorrow."

"Open house again on Sunday?"

Why not? "Sure," I said. "It'll give me something to do other than worry about serial killers and stalkers. And now I really have to go. He's coming toward the car."

"See you in the morning," Charlotte said and hung up. I dropped the phone back into the console in time to unlock the doors before Rafe started yanking on the handle.

He slid behind the wheel with an irritated grunt, and a look into the back seat at the baby. She was still there, of course, and no reason he'd have supposed otherwise, since I'd been out here with her since he left the car, but I guess he wanted to reassure himself she was still present and accounted for.

"Anybody hurts her," he informed me, "I'm tearing them limb from limb."

No question. "I'll help you." I don't really have limb-tearing in me the rest of the time, but I'd realized that when it came to my daughter, there wasn't much I wouldn't do.

Rafe smiled faintly, and some of the tension left his face. He leaned his head against the seat and closed his eyes. "Christ. I went in there looking to kill somebody."

I was well aware of that. I'd seen his face. "She wasn't there, right?"

He shook his head. "And nobody could identify her, either. Not a regular, they said. Nothing special. She came in a little after we did, so I guess she musta followed us there."

Guess so. All the way from the police station to Aunt Regina's house and back to Beulah's. "How come you didn't notice her?"

"No idea," Rafe said. "I usually keep track of stuff like that. Maybe I'm losing my edge."

Maybe. "Is there any reason I would need to call Aunt Regina and make sure she's all right?"

"I don't think so." He finally turned the key in the ignition and brought the car to life. "She's got no reason to be interested in your aunt."

No. Whereas Carrie… "That might not have been a threat, you know. It probably wasn't. She just had a chance to take a picture of your baby and post it online. And she does look like you. Carrie does. That might be all it is."

"Prob'ly is all it is," Rafe nodded, as he took the turn onto the Columbia Highway with a lot less panache than he'd taken the turn into the parking lot ten minutes earlier. "No reason to assume the worst. Just because she thinks our baby's beautiful and looks like me, don't mean she's gonna want her. Or gonna wanna hurt you to get at her."

That second idea hadn't occurred to me yet, in the panic over Carrie. Now it did. And Rafe let me sit with it for a few seconds longer than strictly necessary before he added, "But no reason to assume good intent, either. Better safe than sorry and all that."

"I'll be careful," I said.

He nodded. "I want you to promise me you won't go nowhere alone for the next few days. Take Charlotte with you, or your mama, or Dix or Darcy. And keep Pearl by you when you're home alone. Make sure all the doors are locked and don't open 'em to strangers."

I promised I wouldn't, even as I hated the idea of becoming a prisoner in my own home. "Just a few days?"

"I don't imagine it's gonna take much more time than that to figure out who this is and what her intentions are," Rafe said. "You said Vasim was gonna work on the video?"

"Officer Rehman? Yes. He thought he might be able to make out at least part of the license plate. And if we have that, we can probably track her down."

"Unless she's using someone else's plate."

Yes. But— "Surely that isn't something that occurs to normal people? If she's truly just someone with a crush on you who's following you around because she thinks you're hot, she wouldn't really think about trying to hide her identity, would she?"

"Depends," Rafe said, slowing the car down as we approached the driveway for the mansion, "on what her end goal is. If she just wants to look at me, she'll probl'ly get tired of it sooner or later."

I hadn't. And I couldn't really imagine anyone else getting tired of looking at him, either. But it was a nice idea. "She knows you're married. And that we have a baby. That doesn't seem to have cooled her interest any."

"It's too soon to say that," Rafe said and pulled the car to a stop at the bottom of the steps. "You OK with me parking here for the night?"

"It's your car," I said, "you can do what you want. Just be careful getting out."

He cut the engine and glanced at me. "She ain't gonna

shoot me. She prob'ly don't even own a gun."

Probably not. It was the 'probably' part that worried me. This was the sticks, and all sorts of people have guns here.

"You wait for me to get there before getting out, though." He opened his door and slid down before I could answer. I held my breath—it wasn't that long ago that he'd done this very thing one night: stopped in front of the steps and been taken down by a rifle shot from across the fields—but tonight, nothing happened. He slammed the door and jogged around the car and pulled my door open. "C'mon."

He handed me out, and then reached in for Carrie and the seat. A few seconds later, we were on our way up the stairs to the front door. He stayed between me and danger every step of the way. I let him unlock the door while I turned around and surveyed what I could of the area in front of the mansion over his shoulder.

Nothing stirred, and if anyone was looking at us—you know that prickly feeling you get sometimes?—I couldn't tell.

"Go on," Rafe told me, and gave me a nudge across the threshold. I scrambled inside, and turned to shut the door behind him after he had moved Carrie to safety inside the foyer. Down the darkened hallway, the scrabbling coming toward us was Pearl's nail clicking on the hardwood floors.

"This is crazy," I said. "Hello, Pearl. Yes, I know you have to go outside, sweetheart. Just let me—"

"I'll do it," Rafe said and turned back to the door.

"Go out the back," I told him. "Less chance anyone's going to take a potshot at you."

"This woman don't want me dead," Rafe said, but he snapped his fingers at Pearl and headed down the hallway toward the kitchen. She followed, prancing excitedly and getting in his way. His voice faded as he moved away. "Take the baby upstairs. I'll be there in a minute."

A bit longer than that, if I were any judge. But I gathered

the carrier, the diaper bag, and the baby, and hauled them all up the central staircase to the second floor. I was in the process of changing Carrie's diaper and wrestling her into her pink pajamas when he stuck his head through the door. "I'm gonna rinse off."

Pearl was with him, tongue lolling in a canine grin. She'd spent her formative years chained under a camper up on the Devil's Backbone, and while she's gotten used to, and pretty happy about, living inside, she isn't all that keen on those things called stairs. In this case, Rafe must have cajoled her upstairs with a doggie biscuit, because it was still in his hand.

"Here you go."

He handed it over. Pearl took it daintily and then crunched into it. I had my mouth open to protest—"Not in the nursery!"—but it was already too late. Crumbs scattered on the floor, and Pearl proceeded to demolish her bone, stubby tail wagging. Rafe headed for the bathroom.

By the time he came out, I had put Carrie on the floor for some tummy time. She's spent a large part of the evening cooped up in her seat, and it's good for her to move around. Since she'd figured out how to roll over once, she was trying to do it again, her small, pink body rocking back and forth with the effort. Pearl had licked up the remaining crumbs from the floor and was prone across the threshold with her big head on her paws, watching Carrie intently. I was always a little bit worried that Pearl would see Carrie as prey, but so far she seemed clear on the fact that Carrie was human, and part of the family, and not a chew toy to be demolished. I hovered pretty close, though, I'll admit that.

Rafe leaned a shoulder in the doorway and watched. "She's gonna do it again."

I nodded. She probably was. "You look better." And not just physically, although he did look quite nice, in faded jeans and a comfortably soft T-shirt that molded his upper body, with his feet bare and moisture still clinging to the roots of his hair. But the shower had beaten some of the tension from his face and body, too. He looked more relaxed, not so braced for battle.

He shrugged. "We're home and safe. I guess that helps."

Yes, it did. "How long do you expect it'll take to find this person and stop her?"

"Not long," Rafe said. "I just called Vasim—"

"At home?"

"He's still at the police station," Rafe said. "He's on second shift this week. Gets off at eleven."

Ah. "And did he have anything to report?"

"No," Rafe said, "but I lit a fire under his ass so he can get me something soon."

Lovely. "He's doing us a favor, you know. He doesn't have to spend his time doing this. It isn't his job."

"It is now," Rafe said. "Tammy's making it Vasim's mission in life to get that license plate. And he's getting paid, remember."

I remembered. But still. "You were nice to him, weren't you?"

"I'm always nice," Rafe said, with blatant disregard for the truth. He had absolutely no reason not to be nice to Officer Rehman, though, so if he said he had been, he probably had. "You ready for bed?"

I wasn't, particularly. It was a little earlier than usual. But I recognized the gleam in his eyes, so I told him, "Just let me feed the baby. I'll be in in a few minutes."

"I'll be waiting," he told me, and pushed off from the door jamb. "Don't linger."

No. I plucked Carrie from the floor and headed for the rocking chair in the corner so I could get her taken care of and get to my husband's needs as quickly as possible.

Charlotte picked me up bright and early the next morning, and by the time Rafe pulled up to the front of the police station, we were parked nearby, keeping watch.

There was no sign of the compact from yesterday. "Maybe she knows you spotted her and she's using another car," Charlotte suggested.

I nodded. "Maybe. Although she came back after I followed her out of town yesterday morning. That's when the video of Rafe kissing me was taken. After I had already followed her car down the street and around the corner. If she'd come back then, why wouldn't she do it now?"

"Maybe she figured you wouldn't think she'd be back yesterday?" Charlotte said. "Maybe she thought it would be safe to double back because you wouldn't be on the lookout because you'd already run her off?"

Maybe. "There he is." I gestured to the Chevy that pulled past us and to a stop outside the police station. A second passed and Rafe got out. Like last time, he stood for a few seconds and looked around, and like yesterday, I knew that he spotted us. Like yesterday, he didn't give any indication of it. After a moment, he headed up the stairs and into the building. Unlike the first morning, no one called out to him today.

"Yesterday," I told Charlotte, "she was parked up there and left this way. But when Vasim ran the video footage for later, after she came back, she was parked down on this side of the hill, and drove up onto the square and away in the other direction."

"Maybe she knew you were here," Charlotte suggested, "and decided to draw you away the wrong way."

Possible. "In that case, she lives up on the north side of Columbia."

"Or farther north."

I nodded. "But probably not too far. She's around this area too much to be driving in. If she's outside the police station before eight in the morning, and at Beulah's, on the south side of Columbia, at eight at night, she probably doesn't live in Franklin or Nashville."

"No," Charlotte admitted. "Although she could work here and live somewhere else. Did you get a good enough look at the license plate to tell whether it was local?"

I hadn't. Or rather, I hadn't looked. I'd been focused on making out the numbers. So had Vasim, I assumed. Neither one of us had commented on whether the plate was from Maury County or elsewhere. I'm not sure we would have been able to tell. "Maybe Vasim noticed."

"Do you want to go ask him?"

"He worked second shift yesterday," I said. "Three to eleven. I'm sure he isn't back yet."

Charlotte shrugged. "Well, I don't see anything moving around."

I didn't, either. The small, pale car was nowhere in sight. "I guess we go home."

Charlotte put the hybrid in gear and we rolled backwards out of the parking space. "Maybe she has something else to do on Saturday mornings."

Maybe so. Or maybe she just wasn't out of bed yet. But I had better things to do than to stalk my own husband in the event that she'd show up. "Just take me home. Maybe the photographs have arrived, and I can get the listing up and promote the open house for tomorrow."

"Works for me," Charlotte said happily and headed up the hill toward the courthouse to circle around and go back home.

We were halfway around when I looked out the window and squealed. "Stop! There! You see that?"

It was a small, tan car with a Smoky Mountains license plate—the purple mountains, orange sky, and black bear I had seen in black and white in the video yesterday—and it was parked on the opposite side of the courthouse from the police station. "That's it. I'm sure it is. Yes... I can see the Mardi Gras beads around the mirror!"

The hybrid kept going, though, and Charlotte said tensely, "I can't stop. There's a car behind us. And he's in a hurry."

I glanced in the mirror. There was a car behind us, or more accurately a truck. And it was so close to the hybrid's bumper that all I could see of it was the grill and the top of the hood. If the guy behind the wheel was impatient—and it had to be a guy; the truck had testosterone written all over it—I had to take Charlotte's word for it.

"We'll go around," she said, without slowing down. "It'll only take a minute to circle the courthouse. Just keep your hair on."

My hair was in no danger of going anywhere. My butt was, though, or would have been, if she'd slowed down long enough to allow me to jump out. She didn't, so I kept an eye on the quarry in the side mirror until we'd circled too far for me to be able to see the tan car anymore. And then I turned to Charlotte. "Hurry up. By the time we get around to the other side, she might be gone."

"The square isn't that big," Charlotte said, her hands tight on the wheel. "And this guy behind me is making me nervous. I keep expecting him to beep at me so I'll go faster. Look, there's an empty parking spot. Want me to pull in?"

"Yes," I said.

Charlotte turned the wheel, and the truck behind us hit the back corner of the hybrid and knocked us a good ten feet sideways. It would have been farther if Mrs. Albertson's car hadn't hit the car parked next to the empty spot and been forced to a stop. Charlotte and I both squealed, with the first impact and the second, and once we came to a quivering stop, Carrie let out the scream that had been building in her little lungs.

"Oh, God." I fumbled for my seatbelt, only faintly aware

that my hands were shaking and my neck hurt.

The truck stopped behind us, and a large and angry man jumped down from the cab. "What the bleep bleep bleep…!"

I left Charlotte to deal with him, and tuned out as I pushed my own door open, and then took the couple of wobbly steps to the back door—it was crunched in; Mrs. Albertson wasn't going to be happy about that—and wrenched at the handle.

At first it wouldn't open, and I felt panic rising in my chest. I knew nothing was likely to be wrong with Carrie. Nobody who could scream like that could have anything seriously wrong with them. But we'd been in a (minor) accident, and she was back there, and the door wouldn't open, and I couldn't get to her… and then I realized that the reason the door hadn't opened under all my frantic yanking was because the mechanism for the lock must have been impacted by the… well, the impact of the truck, and when I snaked my arm through the front opening and pulled the button up manually, the door opened, and I was able to grab to Carrie and lift her out of the seat and cradle her against my chest and see for myself that she was all right.

My pulse quieted after that, and so did her screams. My heart slowed to a rate that wasn't likely to throw me into cardiac arrest, and I was able to look across the roof of the hybrid and figure out what was going on with Charlotte.

The driver of the truck had stopped berating her while I'd worked on getting Carrie out of the back seat, and now he was standing, hands on hips, scowling down at her. At Charlotte. "Now listen here, young lady—!"

"I am not," Charlotte informed him, through gritted teeth, "a young lady, and if you don't stop talking to me like that, I will prove it."

I smirked, and then did my best to hide it. She wouldn't appreciate me laughing at her attempt to sound fierce.

By now, people—the few who were abroad at this time of

the morning—had started coming out of the various shops and offices around Main Street. Several of them had paper cups of coffee in their hands from the coffee shop on the corner. And I recognized a woman I'd spoken to briefly last spring, a friendly lady named Becky who worked at the tourist office on the other side of the square. She didn't seem to recognize me, though, just hurried over to where Charlotte was sitting, still in the front seat of the hybrid. "Are you all right, honey? Do you need an ambulance?"

And someone must have called the police. Since they were so close, several of them were on their way up the hill almost before the hybrid had come to a standstill. One of them must have recognized me and notified Rafe, because when I turned, there he was.

"You all right, darlin'?" His eyes were intent on my face.

"Fine," I said. My teeth were still chattering, so I made an effort to breathe deeply. "We're both fine."

Carrie had gone from shrill shrieks to sobs during the minute I'd been holding her, and now the sobbing turned to delight at the sight of her father.

"Hey, pretty girl." He stroked her cheek. Tears were still stuck in her eyelashes, but that was long forgotten in her excitement to see her daddy. He chuckled. "C'mere, sugar. Daddy'll hold you."

He plucked her out of my arms and cradled her in the crook of one arm while he tickled her tummy with the other. She giggled.

"There goes every ovary on the town square," I muttered, working the kinks out of my neck.

He gave me a jaundiced look, and then a more concerned one. "Neck all right?"

"Fine. We were barely moving when he hit us. I'm just stiff."

He nodded. "The car looks all right. Gonna need a little

body work, but it don't look too bad."

No. Some of the metal had crumpled, but it wasn't anything to worry about. The car on the other side of the hybrid, the one that had stopped our passage, had gotten off with a few minor scratches. And the truck, of course, was unharmed. On the other side of the car, Charlotte and the other two drivers were exchanging insurance information under the watchful eye of a couple of uniformed officers. It was amazing how quickly the guy from the truck had calmed down once the police showed up on the scene.

"Go on home," Rafe told me when that was taken care of. Most of the bystanders had disbursed by then, and so had most of the cops. The driver of the truck climbed back into the cab, and as we stood there, the engine came on with a roar. We watched as he crept around the rear of the hybrid and from there, around the courthouse. "Go home and relax. Take care of yourself and Carrie."

I nodded. "That's the plan. Although I forgot to tell you… I think Jessica Rabbit's car is sitting on the other side of the square." Or was, before all this happened. "We were just about to park and get out and take a look when this happened."

"Over there?" He glanced past the courthouse.

I nodded. "Small, tan compact with a Smoky Mountains license plate."

"D'you happen to write down the license plate?"

I hadn't, of course.

"Here." He handed me the baby. She protested at being dumped by her daddy, but by then he was already gone, jogging across the square toward the other side of the courthouse.

I spent the time while he was gone getting Carrie back into the hybrid and strapped in. Charlotte arranged herself behind the wheel, not without a grimace. "I'm not looking forward to explaining this to my mother."

No, I wouldn't be either, if it had been Mother's Cadillac getting creamed. "It wasn't your fault. The guy in the truck acknowledged that he'd been following too closely, didn't he? I mean, he was."

Charlotte nodded. "Get in. What are you waiting for?"

"Rafe," I said. "He went across the square to look at the car." There was no need to specify which car. "Here he comes now."

And he wasn't looking particularly happy. I knew, before he stopped beside me, what he was going to say. "It ain't there anymore."

No, of course it wasn't. "Maybe my subconscious noticed the license plate. Maybe hypnosis would work." A hot bath, lots of bubbles, candles and soft music...

"Sounds like a plan." He dropped a kiss on my mouth before helping me into the car. "Drive carefully."

Charlotte assured him that she planned to, and we rolled off down the hill under the Martin & Vaughan mural toward home.

We were halfway there when Charlotte's phone signaled an incoming message. She glanced at it. "There's a new video up."

Of course there was. "I'll look."

I pulled the phone toward me and pushed the appropriate buttons. In the backseat, Carrie cooed, the trauma of being in a (very minor) car accident already forgotten.

The video started playing, and I sighed.

"What?" Charlotte asked.

"She was there. Couldn't have been more than ten or fifteen feet away from us." I showed her the screen, where Rafe had just plucked Carrie out of my arms and was cradling her. "I was too shook up to realize it, I guess. It didn't even cross my mind to scan the crowd for anyone filming."

"Mine, either," Charlotte said. "What are you going to do?"

"Go home, send it to Rafe, and let him and Vasim Rehman worry about it." I shut the phone off with an irritated click and handed it back to her. "I've got a job of my own to do. I'm going to upload the new listing with the new photographs and schedule an open house for tomorrow. And let the police deal with the stalkers and serial killers."

"Works for me," Charlotte said, and turned the hybrid in the direction of Sweetwater.

Thirteen

She dropped me at home, and I spent the next hour or two doing what I'd said I'd do: track down the new photographs, create a new home listing, and scheduling the open house. While I did all that, Pearl snored on her pillow and Carrie moved around on the floor. She'd gotten the rolling over thing down well enough that she could now move from one side of the room to the other like a sausage. Eventually she got tired, though, and banged her nose against the floor. The resulting cry made Pearl wake with a startled bark, and that made Carrie cry harder.

I rocked the baby and let the dog out and gave her a treat, and was just about to feed Carrie and put her down for a nap when the phone rang. "It's me," Grimaldi said. Unnecessarily, since I have her number plugged into my phone, and it comes up when she calls.

"What can I do for you?" I whisked off the wet diaper with one hand and reached for a wipe with the other.

"I want to go talk to the Drimmels."

It took me a second to place the reference. "Laura Lee's parents?"

Grimaldi nodded. Or at least she made a nodding sort of sound. "M-hm. They live in Sunnyside."

A neighborhood on the southwest side of Columbia, full of winding roads and trees and large lots with mid-century ranches and split-levels.

"Let me guess," I said, wrapping a diaper around my daughters hips and fastening the sticky straps, "you got Frankie Matlock's prison record, and he could have committed the murders."

"Your friend Ms. Durbin exaggerated a smidgeon when she said he was in and out of trouble all the time," Grimaldi said. "But he's done a few stints behind bars. None of them long enough to stop him from killing eighteen women and dumping their bodies."

"I guess he's still in the area?"

"I don't know where he is," Grimaldi said, "he's someone else who doesn't pay taxes, but I figure the Drimmels can tell us that."

Maybe so. Or maybe not. If they'd lost contact with their deceased daughter's husband, he could be anywhere.

"They had custody of the kids," Grimaldi said. "Still do of the youngest, since he isn't eighteen yet. I'm hoping Frankie stayed in touch with them, and they can tell us where he is. Do you want to come?"

"Of course I want to come. Just let me get Carrie fed, and then she can take her afternoon nap in the car today."

"I'll be there in fifteen," Grimaldi said, and hung up. The implication was that I'd better be ready at that point, whether Carrie had finished eating or not.

She refused to let me drive again, of course, so we had to move the car seat back into the SUV. That done, I crawled into the passenger seat and Grimaldi arranged herself behind the wheel, while in the back seat, Carrie sucked on her pacifier as her lids got heavy. By the time we were halfway to Sunnyside, she was sleeping.

By then, Grimaldi and I were deep in a conversation about Frankie Matlock and his various deeds and misdeeds.

"The first time he went to prison was the time when Laura

Lee was killed," Grimaldi said, as she zoomed up the highway in the direction of Columbia. "Eight months for check kiting. He was in prison while Laura Lee was killed, so we know he wasn't responsible for that, but he got out in time to kill the second woman. Her name was Julie Green, and she was picked up and dropped in Kentucky."

"So outside of the jurisdiction of Maury County," where Laura Lee's murder had been investigated as a single crime, if it hadn't gone cold already, "and also not the same jurisdiction as the third victim."

Who happened to be Grimaldi's mother. I remembered it a second too late to bite my tongue.

She shook her head. "Nobody had made that connection yet then. That didn't happen until a year or two later."

Right.

"Frankie Matlock was out of prison when my mother was killed," Grimaldi added. "I don't know if anyone's tried to put him in Kentucky at the time of Julie Green's murder, or in Indiana at the time of my mother's, but we're going to attempt to do that today."

"That's a long time ago. Might be hard for anyone to remember dates and times so many years later."

Grimaldi nodded. "We're going to give it a shot, though. He wasn't in prison, so we know that much. And if we can put him somewhere else, somewhere that isn't Kentucky or Indiana, we can eliminate him."

"You're absolutely sure we're talking about one killer and not several?"

"I'm not absolutely sure of anything," Grimaldi said, steering the SUV up the street. "We know, from the numerals, that all eighteen victims are part of the same series. Whoever killed them, whether one or more killers, had to be aware of the others. The numbers—numerals—are chronological. And the victims are all the same type. So my first guess is a single perpetrator. That's what the FBI's profile says, too. Someone who likes to work alone."

"So Laura Lee…"

"Was either the first victim of the same killer, or killed by someone else." Grimaldi turned the SUV in the direction of the signs for Damascus. It looked like we'd be approaching Sunnyside from the south instead of through Columbia. "It's possible that the origin kill was made by one person, and it was a trigger for someone else, who went on to kill the other seventeen."

"Like Frankie. If some random trucker killed Laura Lee, and Frankie, when he got out of prison, killed the others."

"That's one theory," Grimaldi said.

"What about DNA?" This was an uncomfortable subject when one of the victims was her mother. "You said they were raped and strangled. There must have been DNA on someone. After eighteen victims, surely he must have left a hair or a drop of sweat or semen or spit, on at least one of them."

"There's too much DNA," Grimaldi said flatly. "A lot of these women turned tricks. Several of them hadn't showered between the last time they worked and when they were killed."

"No overlapping DNA? The same DNA found on more than one victim?"

"There's been a few instances of that." She turned off the main road into one of the meandering lanes that cut through Sunnyside. The yards immediately became bigger with the houses sitting farther back from the street. "One set, on three different women, turned out to belong to a truck driver from Louisville who liked the company of prostitutes when he was away from home."

Her voice was even, without any hint of judgment. I wasn't so sanguine.

"He had sex with three different women who happened to get murdered within a few hours of him sleeping with them?

And in addition to that he has a wife at home?"

"Truckers can live very different lives on the road and at home," Grimaldi said noncommittally. "This is the street. We're looking for number 739."

I peered out the window on my side of the car while the conversation continued. "But this guy didn't kill any of them?"

"He had an alibi for several of the others," Grimaldi said, peering out the other side. "So if we're looking for a single perpetrator, it won't be him."

She continued, without changing her tone, "The house is going to be on your side. These are all even numbers."

"I'm looking. What kind of alibi did he have? The guy from Louisville?"

"He was driving south through Alabama at the time when another victim was killed in North Indiana," Grimaldi said. "He couldn't have been in two places at once."

"But if there are more than one of them? Some sort of conspiracy..."

I trailed off, thinking about the ramifications of a band of murderous truckers, raping and killing women all over the country, and communicating on their CB radios, if truckers still used those...

Except these women hadn't been killed all over the country. They'd been killed in a pretty narrow corridor, especially considering the size of the rest of the country. So if there was a conspiracy of truckers, it only involved interstate 65...

"The FBI isn't taking that angle seriously," Grimaldi said. "Their profile indicates someone who likes to work alone."

So no conspiracy of truckers. I wasn't sure whether I was happy about that, or the opposite. It was probably a good thing. If there was just one killer, it would be easier to convict him. Probably.

"There's number 739," I said, "coming up. The blue mailbox."

Grimaldi nodded and aimed for the driveway.

"Was there any DNA found on Laura Lee?"

"There was," Grimaldi said, as she maneuvered the SUV up the curve of the driveway, "but not from that guy. We haven't identified it yet. So far, it isn't a match to anything else, in this case or any other."

I nodded as she pulled the car to a stop on the parking pad outside the double garage, and looked around.

Laura Lee's parents lived in a low-slung, mid-century cottage, built between the war years and the time when streamlined, atomic ranches became popular. It had the peaked entrance of a cottage, but in every other way it was a ranch: long and low, built of red brick with touches of orchard stone around the door and chimney.

"Decent place," I told Grimaldi, who nodded. "Who lives here?"

"According to the census, Mr. and Mrs Drimmel and two grandchildren. The elder, a daughter, graduated from high school, so she might be in college."

And still have her official address here. I nodded. "Do they know we're coming?"

Grimaldi shook her head. "They're both retired, though. I'm guessing at least one of them is home. Hear the music?"

I did hear the music. Nineteen-forties Big Band; nothing I could imagine either of the kids listening to. If Laura Lee had been dead for sixteen or seventeen years, her youngest couldn't be any less than that, and Grimaldi had just said the girl might be in college.

"Let's go." She pushed her door open.

"Carrie's asleep," I said. "Do you want me to stay in the car?"

She gave me a look. "No. I want you to come with me, in case you notice something I don't. Besides, it's rarely a good idea to interview people on your own. Not until you know they aren't suspects and won't come at you with a carving knife."

"These are the first victim's parents," I pointed out. "Carving knives aren't likely to come into play."

She just shrugged, and I added, "I have to bring Carrie. After last night, I'm not letting her out of my sight."

Grimaldi nodded. "Your husband told me what happened. Just grab her and let's go."

The music turned out to be coming from inside the garage, that was why we could hear it so clearly. As we passed the garage windows—that looked like regular windows from the front—the music became more pronounced, and I realized that what I had taken for some weird percussion beat, was actually the sound of metal on metal. Someone was inside the garage working on a car. The lights were bright, but all I could see were a pair of shoes and the bottoms of a pair of pants, or maybe overalls, sticking out from underneath an antique car, the kind with pronounced fins.

"Come on," Grimaldi waved. She was already up on the stoop. I abandoned the window and hoofed it up next to her. By then, she had pushed the doorbell and was waiting for sounds of life inside.

"There's somebody in the garage," I informed her, "working on a car. But between the music and the noise, he might not be in a position to hear the bell."

"If nobody answers, we'll go knock on the window." But she didn't sound concerned, just looked around. "First impressions?"

"Of the house?"

"That's your business, isn't it?"

It was, now that she mentioned it. "Reasonably well-maintained," I said, "but a little old-fashioned. We already know they're older people, but I would have guessed that anyway, from the finishes."

I touched the iron fretwork holding up the porch with my

free hand. It was wrought iron with little leaves, painted white. "Most young people would have taken this out, or built a box around it, or at least painted it black or something." Here, it matched the shutters, which would also have been painted a different color if I'd been renovating this house.

I had my mouth open to comment on the vinyl siding on the underside of the porch ceiling when Grimaldi raised her hand. After a second I heard it, too: footsteps from inside the house. A moment later the door opened a crack. "Yes? Can I help you?"

The face was as round and friendly as Millie Ruth Durbin's, and of around the same vintage. Seventy, give or take a year or two. She had white hair, cut short into soft little curls, and she was dressed in a pair of pink velour pants and a matching T-shirt. They brought out the roses in her cheeks.

The eyes were blue, and they went big when Grimaldi flashed her badge. "Oh, Lord. My kids. Something's happened to my grandkids—!"

"No." Grimaldi held up a hand, and stopped Mrs. Drimmel in mid-shout. "No, ma'am. Nothing's happened to anyone. Not recently. It's about your daughter."

"You found him," Mrs. Drimmel said.

"No. I'm afraid not. But there's been another murder..."

She sighed. "You'd better come in."

She stepped back. Grimaldi crossed the threshold into a foyer paved with yellowed marble. I took a better grip on Carrie's seat, and followed.

Mrs. Drimmel looked askance at us. Grimaldi looked official, in her dark suit and with her badge. I didn't, in my blouse and flowery skirt and with a baby in my hand.

"The babysitter canceled," I said. It wasn't true, of course, but I didn't want Grimaldi to seem unprofessional for showing up with a woman with a baby. And there was absolutely no way I'd leave Carrie alone in the car. Not even a police car with the doors locked.

Mrs. Drimmel nodded, as if my statement had actually made sense. "Have a seat. Through there."

She gestured to the room to the left of the foyer. It turned out to be a formal living room, with wall to wall carpet covering the floors—another thing I'd change if I were renovating this place—and a fireplace flanked by bookcases, with a mantel full of what looked like family photographs.

Grimaldi waited for Mrs. Drimmel to take a seat on one of the chintz chairs before she lowered herself to sit on the sofa. I took a seat next to her and put Carrie and her carrier on the floor.

"Pretty baby," Mrs. Drimmel said, peering at her.

"Thank you." I stared at her, for some sign of prejudice over the fact that I was sitting here with a brown baby, but there was none visible. "She takes after her daddy."

Mrs. Drimmel nodded. "I can see that she don't favor you much."

The niceties over with, Grimaldi cleared her throat. "I'm Tamara Grimaldi. I took over as chief of the Columbia PD in January."

"We heard what happened to Carter," Mrs. Drimmel nodded.

"You probably also heard that there was another woman found at the truck stop down by the interstate a couple of days ago."

"My husband mentioned it. But that's the sheriff's job, isn't it?"

"We're working together," Grimaldi said blandly. "I wanted to ask you a couple of questions about your daughter, Mrs. Drimmel. Or more specifically, about your son-in-law."

"Frankie?" She sounded surprised. "I haven't seen him in donkey's years."

"But they were still married when your daughter died."

"Sure." She nodded. "Frankie was in prison then, though. No better than he ought to be, Frankie. I told her over and over, she oughta leave him, that one day he was gonna come to a sticky end, but instead of Frankie, it was Laura who died…"

She trailed off.

"I've looked at his prison record," Grimaldi said, yanking the conversation back on track. "There was no question at all that he wasn't the one who killed her."

She hadn't presented it as a question, but Mrs. Drimmel shook her head. "No. He wasn't violent, Frankie. Never raised a hand to her, or to the kids. Just lazy and weak minded. Couldn't be bothered to work for a living when taking other people's stuff was easier. But he wasn't violent."

"Would you happen to know where I could find him these days?" Grimaldi asked. She obviously wasn't convinced by Mrs. Drimmel's description of Frankie. "He finished his parole from the last time he was in prison—he was living in Birmingham at the time—but that was two years ago, and there's no record of him anywhere at the moment. I've looked, but I can't find him."

"We haven't seen him in longer than that," Mrs. Drimmel said, frowning. "Jacob—that's my husband—warned him not to come around here no more, asking for handouts. That musta been five or more years ago."

"And you haven't seen him since?"

Mrs. Drimmel shook her head. "That's when he went to Birmingham. I gave him a hundred dollars from my rainy day fund and told him he'd better not come back, or Jacob'd whop him."

I guess Jacob didn't share Frankie's laziness and weakness, if he could whop his son-in-law when necessary.

"So Frankie went to Birmingham five years ago," Grimaldi picked up the story.

Mrs. Drimmel nodded. "That's the last we've seen of him.

He don't write and he don't call."

"No contact with his children?"

"Not less'n he wants something from them," Mrs. Drimmel said. And added, "He never even tried to get'em back after Laura passed. Told us we could keep'em, and with his good wishes."

She shook her head. "I don't hold with a man who won't step up and take care of what needs doing."

"You were taking care of them when Laura Lee died," Grimaldi nudged.

I got to my feet with a murmur and drifted toward the fireplace. Mrs. Drimmel gave me a distracted nod. "That I was. Frankie had finally gone too far and gotten himself caught and thrown in prison, and Laura had the hardest time making ends meet. We offered to help her, but after all the things we'd said about Frankie—"

She didn't finish the sentence, but it wasn't necessary. I could read between the lines, and I'm sure Grimaldi could, too. Mr. and Mrs. Drimmel had given Laura Lee a hard time about getting involved with Frankie, and when they turned out to be right, pride had made her refuse their help.

"So she took a second job at the truck stop at night," Grimaldi said, to get Mrs. Drimmel going again.

The older woman nodded. "She was waiting tables, and maybe she did some other things, too, to pick up a little extra money…"

The bookshelves were full of what looked like old, leather-bound reference volumes, and issues of *Car & Driver* magazine for at least the past couple of decades. I ran my eyes over the photographs ranged on the fireplace mantel.

A black and white wedding picture of a young man and woman in what I guessed were the late nineteen-sixties garb must be Mr. and Mrs. Drimmel. Jacob was big and broad-shouldered in a suit and tie, while his petite wife tried to make up for the difference with a bouffant hairdo that probably owed some of its height to a pair of socks or the heel of a loaf of bread balanced on her head underneath the hair. Her shoes were slingbacks with skinny, two-inch heels and toes so pointy they could have served as deadly weapons. They both looked solemn and a little scared, like the future was a scary place. And seeing as how they probably got married during the worst of the Vietnam War, who could blame them?

A later photo of a brown-eyed girl with the big hair of the nineteen-eighties had to be Laura Lee; probably a high school graduation photo. She was more striking than pretty, with a slightly oversized nose she might have grown into before she died, but that rather dominated her face at the tender age of eighteen or so.

"Who told you about the other things?" Grimaldi wanted to know. "The police?"

"Jacob," Mrs. Drimmel said. "I guess he heard about it from the police."

"But Laura Lee hadn't talked to you about it herself?"

I glanced over my shoulder as Mrs. Drimmel blushed. "Maybe she had. Just in passing, you know? That once, this guy—this trucker—had gotten the wrong idea and made a pass—"

This was a polite euphemism for soliciting sex, I assumed.

"—and Laura told him she'd go with him for fifty dollars, and that it was the easiest fifty bucks she ever made."

I turned back to the mantel and the pictures. There was no wedding photo for Laura Lee and Frankie, so either they must have eloped, or the Drimmels had taken it down after Laura Lee died. They had no reason to remember Frankie fondly, I guess.

There was a snapshot of an older Laura Lee holding a bundle containing a baby, though, with a slightly older child standing next to them. I leaned closer and squinted.

"…nothing I could do!" Mrs. Drimmel said. "She was an adult, and I didn't have any money to give her. I knew Frankie would be angry, of course, but he was in prison, and anyway, it was his own fault for getting himself arrested and leaving her with nothing…!"

"Did she name any of these men?" Grimaldi wanted to know. There was no point in pursuing Frankie's anger with Laura Lee, since he'd been in prison when she died and couldn't have killed her.

Mrs. Drimmel shook her head. "She said it was easier if she didn't know their names."

I could well believe that. I abandoned the picture of Laura Lee and her kids, and went on to the next photograph. And found myself face to face with a face I knew.

My jaw dropped. "Excuse me." I picked up the photograph and turned to them. Mrs. Drimmel stopped speaking in the middle of a sentence. Grimaldi looked annoyed. I ignored it. "Is this your grandson?"

Mrs. Drimmel nodded. "That's Curtis. Laura's boy."

I looked at Grimaldi. She looked back at me.

"Frankie's black," she said.

Mrs. Drimmel looked surprised. "Yes'm."

"You didn't check?" I asked Grimaldi.

She shook her head, looking chagrined. "It never crossed my mind. If there'd been an arrest photo attached to the file I pulled, I would have noticed, but…"

But there hadn't been. Obviously.

Mrs. Drimmel was looking from one to the other of us. "Does it matter?"

Grimaldi pulled herself together. "Not to your daughter's murder, no. He wasn't involved in that. But for the others, the profile indicates someone Caucasian."

Mrs. Drimmel blinked. "Oh."

"Most of the victims have been Caucasian," I explained, as I put the picture of Curtis back on the mantel and drifted toward them. "The couple that haven't been were light-skinned. It indicates a white killer."

Mrs. Drimmel nodded. "I don't imagine it would matter to Laura what color someone was. She married Frankie, and he was black. Her boyfriend before Frankie wasn't."

"Who was her boyfriend before Frankie?" Grimaldi wanted to know. It was hard to believe the police hadn't covered that back then, but maybe she just didn't remember the details.

"You wouldn't know him," Mrs. Drimmel said. "His name was Noah."

"Trent?"

She gave me a look of surprise. "How d'you know?"

"Someone mentioned him," I said, avoiding Grimaldi's accusing stare. "It was in a different context. Nothing to do with your daughter."

Mrs. Drimmel nodded. "Why would you wanna know about Noah? That was a long time ago."

"Just tying up loose ends," Grimaldi said lightly. "Noah Trent, you said? Where can I find him?"

"The cemetery down in Sweetwater," Mrs. Drimmel said. "Killed himself around ten years ago, Noah."

Grimaldi stared at me. I grimaced. In the silence, we heard the faint music and clanging of metal on metal from beyond the wall. "Is that your husband?" I asked.

Mrs. Drimmel nodded. "He's picked up an old car he's working on. I never thought he'd retire—he worked until he was seventy-two—and now that he has, he's still at it."

I smiled. "Was that his job before he retired?"

"Diesel mechanic," Mrs. Drimmel said, and shook her head. "I should have figured he wouldn't be able to leave it alone. I thought after he retired, he'd settle in to play golf and tool around the house, but no. He went out and found himself an old car to tinker with. But at least he's doing it here, so I get to see him more."

Good for Mrs. Drimmel.

Grimaldi shot me a look and pushed to her feet. "Thank you for your time, Mrs. Drimmel."

"Happy to help," Mrs. Drimmel said while I grabbed Carrie's car seat. "You working on Laura's murder again? They never did arrest anybody for that…"

"We're looking at it again," Grimaldi assured her as we made our way toward the door. "I'll be in touch."

Fourteen

"What's this about Noah Trent?" Grimaldi wanted to know as soon as the car doors were shut behind us. She inserted the key in the ignition and started the car.

"I'm sorry," I said, pulling the seatbelt across my body and fastening it. "I assumed Rafe had told you. When we were at Beulah's last night, before all the hoopla with the video and then the picture of Carrie—"

She nodded.

"We asked Mo—Maureen, the waitress—if she knew anything about Jurgensson and the kid he had the affair with. She's around the same age Laura Lee would be, so we figured she might have attended Columbia High around that time, too."

"And she named Noah Trent." The SUV rolled down the long driveway to the street.

I nodded. "And told us he couldn't be involved in the murders because he's dead. And has been for about a decade."

"That does seem like it would give him an alibi," Grimaldi agreed, "at least for two -thirds of the victims. I can't really see how he would be connected."

I couldn't, either. If the thing with Jurgensson had happened twenty-five or thirty years ago, and Laura Lee's murder had happened sixteen or seventeen years ago, and Noah had killed himself ten years ago, there was no connection there that I could see. The incident with Jurgensson hadn't triggered Laura Lee's murder, and her murder hadn't triggered Noah Trent's suicide.

"We can probably eliminate Noah Trent from suspicion," Grimaldi agreed. "Although I'd still like to track down Jurgensson. If nothing else, I'd like to make sure he's still alive and nobody did away with him."

"My uncle said he used to play golf with Jurgensson occasionally. And that one of the others kept in touch with him for a while after he left. Uncle Sid said he—Jurgensson—worked some menial job in Tucson or Tupelo last he heard."

"What's your uncle's friend's name?"

"Art Mullinax," I said. "He lives north of Columbia somewhere, not too far from Fulton Street. That's what Uncle Sid said. On something called Daffodil Hill Farm. I've never heard of it. But you should probably check with Rafe before you go over there. He went with me to Aunt Regina's and Uncle Sid's house yesterday, so he knows about Mullinax already." And unlike Grimaldi and me, it was his actual job to follow up on leads.

"Call him," Grimaldi said.

I resisted the urge to salute, but just barely. "Yes, ma'am."

She gave me a look, but didn't comment. I pulled my phone out and dialed my husband's number.

It took a few seconds, but then he picked up. "Darlin'."

"Quick question," I said. "Grimaldi and I have been to see the Drimmels, Laura Lee Matlock's parents. Turns out Curtis—the kid from the other night—is her son."

Grimaldi took her eyes off the road to stare at me. Rafe just sounded amused. "No kidding?"

"No. Mrs. Drimmel has a photograph of him on the mantel. I recognized him. Besides, same name."

"Small world," Rafe said.

"Small town. Anyway, Noah Trent's name came up. Turns

out he was Laura Lee's boyfriend at some point."

"The kid who was involved with the Latin teacher?"

"The same. Grimaldi wants to go talk to Uncle Sid's friend, the one who was in contact with Jurgensson after he left here. Mullinax."

"OK," Rafe said.

"We're making sure you haven't already done that."

"No. I'm working on the last murder. Not the first."

Of course. "Are you getting anywhere?"

"We're still making lists of trucking companies," Rafe said, "and drivers. Right now, we have about thirty suspects who came through the truck stop in the time period we figure Ramona's body was left. Now we gotta cross-check their schedules with the other murders."

Some of which went back more than fifteen years. "It sounds like a big job."

"They don't come much bigger. Go on and have fun. I'll be at the sheriff's office if you need me."

He sounded ready to hang up. "Just one more thing," I said quickly.

"Yeah?"

"Anything on the stalker? Did Vasim Rehman manage to figure out the license plate?"

"Not so far as I've heard," Rafe said, "but he's in Columbia and I'm in Sweetwater. I'll check with him."

I told him I'd appreciate it. "I don't want to pile anything more on your plate—"

The silence was loud.

"—but have you considered whether you ought to call Ginny and Sam?"

The silence got even louder for a few seconds. Then it exploded. "Shit."

"Relax," I told him. "Chances are this person doesn't know you well enough to know you have another child, let alone who David is or where to find him. We haven't made a big deal out of his relationship to you."

"No," Rafe agreed, but he sounded distracted.

"But like you said the other night, better safe than sorry. They should probably hear what's going on. And from you." Or I'd call David's parents myself.

"Sure thing, darlin'. I'll call 'em right now."

He was gone before I could say goodbye. I turned back to Grimaldi. "You heard him, right? We can go ahead and talk to Mullinax."

She nodded. "You two worried about the kids?"

I nodded. "Rafe showed you the social media post, right? All it said was *beautiful baby* and *she looks just like her daddy,* both of which are true. And that's not exactly threatening, I guess..."

"Not exactly," Grimaldi agreed, stabbing at the computer screen extending from the dashboard of the car.

"But I don't like how this woman is zeroing in. Following Rafe around and taking pictures of him is one thing. Posting pictures of his baby online is something different. I realize that everybody knows everybody in a small town, pretty much—"

I'd grown up in Sweetwater, and I had a pretty good idea who all of Sheriff Satterfield's deputies were and where they lived.

"—and Rafe being who he is, and me being who I am, everybody would know where to find him anyway—"

Aunt Regina had done a spread of our wedding in the *Sweetwater Reporter* last year, so the whole town—or at least everyone who subscribes to the *Reporter*—knew that Margaret Anne Martin's younger daughter had married Sweetwater's black sheep.

"—but I don't like all this personal information getting out. Even if this fruitcake isn't a threat to Carrie, and just thinks she's a pretty baby who looks like her father, there are other people out there who might not mind an opportunity to hit Rafe where it hurts." And I wasn't talking about Sergeant Tucker.

"Your husband did a lot of damage to some very bad people," Grimaldi nodded, "as you well know. We're not taking this lightly at all, I promise. Officer Rehman is trying to track down the car. And the TBI is involved now. Your husband called Mr. Craig this morning."

Good to know. That hadn't occurred to me—Wendell and Jamal were in Nashville, and probably wouldn't be able to come down here for this; not when there wasn't a specific threat of any kind—but I was glad they knew. Wendell was the closest thing to a father Rafe had, and he had spent a lot of years making sure Rafe survived whatever sticky situation he was in.

"Your husband's going around with Agent Yung," Grimaldi added, "and she's been apprised of the situation. She's trained at Quantico and she'll give him any kind of backup he needs."

Hard to imagine, considering how she'd probably still like to slap him behind bars. "You don't suppose Agent Yung..."

I didn't have to finish the sentence.

"No," Grimaldi said, so the idea must have crossed her mind, too. "At least one of the videos was taken when she was inside the police station with me. And besides, you would have noticed her at Beulah's yesterday. You might not have paid attention to some random woman, but if Agent Yung had been there, you would have seen her."

True. "I guess the FBI trains their agents well."

"They can usually hit what they're aiming for," Grimaldi said and turned off the main road onto a much narrower one that meandered into the sticks on the north side of Columbia. I looked around.

"Is there where Mullinax lives?"

She had both hands on the wheel as we bumped over ruts and rocks. The road wasn't even paved. "According to his driver's license and my GPS."

No sooner had the words crossed her lips than the road opened up and we saw a big, turn-of-the-last-century Victorian sitting on a carpet of green velvet up against a backdrop of spring-fresh trees. Daffodils and tulips bloomed in riotous color along the porch, and two flowering trees—ornamental Bartlett pears or dogwoods, probably—flanked the path to the front door.

"Wow," I said.

Grimaldi gave me a sardonic glance. "Not what you expected?"

"I expected a doublewide trailer and a toothless old redneck at the end of a road like that one," I said, honestly, "although given that the man plays golf with my uncle, I probably shouldn't have..."

There were three vehicles parked outside the garage, and there might have been three more behind the doors. One car was a prosaic gray sedan, a few years out of date. One was a silver SUV, ladylike and dainty, not dissimilar to the one we were pulling up in. The last was a golf cart. I guessed Mr. Mullinax might use it to travel around the property and maybe down to the main road to pick up his mail. It was a long trek on foot.

Grimaldi pulled our SUV to a stop and cut the engine. Silence descended. "Hard to believe we're inside the Columbia city limits," she said.

It was. The place looked like it belonged way out in the country, and it had probably been well outside town when it was built. But that was a century and a quarter ago, maybe even more, and the town had steadily encroached.

"I've heard of Daffodil Hill Farm," I said, looking around. "I knew it was up here somewhere, but I've never seen it before."

"No reason why you would, I imagine." Grimaldi pushed her door open. "Mr. Mullinax seems to like his privacy. Let's go see if he's in residence."

Sure thing. I climbed out and reached into the backseat for Carrie.

Like at the Drimmels' much humbler home, it was Mrs. Mullinax who answered the door. Or so I assumed, until she introduced herself as the housekeeper. Mr. Mullinax was in the study. Would we like to see him?

Grimaldi indicated that we would, and we were shown into a spotless parlor with a stunning Victorian fireplace—all dark wood and glazed green tile—and offered refreshments. Grimaldi said no for both of us. I smiled apologetically. "That's a lovely fireplace. Would you mind if I took a closer look?"

The housekeeper waved her hand at it. "Help yourself. I just dusted it this morning."

It looked freshly dusted. And unlike the Drimmels' fireplace, it sported no family photos. Instead, the mirror behind the mantel reflected stubby candles in silver holders, and a matching vase holding a spray of glossy magnolia leaves and waxy flowers.

Mother would have approved. I guess I did too, or at least the professional part of me did. Although I have to admit Mrs. Drimmel's family photos had set a much friendlier tone.

The housekeeper wandered out, presumably to let Mr. Mullinax know we were there, and Grimaldi arched her brows at me as I ran my fingertips over the carved wood of the mantel.

"Nice workmanship," I said apologetically. "And I love the original wood. This is old mercury glass. See how wavy it is? And look at the tile. Isn't it gorgeous? And it's in pristine shape. Not a chip or crack in any of them."

I looked around the rest of the room, with the dark hardwood floors and eleven foot ceilings and narrow windows tall enough that either one of us could have stood upright on the sill and not come anywhere close to cracking our heads on the round top. "This is a gorgeous room. If the rest of the house looks like it, it must be worth a fortune."

"You'd know," Grimaldi said.

I shrugged. "It's my job. And I grew up in the Martin mansion. I know the value of old houses. This is a beautiful one."

"Thank you, young lady."

The booming voice came from outside the door. A moment later, a man—Mr. Mullinax—sailed through.

He must have been about a decade older than Uncle Sid. And he was as jolly as Santa Claus. The only thing missing was the white beard. The hair was white and fluffy, like down, the cheeks were rosy red, and the twinkling eyes were blue, but he was clean-shaven.

"Mr. Mullinax." I flushed. Mother would not be happy to hear that I'd been calculating the man's value in his hearing, and given the probable antecedents and bank balance here, Mrs. Mullinax and Mother were most likely friends. It would undoubtedly get back to her. Since I had to tell him who I was and why we were here, there was no way to pretend I was some uncouth bystander, either. "I'm Savannah Martin. Collier. My Uncle Sid told me about you."

"Regina's niece." He grabbed my hand and patted it. "You married the cop."

I had. And Art Mullinax was nicer about the description of Rafe than some I've heard.

"This is Police Chief Grimaldi," I said, gesturing with my free hand. Mr. Mullinax dropped me like my hand was hot and turned to her, looking her over.

"Charming," he said.

It was the first time I'd heard that word applied to Grimaldi, and from her expression, it might have been the first time she'd heard it applied to herself, too. "Mr. Mullinax."

When he snatched for her hand, she snatched back, and gave his a good shake before dropping it. "I wanted to ask you a couple of questions about Kent Jurgensson."

Art Mullinax's blue eyes went sorrowful, and he shook his head, clucking. "Terrible tragedy. Just terrible what happened."

"Uncle Sid said you played golf with him," I said.

He turned to me. "Indeed, young lady. Sid, Kent, me, and Jacob Drimmel when he was available."

"Laura Lee Drimmel's father? The same Laura Lee who used to date Noah Trent?"

Mullinax nodded. "The very same. Now, what do you know about Noah Trent?"

His eyes were still twinkling, but the look was intent.

"Not much," I admitted, with a glance at Grimaldi. This was her interview; shouldn't she be asking the questions and answering them?

She didn't say anything, though, just arched her brows at me, so I added, "Someone told me he was the boy involved in the… um… incident with Mr. Jurgensson."

Mullinax nodded. "So he was. But he's dead now, rest his soul. And we shouldn't speak ill of the dead."

No, we shouldn't. Or so Mother had always told me.

I glanced at Grimaldi. She still wasn't speaking up. "Uncle Sid said you'd been in touch with Mr. Jurgensson since he left here. We thought maybe you'd be able to tell us where he is."

Mr. Mullinax tilted his head to look at me, like a plump sparrow. "Now, why would you be looking for Kent?"

"We have some questions," Grimaldi said, finally. Mullinax turned to her, and she added, "Not about what happened back then. Or not specifically."

"About what, then?"

"Another case," Grimaldi said. "With a Latin connection."

Mullinax's bushy eyebrows rose. "A Latin connection?"

"We just wanted to discuss some former students with him." After a second she added, "Not Noah Trent."

Mullinax nodded and looked thoughtful.

"Uncle Sid said he heard that Jurgensson worked some menial job in Tupelo or Tucson," I contributed. "I guess it must have been you who told him that?"

"I imagine it might have been. Although it might just as well have been Toledo or Toronto as Tucson. It's a long time ago. Not sure I can remember the particulars."

"I don't suppose you have any letters or postcards he might have sent you?"

"Oh, I don't imagine I do," Art Mullinax said cheerfully. "The last time I heard from Kent... it must be a dozen years ago, at least. Probably more. Just Christmas cards, you know, or a note whenever he moved to a new place. He found it hard to find employment that lasted, poor bastard. And not surprising, either."

No, it wasn't surprising. Even if he had avoided being listed on the Sexual Offender registry, the kind of thing that had happened here is apt to follow a man around. People talk.

"So you have no idea where we'd be able to find him," Grimaldi said.

Mullinax shook his head. "I'm afraid not, my dear. Chief Inspector. Um..."

"Chief is fine," Grimaldi said. "We appreciate the time."

She gave me a look. I smiled politely. "Thank you, Mr. Mullinax. Our best to your wife."

Mullinax beamed pleasantly as he let us out, and then he stood in the open door and waved as we piled back into the SUV.

"Nice place," I said, giving it one last look as Grimaldi put the SUV in gear and we rolled off down the track toward town. Behind us, Art Mullinax disappeared inside the big, white house and shut the door.

Grimaldi grunted.

I turned in my seat and looked at her. "What's wrong?"

She glanced over before she turned her attention back to the—I use the word in its loosest sense—road. "Just wondering which part of the acreage I'd have to dig up to find what's left of Jurgensson."

My jaw dropped, and it took me a few seconds to hike it up. "You're kidding. Right?"

She didn't answer, and I repeated it. "You're kidding. You must be."

"I'm not sure what I am."

The trees closed behind us, and we drove on in a tunnel of green leaves. The sun, starting to wane now, slanted late-afternoon spears of light through the branches in front of us.

"You think he killed Jurgensson? Why? He didn't say anything suspicious, did he?" If he had, I hadn't noticed. "What makes you think he killed Jurgensson?"

She didn't say anything, so I continued, figuring it out in my head as we went down the track. "It makes for a nice theory. I'll give you that. He's the only one who's heard from Jurgensson since he—Jurgensson—left. If he left. There's no real proof that he ever heard from him at all. If anyone killed Jurgensson and buried him, Mullinax is at the top of the list. But you have no reason to suspect that he isn't telling the truth. Jurgensson could be bagging groceries in Toledo or Toronto or Tucson as we speak."

"Not Toronto," Grimaldi said. "He'd have had to make it across the border to Canada, and there's no record of that."

"Surely there are ways to sneak across the border where nobody will check your papers? People come across the border from Mexico all the time."

Grimaldi shrugged. "He could be in Toledo or Tupelo or Tucson. Or somewhere that doesn't start with a T. Or he could be buried on Art Mullinax's back forty."

The track ended and we reached the paved road again. The SUV picked up speed heading back to downtown Columbia. I settled a little more comfortably into the seat and added, "Why would Art Mullinax kill Kent Jurgensson?"

"Motive's easy," Grimaldi said, and brought on an echo of Rafe, who had told me the same thing, not just once but multiple times. "Maybe he knew the Trent family. Or maybe he was just disgusted that Jurgensson committed statutory rape in general. Maybe he has sexual abuse in his own past, and this brought it back. Maybe he was angry because he and Jurgensson—and your uncle and Laura Lee's father—played golf together, and Jurgensson had fooled them all into thinking he was a nice guy. Any one of those might be reason enough to kill him."

I supposed. But— "There's no way to prove any of that." Except maybe for a connection to the Trents, if one existed. Or any sexual abuse, if it had happened and there was a record of it. But even if a connection to the Trents or a record of sexual abuse existed, it wouldn't be proof of murder.

"No," Grimaldi agreed. "And I'll never get permission to dig without more than I've got."

"But you think he did it. Why?"

She shrugged. Or maybe it was more like a squirm. "It might just be that I want to find someone guilty of something. I'm not any closer to figuring out who killed Laura Lee Matlock, and my mother, and Ramona Mitchell, and everyone in-between. We don't know who's stalking your husband— although we will figure that out eventually. But if Mullinax killed Jurgensson, at least that'll be one thing I'll know for sure."

"Except there's no proof."

"No," Grimaldi said regretfully, as the first stoplight in Columbia rose up in front of us. "And after so many years, it's not likely I'll find any, either."

Probably not. Especially if no one had suspected anything back then.

"I guess you'll be going back to the police station and digging up the old files on Jurgensson."

"I already have them on my desk," Grimaldi said. "Now I'm going to look at them again and see if Mr. Mullinax's name shows up anywhere."

Better her than me. "Drop me off at home first," I told her. "I have some work of my own to do."

She glanced over, and I added, "Nothing to do with this. We've got an open house scheduled tomorrow on Fulton. I should print out some fliers and sign-in sheets, and make sure we're ready."

And I should also prepare some dinner for my husband, so he wouldn't suggest going to Beulah's again. At this point, my instinct was to keep Carrie under lock and key and out of the public eye as much as humanly possible.

Fifteen

Rafe made it home in time for dinner. The fact that he was able to stop working to go home for a meal with his wife probably indicated that the case was going cold, as the previous seventeen had done.

He grunted when I said so. "We're trying."

"I'm sure you are," I said, ladling out chicken and broccoli. "We didn't do any better. The biggest surprise of the day was that Curtis is the first victim's son. Although I don't see where that could have anything to do with anything."

"No," Rafe agreed, picking up his fork.

"If Frankie was black, though, I guess he's off the suspect list for the other murders. Grimaldi said the profile Agent Yung provided said the killer is definitely white."

"Not sure there's anything definite about it." He poked at some of the chicken before he stabbed a piece of broccoli. Instead of lifting it to his mouth, he added, "Look at me."

"I am looking at you. You're not eating."

He popped the broccoli in his mouth and chewed. "What I meant," he said when he'd swallowed, "is that I'm black."

I opened my mouth to say that he's as much white as he's black, maybe more, and he added, "Or as near as makes no difference."

Maybe so. At any rate, I didn't debate it, because I knew what he was getting at. "And most of the women you've slept with—at least the ones I know about—have been white. Or Hispanic, in Carmen's case."

Yvonne, Elspeth, me, Carmen, me again... And I knew there had to be others, even if I couldn't put names or faces to them. The ones I knew about were one redhead, two blondes, and Carmen. The pinup girl he'd had on the wall of his bedroom in the trailer in the Bog growing up, she had been white, too. A platinum blonde with china blue eyes and lacy white lingerie.

"If somebody tried to make a profile of me," he said, "based on the women I've taken to bed, they'd prob'ly conclude that I'm white, too."

"And they'd be half right."

He shrugged.

"So what are you saying? That it could be Frankie after all?"

"'Course it could," Rafe said, sounding irritated. "He married a white girl, didn't he? Don't that tell you what his type is?"

I guess it did, now that he mentioned it. "So we throw the profile out?"

"Not necessarily. I'm just saying that sometimes the profile's wrong. Or sometimes people interpret things wrong. A lot of people don't think outside the box."

He forked up another piece of broccoli.

"I guess that's true," I said slowly. "And speaking of thinking outside the box..."

"Yeah?"

"Grimaldi and I went to see Art Mullinax. He lives on the old Daffodil Hill Farm, up on the north side of Columbia. You should have seen it, Rafe. It was gorgeous. This big, white Victorian house, and flowers and flowering trees everywhere..."

His lips curved. "We got a big, white house and flowers

and flowering trees, too, darlin'."

I guess we did. Even if it wasn't, technically, our house.

"He say anything helpful?" Rafe wanted to know, and I dragged my mind from architecture and landscaping back to the case—or cases—at hand.

"Mullinax said he hadn't heard from Jurgensson for years, and he wasn't sure whether Jurgensson had been in Tupelo or Tucson or Toledo or somewhere else the last time he wrote. He didn't hang onto any of the letters or cards, of course."

"No reason why he'd keep'em," Rafe said.

"That's what I thought. But Grimaldi was acting a little weird when we drove away, so I asked what was wrong. And she told me she was trying to figure out which part of the property she'd have to dig up to find Jurgensson's remains."

Both Rafe's eyebrows elevated this time. "She got a reason for thinking that?"

"Nothing beyond an evil mind," I said. "Or a lot of experience. And that might be enough. I didn't hear Mullinax say anything suspicious. But she might have heard something I didn't. And even if she didn't notice anything specifically..."

Rafe nodded. "It makes sense. If anybody did away with him, it'd be the guy who claimed to have heard from him."

"There's no reason to think he's not alive and well somewhere, though. Is there?"

"Not other than that his social security number ain't been used in thirty years," Rafe said.

Well, yes. There was that.

"Well, it's a big property. And Grimaldi said she wouldn't get permission to dig any of it up unless she had more evidence than she has currently. So she went back to the police station to read the file again."

"She musta taken it home," Rafe said, "'cause she was gone when I got there."

"It's not even her case. Or for that matter a case at all.

You'd think she'd have enough to keep her busy between the serial killer and your stalker, and she wouldn't need to invent more murders."

"Speaking of my stalker," Rafe said, and forked up another piece of chicken. "Vasim's cleaned up the video. He's spending second shift trying to match the license plate to a car."

Great.

"Problem is, it's Saturday night, and things can get a little rowdy. So he might not have time. But if we get lucky, by tomorrow we could have a name and address to go with the car."

"That would be great," I said enthusiastically. "It's probably nothing to worry about." Or at least I kept telling myself that, repeatedly. "It's probably just some woman with a crush on you. But I'd feel better if we can figure out who she is and warn her off. I don't want to have to keep looking over my shoulder for the rest of my life, just in case someone's trying to sneak up behind me."

"You won't have to. Another day or two at the most, and we'll have her." He plunged the fork back into the casserole. Now that he'd started eating he must have realized he was hungry.

"Just out of curiosity," I said, as I picked at my own food and as Carrie kicked her feet in the bouncy seat and Pearl snored on her pillow, "what'll happen when you figure out who it is? I mean… you can't really arrest her, right? Is it illegal to take pictures of other people and posting them on social media?"

"Gray area," Rafe said. "If they're in public, you don't need permission. There's no reasonable expectation of privacy."

"So someone could take a picture of us holding hands at Beulah's because they thought we were cute, and that'd be OK."

He nodded. "But anybody standing outside the house right

now, shooting through the window, would be violating our privacy. We're in our own home and have the right to expect to be by ourselves."

Not an issue so far, although I cast a nervous glance at the back door. "You don't think anyone's out there, do you?"

"You'd see 'em if they were," Rafe said calmly. "It's still light out. Besides, Pearl would be having a fit."

And she was lying quietly on her pillow, napping.

"All of the pictures and videos so far were taken in public places. So it wasn't illegal to take any of them. And I guess, if it's legal to take them, it's legal to upload them to social media?"

"More or less," Rafe said.

"So she hasn't done anything illegal."

"Depends on your definition of illegal. And on the DA. I'm sure Satterfield'd be happy to charge her with something if you asked him to."

Perhaps. Perhaps not. Todd wasn't so enamored with me anymore, now that I was married to Rafe and he was engaged to Marley.

"What we can do," Rafe said, "once we figure out who she is, is we can get a protection order and tell her to cease and desist. Once she's been served, if she keeps doing what she's doing, it'll be felony stalking, and she can go to prison."

"That'd work." She'd be behind bars, and I wouldn't have to worry about anyone trying to take my baby away.

"That's unless she does something more now."

Right. I grimaced.

We had finished eating and Rafe had taken Carrie into the parlor and was playing with her while I was filling the dishwasher under Pearl's watchful eye when we heard the sound of tires on the gravel outside.

Or rather, what I heard—and saw—was Pearl's ears twitch

before she took off like a bullet across the kitchen and down the hallway toward the foyer, barking hysterically.

I grabbed a dish towel and followed. By the time I was halfway down the hall, Rafe had emerged from the parlor. Pearl was dancing in front of the door, her barks reverberating through the house.

"Knock it off," Rafe told her, sternly.

She danced out of the way, still yipping. By now, I was close enough to hear the sound of a car door slam outside. When I peered through one of the sidelights, I saw a small, blue car pulled up to the bottom of the stairs, and a man starting to climb.

He wasn't anyone I knew. Medium height and sort of weedy, he might have been in his mid-twenties, with a scrubby little goatee and a faded T-shirt sporting a picture of the Beatles.

"Hold the dog back," Rafe told me.

I wrapped my hand around her collar and held on. "It's OK, sweetheart. Daddy'll take care of the bad man."

She stopped barking, but the rumble in her throat made my hand vibrate.

Rafe, meanwhile, pulled the door open and blocked it. "Something I can do for you?"

The young man looked at him, up and down, and rather than look intimidated, he grinned. "Got a kid in the car who says you'll pay the fare."

I peered through the window again while I held onto Pearl. She had stopped growling now, so I thought it might be safe to let her go. As soon as I did, she bulleted up next to Rafe and stuck her face outside.

"Whoa." The guy outside took a step back.

"Thought I told you to hold her," Rafe said without turning his head.

"You did. But I figured he wasn't a threat." I stuck my head outside, too. "Uber?"

He nodded.

"Let me guess. The kid looks like him," I gestured to Rafe, "only smaller."

He gave Rafe another up and down. "Pretty much."

"How'd he con you into driving him from Nashville to Maury County?" Rafe wanted to know. He was already reaching for his wallet, but it didn't keep him from adding, "It'd serve the little bastard right if I refused to pay and sent him back home."

"Then Ginny and Sam would have to pay," I pointed out, "twice the distance."

"That's the only reason I'm not doing it." He held out his card.

The young man shook his head. "It's gotta be cash, man."

Rafe sighed. "'Course it does."

"I'll go get some," I said. "How much is the fare?"

The driver mentioned an amount that made me wince, but I nodded gamely. "I'll be right back."

"You can let him out," Rafe said, as I headed toward the kitchen, where we keep the emergency stash of money.

By the time I got back, with the exorbitant fare plus tip, David had been rescued from the confines of the small compact and was standing in the foyer grinning up at Rafe. Not for the first time, the resemblance between them struck me. David looked very much like Rafe had when we'd gone to high school together, and the older he got, the stronger the resemblance became.

If he felt bad for showing up unannounced and setting us back several hundred dollars, he showed no sign of it. "Hi, Savannah," he told me, with a flash of that grin that wasn't just his own.

"David." I tried to sound stern as I handed the driver the money we owed him and watched him take off down the stairs like he was afraid we were going to call him back. "Did you tell your parents you were leaving?"

It was hard to be firm, though, when he looked so much like Rafe.

The latter had no such problems. "You little delinquent," he told his son, "why do you keep doing this to your parents?"

He wasn't talking about us. I didn't feel like David's mother, and although Rafe was, biologically, his father, I'm not sure he felt much like it, either. Their relationship, since they first met a year and a half ago, had been more fraternal than fatherly.

No, Rafe was talking about Ginny and Sam, David's adopted parents. This wasn't the first time David had left home on his own to visit us here, without his parents permission or knowledge. Each time, Ginny had called me in hysterics, letting me know he was gone. I wondered why I hadn't heard from her this time.

"They don't know I'm gone yet," the delinquent said calmly. "They don't even know I know enough to leave."

Rafe sighed. "What d'you do? Eavesdrop?"

David shrugged, not the least discombobulated. "How else am I going to find out what's going on? Nobody ever tells me anything."

If this was a dig at Rafe (as well as at Ginny and Sam) it didn't come off. "That's because there's nothing going on you need to worry about," Rafe told him, sternly.

David scowled up at him. He was almost as tall as me now, but had quite a few inches to go before he reached Rafe's height. And he might never get there. Elspeth had been on the short side. "Dad told Mom you have a stalker. '*Again*,' they said. And that this somebody's talking pictures of you, and of Savannah, and of Carrie, and posting them online."

"I suppose you looked 'em up?"

"You suppose right," David said. "What did you think I'd

do, ignore it? You're my dad, whether you like it or not, and Carrie's my sister. If something's happening, I want to know about it."

"So you can put yourself in danger, too?" Rafe didn't give him a chance to answer, just went on, "You moron, the reason I called Sam is so he and Ginny could make sure you were safe. The last thing I wanted was for you to show up here. We were all much better off with you in Nashville."

"I can take care of myself..." David began.

"You think I don't know that? So can I. That don't mean I put myself in danger when I don't have to. That's not brave. That's stupid."

David flushed, and until he spoke I wasn't sure whether it was from embarrassment or anger. Once he opened his mouth, there was no doubt. "You think you're in a position to lecture me on stupidity? Or weren't you the one who—?"

"Enough," I said. With enough force to shut him up. Or maybe he'd just been brought up to be quiet when a lady's talking. Rafe looked at me, too, and I was happy to see enough amusement in his eyes to know that he wasn't really angry. "Go sit in the parlor. Both of you. Have you had dinner, David?"

"No," David said, with his lower lip stuck out. "I had to cause a scene and be sent to my room without supper in order to get away."

"Of course you did." I resisted the temptation to roll my eyes, but just barely. "For the record, I hope Ginny and Sam ground you for real when they find out what you've done. Is chicken and rice all right?"

"Fine," David said, with another of those angelic smiles that popped out every so often. "I'll eat anything."

"Then go sit in the parlor and I'll bring you a plate. Are you going to call Sam, Rafe?"

Rafe sighed. "I guess I'd better." He glanced at David, who

was smiling brightly as if all was well with the world. "And I agree with Savannah. I hope your parents ground you for a month when you get back home."

"That's mean," David said, but without rancor. The two of them headed for the parlor, with Pearl dancing in front of them, while I walked back toward the kitchen to dish up another plate of chicken casserole.

David bedded down in Dix's old room for the night. By then, he knew as much about the case—as he called it—as we did. He realized, because Rafe had taken pains to explain it to him, that his showing up here tonight had made him more of a target rather than less, but that didn't seem to faze him much.

"She's not going to be interested in me," he'd said confidently. "I'm bigger, and hard to manhandle, and I know who I am. I can tell anyone who asks my name and my social security number and who my parents are and where I live. If she's after anyone, it's Carrie."

We all looked at the baby, who was kicking her feet on the floor. Small, easy to grab, and with idea who she was or who she belonged to. If someone wanted to take her, there'd be nothing stopping them. Except us.

"Nonetheless," Rafe told David, "I'm taking you back home tomorrow, and I want you to promise me you'll stay there."

He waited. David squirmed. "Fine," he said eventually, when it became clear that Rafe wouldn't accept any other answer. "Can I at least stay long enough to see the rest of the family? I don't have to be back at school until Monday morning."

We agreed that that would be acceptable to us if Ginny and Sam said it was OK, and Rafe got on the phone.

"They already knew he was gone," he told me later, after David had been installed in Dix's room and we were in our own, getting ready to sleep. "They were about to call, since they figured he'd be on his way here."

"It's not exactly the first time he's pulled this stunt."

Rafe shook his head. "He's getting better. Or more diabolical. Before, he always left on foot, or on his bike, and it would take him hours, if not days, to get here. This time he called a car, and was here in an hour. They barely had time to figure out he was missing before he arrived."

"He's a smart kid." I lifted the comforter and crawled in before I added, "A little too smart for his own good, maybe."

Rafe nodded gloomily. "I'm gonna leave the door to the hallway open. Just in case he's in there thinking about sneaking out. I don't think he wants to go back to Nashville before this is over."

That was the very distinct impression I'd gotten, too. And he might be thinking that he could run away from us and go to ground somewhere and flush out the stalker himself. I wouldn't put it past him. "He's amazingly like you for having been brought up by someone else."

"All my worst qualities," Rafe said, and climbed into bed next to me after leaving the door ajar.

"I wouldn't say that. He's brave, and clever, and determined—"

"And stupid," Rafe said, "if he thinks he can get past me and outta here."

Right. "There's a back staircase, you know. The servants' stairs. They fetch up in the kitchen. He doesn't have to come this way to get downstairs."

"Dammit," Rafe said. "He wouldn't know about those, though."

"Actually—" I sounded apologetic, even in my own ears, as if the servants' stairs were my fault, "I think he does. Back in June, when Hernandez had David and my mother tied up in the master bedroom, I'm pretty sure the servants' stairs came into play."

Rafe was flat on his back staring up at the ceiling. "Well, I can't lock him in."

No. "We could rig a warning system," I said. "Tie a thread to his door knob, and a bell to the thread, and if he pulls his door open in the middle of the night, the thread will snap and the bell will fall…"

"And Pearl will give us both a heart attack when she goes after what she thinks is a burglar." He turned and gathered me in.

"She wouldn't hurt David," I said sleepily, as I found a comfortable spot for my head against his shoulder.

"She might bite first and ask questions later. Better not risk it." He still sounded wide awake.

"You *are* going to go to sleep," I asked, "aren't you?"

Because if he wasn't, I would feel compelled to stay awake and keep him company.

"Sure, darlin'." He ran a hand up and down my back, warm and hard under the blankets. "Don't worry about it. I'm a light sleeper. I'll hear him if he tries to leave."

I didn't doubt it. I don't sleep that heavily myself these days, what with having to wake once or twice a night to feed Carrie.

"Good night," I told him sleepily.

"Night, darlin'." The last thing I remember is the feeling of his lips against my forehead.

Sixteen

David must either be OK with the status quo, or else all the activity—Pearl walking around, Carrie waking up in the middle of the night, me getting up to feed her—dissuaded him from making a break for it during the late hours. He was up at one point, and stuck his head through the nursery door when I called out to him, to tell me he was thirsty and was going downstairs for something to drink. I told him to be careful of the dog, and three minutes later he was back upstairs. Of all of us, Rafe was the only one who spent a quiet night. He bounded out of bed bright and early, and headed down to the kitchen for his first shot of caffeine. I stayed in bed until I heard Carrie wake up, and by then David had gone downstairs, too. The two of them brought me pancakes—a little burnt, but otherwise not bad—in bed while I fed Carrie.

It's family tradition to meet for Sunday Brunch at the Wayside Inn after church. Some of the time we're all there—and there have become a lot of us over time—while sometimes just a few of us show up. Today, Dix was there with his girls, and Catherine, but Jonathan had taken their kids home, since Cole, the youngest, had a stomach ache. Audrey and Mrs. Jenkins graced us with their presence sometimes, but not today, so I suggested that Rafe could take David and Carrie to Audrey's house while I headed to my open house later. Mother was there, though, with the sheriff, and she lit up when she saw David. The two of them had bonded over that experience with the serial killer last June, and she's always delighted to see him.

Rafe and I sat down with Bob while Mother interrogated David about his life and school this year.

"Any progress on the investigation?" I wanted to know.

Bob shrugged. He's a tall, rawboned man who looks like the sheriff in an old Western. "We're whittling it down. Tracking down trucking companies and drivers and finding out who and what they saw, and when. So far, nobody's seen anybody who looked like they didn't belong at that truck stop."

"Were you part of the investigation into Laura Lee Matlock's murder way back when?" I asked, while Catherine descended on the baby, took her out of the car seat, and bounced her. Carrie gurgled.

Bob grinned. "It ain't that long ago, darlin'. Sixteen years? Maybe seventeen?"

Something like that. More than half my life. But maybe it didn't seem that long ago for him. "So you remember it."

He nodded. "Sure. We don't get so many locals murdered that any of them get forgotten. But she disappeared from here, remember, and was found somewhere else. The police there did all of the work on the body and dump site."

Right. "What did you think had happened?"

"The same thing we still think happened," Bob said promptly. "She went out to somebody's truck with him, and ended up dead. At that time, we just didn't see the pattern."

"There wasn't a pattern at that time."

Bob nodded. "Took a couple more victims for that."

"So at the time you just thought it was random."

"At first we didn't know what it was," Bob said. "We checked on her husband, and anyone else she might have gotten involved with while Frankie was inside—"

"Was she involved with anyone else while Frankie was inside?"

"Not like that," Bob said. "Her mama told us that sometimes she went outside with a trucker for a little extra money…"

Mrs. Drimmel had told Grimaldi and me the same thing.

"—but other than that, there was nobody in particular. So we figured she'd gone outside with the wrong guy. That's still what I think."

I nodded.

"You and Tamara getting any closer to figuring anything out?"

I guess she must have run her own investigation by him, to get permission or just to let him know she was asking questions. "Not much," I admitted, as Dix shifted closer, maybe attracted by the mention of Grimaldi's name. "We got off on a tangent about the Latin teacher and the kid he molested."

"Because of the numerals." Bob nodded.

"Grimaldi thinks Jurgensson is buried somewhere on Daffodil Hill Farm."

Bob's eyebrows rose. "What gave her that idea?"

"She didn't tell me. I didn't notice anything suspicious, so it might just be instinct on her part. Or imagination."

"Instinct," Dix said. I glanced at him, but he didn't say anything else.

I turned back to Bob. "I don't imagine there's any reason to think he's dead at all, really, other than the social security business. But if he is…"

"Daffodil Hill Farm's a better place to look than many others," Bob concluded. "Plenty of land up there to hide a body. And Art Mullinax has had plenty of offers to sell off parts of the woods in the past few years, but he's always said no."

"Could be he just wants to keep urban sprawl from creeping in," Dix suggested.

Bob spared him a glance. "Could be. No reason to think otherwise. Except…"

He went into thinking mode, his gray eyes distant. I glanced at Rafe. "What do you think?"

My husband shrugged. "If Tammy says so, I wouldn't be surprised if she was right."

Sure. But… "Surely she isn't in the habit of accusing totally unrelated people of murder? I mean, I get why she might think that Jurgensson is dead. Nobody's heard from him in years, other than Mullinax. Or at least nobody admits to having heard from him. But to go from there to thinking that some random guy murdered him and buried him in the pasture…"

I ran out of breath and had to stop for a moment. Bob shook his head. "He's not just some random guy, Savannah."

"I know he and Jurgensson played golf together. Uncle Sid told me."

"He's Judy Trent's brother," Bob said. "Judy was Noah's mother."

I blinked. "So Art Mullinax is—was—Noah Trent's uncle."

Bob nodded.

"Well, that would explain it." Or would at least explain it better. "Does Grimaldi know that?"

"I don't imagine so," Bob said. "She hasn't been here long enough to know the ins and outs of the personal relationships."

No. Not if I didn't know, and I'd lived here most of my life.

"If Noah and Jurgensson are both dead, though," Dix said, "they can't be involved with your serial killer case."

Rafe and Bob both shook their heads. "We gotta look for those Roman numerals somewhere else," Rafe added.

"You don't suppose Mullinax…?"

I trailed off when the waitress showed up to take our drink orders. "Hi, Lynn. I'll have sweet tea, please."

Lynn nodded. "Did I hear you mention Judy Trent?"

I glanced at Bob, and at Dix and Rafe, before I nodded. "Do you know her?"

"She lives down the street from me," Lynn said, taking down Rafe's drink order. Bob and Dix had been here when we arrived, and were taken care of already. "Everything all right?"

"Fine." The sheriff smiled at her. "Nothing to worry about."

"That's right," I said lightly, "you live in Sunnyside, don't you?" It wasn't really a question. I knew very well where she lived. It was just a couple of months since I'd broken into her house, or at least her garage. "I guess you know the Drimmels, too."

She nodded. "Nice folks. Well, she's nice. I don't know him well. And the kids are OK. Horrible, that video of Curtis the other night. Good thing you got there in time to stop anything from happening to him." She glanced at Rafe from under her lashes.

"He woulda been fine without me being there," the latter said calmly. "Tucker wasn't gonna hurt him. But maybe you have some idea who his friends might be, that ran off and left him there?"

Lynn looked at him for a second before she admitted, "I might."

"If you wanna come to the police station one day and tell me about it, I'd be happy to listen."

"I might do that," Lynn told him. And added, "I'd better get these drink orders in. I'll be right back."

We all nodded, and waited until she was out of range before we went back to the conversation. "You don't suppose Art Mullinax," I said again, "is the serial killer? Maybe he and Noah Trent killed Jurgensson together back when Noah was in high school, and Laura Lee found out about it? She dated Noah for a while, her mother said. I'm not sure exactly when, but

Mrs. Drimmel said he was the boyfriend before Frankie, so it would have been after the episode with Jurgensson."

"And then maybe Noah told his uncle Art what Laura Lee had figured out," Dix added, getting into the spirit of the thing, "and Art decided that Laura Lee had to go. So he killed her, and it either broke him, so he started killing other women too, or he killed the others to cover up Laura Lee's murder."

"To make it look like the work of a a serial killer," I said.

"Darlin'…" Rafe looked at me patiently, "it *is* the work of a serial killer."

"You know what I mean. He could have done it compulsively, the way serial killers do, or he could have done it deliberately, to cover up Laura Lee's murder."

"He'd be a serial killer either way," my husband informed me. "What about Noah? You got an explanation for that death, too?"

Dix opened his mouth, and I got in first. "Noah figured out what Uncle Art had been up to, and was horrified by it, not to mention afraid he'd be implicated, so he killed himself."

"Or Uncle Art killed him," Dix added, "and made it look like suicide."

I nodded. "Mullinax sounds sort of Roman, doesn't it? Like… I don't know, Claudius or Tiberius."

Rafe's mouth curved. "Can't say they sound all that similar to me, but you may be right."

Bob's head had swiveled back and forth as he looked from one to the other of us. "That's a nice theory," he said now, "but you understand there's no proof?"

Of course. "A theory is a good thing, though. Right? Then you can go about trying to prove or disprove it."

"One thing comes to mind," Rafe said, "and I didn't see Mullinax—don't think I ever met the man—how'd he look, driving into a truck stop to dump a victim? Like he'd belong?"

Not precisely. "He's at the upper end of the profile age

wise," I admitted. "Probably more like seventy-five. But he looked like he was pretty healthy. He golfs."

"Healthy enough to strangle a full-grown woman and carry the body?"

Hard to say, really. But he hadn't looked unhealthy, so that was something. Maybe.

When I didn't answer, Rafe went on. "Any reason to think Mullinax would look at home at a truck stop? Did you see a truck? Anything with a diesel engine?"

I shook my head. "It's a farm, though. I wouldn't be surprised if such a thing existed."

"I don't see him traveling up and down I-65 on a tractor, darlin'."

Well, of course not. "I didn't mean that," I said. "All I meant is that there might have been a pickup truck or something in the garage. It was a big garage."

"You didn't look inside?"

I hadn't. "I don't think it had any windows, and the doors were all closed. But practically anything could have fit in there."

Except maybe an eighteen-wheeler. But the cab of one might.

"I guess it couldn't hurt to go out and take a look," Rafe said, with a glance at Bob.

The latter nodded. "We can run out there this afternoon, see what we see."

He shifted sideways as Lynn leaned in to put Rafe's drink on the table.

"Not this afternoon," Rafe told him, leaning the other way as Lynn's hip brushed his arm. "Thanks, Lynn." To Bob, he added, "I have something else I gotta do later."

"I have an open house," I told Bob, leaning too, as Lynn came closer with my iced tea, "at the house on Fulton, and Rafe's taking David back to Nashville. Thank you, Lynn."

She nodded. "You folks ready to order?"

I guess we were. I mean, I hadn't opened the menu, but I've been at the Wayside Inn often enough to know what they serve. "I'll have the savory crepes with a side of field greens, please."

Lynn took the other orders—Rafe was having steak with shoestring potatoes at noon—and then moved on to Mother and David. Catherine had scooted closer to them, still with Carrie on her lap, so both my children, or Rafe's children, were getting quality time with their aunt and grandmother. It was nice to see.

Bob and Rafe decided that they were going to pay a visit on Art Mullinax in the morning, and Dix was angling to be allowed to come. I have no idea why he'd want to, but maybe he'd gotten bitten by the detective bug, too, and wanted to play.

"Can I come?" I wanted to know. "Grimaldi let me."

They looked at one another.

"That'd be quite the delegation," Bob said. "You, me, Yung, Tamara, Dix, Savannah…"

Rafe nodded. "Better not, darlin'. We're just gonna go have a talk with him. If we show up with that kinda group, he's gonna be suspicious. You and Tammy go find something else to do. You, too." He glanced at Dix.

My brother looked mutinous. "I don't see why I can't come. You might need a lawyer."

"I'll make sure he doesn't," the sheriff said dryly. "You do your job, Dixon, and let us do ours."

Dix stuck his lower lip out, but didn't protest. I turned to Rafe, who shook his head. "Sorry, darlin'. If there's anything there, I don't wanna get his back up with a big group. Bad enough that the sheriff and local PD shows up."

"And the TBI." Not to mention the FBI.

"We'll try to keep Leslie out of it," Rafe said. "Nothing to do with her case, after all. And no need to mention that I'm doing double duty with the TBI, either. Better to keep it as low key as possible."

"What are you going to use as an excuse for going out there? Because if he's guilty of anything, he's going to be suspicious no matter what you say."

We discussed it until the food arrived, and then we ate. Once the food was gone, Rafe caught David's eye down the length of the table. "Time we were getting on, if we're gonna have time to stop by Audrey's before we drive back to Nashville."

David looked reluctant to be parted from Mother, but he nodded. "Sorry I can't stay longer."

"From what I understand," Mother told him sternly, "you shouldn't be here at all. Next time, you're to stay home, where you're safe."

"I'm safe here." He grinned at her, before he leaned in and kissed her cheek. "Bye."

Mother looked momentarily stunned, and then pleased.

I took Carrie back from Catherine and we headed out. "We'll take you home and pick up the Harley," Rafe told me when we got to the parking lot, "that way you can keep the Volvo to go to the open house."

"There's no room on the Harley for Carrie," I pointed out, while David's eyes got big. After a second, he started to vibrate with excitement. He'd been on the back of the Harley before, but never for an hour or more on the interstate. "Besides, are you sure Ginny would approve of that?"

"By the time she finds out, it'll be too late," Rafe said. And added, "You suggesting I can't be trusted to get David home safe?"

"Of course not. I know you know how to handle the beast. I just don't know whether David's parents are going to want him riding on it."

"He'll be fine," Rafe said dismissively and opened the Volvo's back door so I could put Carrie's seat inside. David crawled into the back next to the carrier, and Rafe behind the wheel. "Coming?" he asked me when I didn't climb in next to him.

"Just looking around."

"She ain't here," he told me.

No. There was no sign of the tan compact. "I thought maybe Lynn…"

"She drives a blue Volkswagon," Rafe told me. "You saw it back when we were at her house that time."

Of course I had. "She might have switched it out."

"Switched out a nice VW for that old import? Why would she wanna do that?"

"So she could stalk you in peace and we wouldn't recognize the car?" I folded myself into the front seat.

He shook his head as he put the car in gear. "It ain't Lynn. We'd have recognized her at Beulah's the other night. Besides, Yvonne knows Lynn. If she'd been there, Yvonne woulda told me."

"Fine." His arguments made sense. "It's not Lynn."

"No," Rafe said, and left the parking lot for home.

Back at the mansion, I said goodbye to David, since they were planning to head for Nashville straight from Audrey's house, and kissed Rafe. "Drive carefully."

"You too, darlin'. I'll see you later." He swung a leg over the big, black Harley-Davidson and nodded to David. "Get on. Hang on to me. Lean into the curves. You'll be fine."

David didn't look like he needed the reassurance. He was wearing a big grin behind the helmet, and when the bike took off down the driveway with a spurt of gravel, he let out a "Whoop!" I could hear all the way back to where I was standing.

They took a right turn out of the driveway, toward downtown Sweetwater and Audrey's house, and I carried the baby inside to change her diaper and feed her before it was time to head to Fulton Street and the open house.

I was a few minutes late, but nobody cared except Charlotte. She was there before me, but because she didn't have a key, she had to sit in her Jeep and wait. When I pulled up behind her and opened my door, she flung her own open and stalked toward me. "You're late!"

"Sorry," I said. "I had to see Rafe and David off. He showed up late last night, in a rented Uber, after having crawled out his bedroom window."

It was enough to stop her in mid rant, although it took her a second to switch gears. "Oh, my God. Is he OK?"

"He's fine." I reached into the back of the Volvo and pulled out the baby seat. Carrie had fallen asleep on the way here, and looked like a little angel, with long lashes shadowing her cheeks and her little pink pout. "It's not the first time he's pulled something like this. Last time, he was at camp up on the Cumberland Plateau, and he used a bike, and it took him hours to get here. We were all worried sick."

Especially since we didn't know whether he'd actually run away or whether Hernandez had grabbed him.

"He spent the night with us and came to brunch this morning," I added, as I headed up the steps to the front door. "He and Rafe were going to see Mrs. Jenkins at Audrey's before Rafe took him home. On the bike."

I stuck the key in the lock and twisted it.

"How will his mother feel about that?" Charlotte wanted to know.

"I imagine she might have some things to say about it." I pushed the door open and went in. "But as Rafe pointed out, by then it'll be too late. Oh, shit. I mean… shoot."

"What?" Charlotte peered around me, and came up with a

more subdued, "Oh, not again!"

"It's starting to feel personal, isn't it?" I looked around for the baseball, and saw it lying over by the wall, in practically the same spot as it had been the last time.

Charlotte nodded. "Either someone has really bad aim…"

"Or really good aim." I headed for the kitchen and the broom. "I'll get the glass up. You can find something to tape over the hole. And one of us is going to have to go to the hardware store and get another piece of glass before we leave here tonight."

Charlotte nodded, and went to look for a piece of cardboard.

She ended up going to the hardware store while I stayed. It wasn't necessary for both of us to be at the open house, and I was the one with the real estate license. She was more expendable—in this case—because she couldn't discuss price or any of the other official details with anyone who asked.

By then, the first rush of visitors—the one that shows up in the first hour—was gone, and I was waiting for the second rush, the one that shows up in the last fifteen minutes and often stays after the official end of the open house at four. Charlotte had left, and there was a young couple meandering around in the master bedroom. I had told them to give me a holler if they had any questions, but otherwise I was going to stay in the living room, between Carrie and the front door. I had tucked her into a corner of the dining room, below the broken and taped window, as far from the front door as she could get, so nobody would reach in and snatch her.

That was when a young woman with two kids walked through the door. She looked vaguely familiar, and it took me a second to place her. Then it came to me: she lived a couple of houses down the street, and when the roof had blown off last month, she and her husband and the kids had been out in the street, worrying that their little house would be next.

For the life of me I couldn't remember her name, or that of the kids, but I greeted her like I recognized her. "Hi there! How are you?"

"Fine." She didn't look fine, though. She wouldn't meet my eyes, but kept looking down instead. "Jerry has something he needs to tell you."

Jerry. Right. The little boy.

He was about four, and like the last time I'd seen him, he was clinging to his mother's pant leg. This time, there was no explosion to account for the nerves, so something else must be wrong.

I squatted down to his level. "Hi, Jerry. What's up?"

I hope you won't accuse me of arrogance if I say that I thought I might have guessed the problem. It didn't come as a surprise when the kid took his thumb out of his mouth, blinked big, blue eyes, and told me, "I broke your window."

I nodded, since I'd already suspected it. "How did it happen?"

"I was playing with my ball," Jerry said, "and it slipped out of my hand and went through the window."

The window that was five feet off the ground, when the kid was only about three feet tall.

"Twice?" I asked.

"What?" his mother said.

I looked up at her. "It's the second time it's happened this week."

She turned to the kid. "Jerry?"

He clearly wouldn't be growing up to have David's fortitude, because all it took was a frown on his mother's face to make him break down. His little face twisted, and tears filled his eyes. "The man told me to do it," he said.

"The man? What man?"

But Jerry didn't know what man. Just that he'd driven by in

his car, and had told Jerry he'd pay him five dollars if Jerry could get the ball through the window in our house.

"Jerry!" his mother said, appalled. "What have we told you about talking to strangers?"

Not enough, apparently, to outweigh the chance to make five dollars. "Did the man come back again yesterday?" I asked.

Jerry nodded. He was knuckling tears off his face with both fists.

"Jerry!" his mother said. "Don't you know that you're not supposed to break other people's things? Mrs. Collier's husband is a policeman! He can take you to jail for this!"

He probably couldn't, actually. Not for this. But who was I to tell this woman how to parent her child? And clearly Jerry needed incentive, both to keep him from talking to strangers in cars, and from breaking windows.

"Can you tell me what the man looked like?" I asked Jerry when the storm was over and he'd stopped hiccupping. "Or the car?"

But that Jerry couldn't. The car had been big and blue, he said, and the man had been "just a man." He had no real concept of old and young; the one thing he was sure of was that the man didn't have a beard or glasses.

"Was he brown?" I asked. "Or white?"

"Like us," Jerry said.

White, then. So that eliminated Curtis, and Frankie Matlock, who wasn't supposed to be around Columbia anyway, and who wouldn't know that my sister owned the house, and even if he did, would have no reason to vandalize it.

What it didn't do, was eliminate any of the more likely suspects, like the guy who had vandalized the house the first time, or his father, who might be upset that his son and his wife had to pay for damages. Or the family members of the guys who had set the explosion, or even the one young neo-Nazi we knew about who hadn't been swept up in the sting, since he'd testified against his friends, and since he hadn't actually been guilty of anything more than destruction of property. He was only twenty-one or –two, but I wasn't sure Jerry would be able to tell the difference between that and, say, Sergeant Tucker, and there was no point in trying to get him to be more specific.

His mother took him home with the promise that Jerry would come back with the ten dollars he'd gotten for the 'work' so I could spend it on fixing my window. Jerry looked a little mutinous over that, and his lower lip was firmly stuck on truculent when he stomped away. But he did come back ten minutes later with two crumpled five dollar bills that he gave me, with every sign of reluctance. I took them, not because I needed help paying for the window, but because his mother clearly wanted to teach him what happens to ill-gotten gains, and it would do the boy no harm to learn that crime doesn't pay.

By then, the second wave of visitors had started to show up. Charlotte came back with the piece of glass, so we decided we might as well show everyone how capable and responsive we were, in case anyone might want to make an offer. Replacing a broken window isn't a difficult or drawn-out process, and we'd just replaced this window anyway, so we didn't even have to deal with chipping out old, dry caulk. I had to move Carrie into the kitchen, since she'd been parked under the window in question. She was still asleep, and didn't wake, not even when we started messing with the window.

People came and went, a few of them lingering to give us advice about what to do, while the rest just wandered in and out. I don't think more than thirty seconds had passed before I glanced over my shoulder, as I'd done every thirty seconds, and saw that the spot on the floor where I'd put Carrie's car seat, was empty.

Seventeen

I almost dropped the piece of glass. It would have shattered on the floor—for the second time that day—if Charlotte hadn't had a good grip on it. "What?" she wanted to know, irritably, as she juggled the pane.

"Carrie."

I didn't have time to say anything more, since I was already on the move. I just registered Charlotte's eyes opening wide before I was through the door into the kitchen.

There was just a chance that someone else had picked her up and moved her. Or at least that's what I tried to tell myself, to quell the instant panic that someone had left with her.

Surely I would have noticed if someone had walked my baby out of the house?

Surely I would have—

And that's as far as I got—the panic didn't even have time to lodge deeply, and I can only be grateful for that—before I heard loud voices and the sound of activity behind the house.

I'm pretty sure I pushed a couple of prospective buyers out of my way as I careened down the hallway and through the master bedroom to the French doors onto the deck.

And stopped like I'd run into a wall.

Rafe, gun drawn, and Grimaldi—ditto—were advancing from the left and right on a person who stood in the middle of the grass clutching Carrie's seat.

At first, I thought I was looking at a young girl. She was considerably shorter than David—he was there, too, at the corner of the house—and she couldn't have weighed more than a hundred pounds soaking wet.

When I got a better look, I realized she wasn't as young as I'd thought. Younger than me by a few years, sure. Twenty-three, maybe. Or twenty-four. Dishwater blond hair to her shoulders, slight build in a pair of jeans and a pink T-shirt. Nothing even remotely like the busty Jessica Rabbit cartoon. But not a kid.

Although there was something familiar about her...

I squinted, trying to bring it into focus, when Charlotte barreled through the door behind me and knocked me forward a step. Behind her, several of the open house visitors started to crowd into the doorway, while a couple others came around the corner from the driveway and gathered behind David.

The girl was starting to look rattled. Blue eyes in a narrow face flickered from side to side, probably assessing her chances of escape.

They were pretty close to nil, as far as I could see. Both Rafe and Grimaldi had guns trained on her, and I'm sure either of them would fire before they'd let her get away with Carrie.

But she did have Carrie, and while the baby was somewhat protected, at least on the underside, by being in the heavy plastic car seat, I'm sure neither of them particularly wanted to fire, either.

And then the likeness finally registered, and I opened my mouth without really thinking about it. "I know you. You work at the pet emergency clinic."

She spared me a glance, but kept her attention on the guns. I would have, too.

"I remember you." It was all coming back to me now. "You were there that morning I came to pick up Pearl. I made you carry the baby, because you looked too small to handle the dog."

And she must have been there the night before, too, when Rafe dropped off Pearl, because she'd asked me about him. Whether he was my husband.

I'd told her yes, he was, and had refrained from adding that he was *'mine, all mine.'*

Not that I'd been worried. It was hardly the first time some woman had taken a fancy to Rafe because he was handsome, and sexy, and liked to flirt.

"What happened?" I asked. "You haven't been following him around since then, have you? The videos just started a few days ago."

She glanced my way again. "I was there the other night. In downtown. When that horrible policeman had that poor boy down on the ground and was trying to kill him."

Grimaldi opened her mouth, and Rafe did, too. In the end, both of them thought better of speaking.

"Curtis is fine," I said. "Nothing happened to him."

"Because *he* came." She shot a glance at Rafe, and if I hadn't already been chilled to the bone from this woman stealing my baby, that look would have done it. It wasn't just attraction, or even some sort of twisted love. It was obsession, pure and simple. I recognized it, because I'd seen it before.

On Elspeth Caulfield's face.

"But it wasn't you who took the video that night," I said, trying to get her attention back on me. Watching him point that gun at her probably wasn't doing her psyche any good, when she was halfway around the bend already. And while I had no problem with nudging her the rest of the way if the opportunity arose, I didn't want to do it while she was holding Carrie.

She shot me another look. "No. I saw it the next morning, and I thought if she could do it, so could I. And because I knew where he worked, I went there and waited for him."

"And the other night you followed us to Beulah's Meat'n Three."

She nodded. "You didn't even notice me. I sat at the counter, and I filmed you, and when the owner carried the baby past, I took a picture of her, too."

"'She looks just like her daddy,'" I quoted, while my stomach did a sort of unpleasant, soggy flip.

She didn't recognize the quote from her post, or if she did, she didn't comment on it. Instead she looked down at Carrie, and a sliver of that obsessive light came back into her eyes. "Yes."

"You can't have her," I said. It wasn't conscious, and might not have been the psychologically best thing to say. To be honest, I didn't think about that. I didn't think about anything at all. "She's mine."

I'm not sure she even heard me. She did hear Rafe. He shifted his hands just slightly on the gun, which he held in both hands, up at chest level and pointed at her, very businesslike. Her eyes focused on the movement, which was probably what he expected her to do. "Put the baby down," he told her. "Step away from her."

The girl—I didn't even know her name; if she'd had a name badge pinned to those scrubs she'd worn to bring Pearl out of the vet clinic last month, I hadn't noticed—hesitated.

"I'd prefer not to hurt you," Rafe added, "but you've got my daughter. And I'm not letting you walk away with her."

There wasn't much chance of that. Between the crowd in the French doors, and the people thronging behind David at the corner of the house, and Rafe and Grimaldi with their guns drawn, and me, there wasn't anywhere for her to go.

I'm not sure she realized that, though. She glanced from side to side, and then back at Rafe. "I love you," she told him.

I have no idea whether she meant them as her last words or not. She might have, because a second later she threw the carrier with the baby to the left—toward me—and stood alone.

To be honest, it wasn't much of a throw. Carrie was more than four months old, and weighed around fourteen pounds. Add five pounds or so for the seat, and she was shifting twenty. And as I've mentioned before, she wasn't a big girl. She'd also been standing there holding the seat for a while, so she was probably tired. The combined weight of seat and baby wears on the arm after a while, and it doesn't take long, either.

So it was really more of a tumble than a throw. She let go of the seat, with just a little push behind it.

The seat rolled, and I shrieked and threw myself at it. The girl, meanwhile, went in the other direction. A bullet—I'm not sure whether Rafe or Grimaldi pulled the trigger—must have just skimmed past her, because it hit the bathroom window and shattered it into a million pieces. A lot of voices shrieked at the same time, and I imagine a lot of people ducked, even though the bullet got nowhere close to them. Hopefully nobody was left inside the house who could have been hit.

I just had time to think, "Not another window!" before I had the baby carrier in my hands and put it upright. Carrie was screaming bloody murder, of course—the rough handling had woken her from sound sleep—but she was unharmed, strapped in tight, and just upset. Her little face was bright red with her screaming, but there wasn't anything else wrong with her.

I unhooked her and lifted her up, and turned to look at the scene behind me.

The girl had made it maybe two feet before David had tackled her. Now she was flat on the ground with her arms up over her face. I wasn't entirely sure whether she was protecting herself from blows or crying, or maybe both. Rafe was plucking his infuriated son off her, much the same way he'd plucked Sergeant Tucker off Curtis Matlock a few nights ago, and Grimaldi was moving in with a pair of handcuffs.

"She took her!" David bellowed. "She took my baby sister!"

Rafe set him upright and dusted him off and slapped him on the back a couple of times. "Good job. You got her. Good job." He met my eyes over David's head.

"She's OK," I said, patting Carrie's warm little back. The screams were down to hiccupping sobs now, and she was starting to snuffle like she was hungry. "Take care of David. I've got Carrie."

Rafe nodded, and put a hand on David's shoulder. "C'mon, son. Let's finish this up."

David nodded, still vibrating with fury. I made my way over to him and bussed him on the cheek. "Thank you."

He nodded, and his eyes fastened on Carrie. "She all right?"

"She's fine. Just shook up and hungry. She'll never even remember this."

"Not sure I'll ever forget it," David said, and followed Rafe toward the corner of the house. The bystanders gave way for the two of them like the Red Sea before Moses.

Grimaldi, meanwhile, had dragged the stalker to her feet. "You have the right to remain silent..." she began, as she marched the girl toward the street in the wake of the other two. The woman's hands were cuffed behind her, and she had tears streaking down her face.

Charlotte crept out of the crowd inside the French doors and made her way to me. "What the hell, Savannah?"

Blame the reaction of coming off an adrenaline high, but it sounded like such an unlikely thing to come out of her mouth that I snorted, and then started to laugh. After a second, the laughter turned to sobs—blame that on the reaction, too—and Charlotte put her arms around me, and around Carrie, as well. Some of the bystanders shuffled their feet awkwardly, and some started to drift away.

"Show's over," I managed. "If you're interested in making

an offer on the house, my number's on the sign out front."

"We'll fix the bathroom window," Charlotte added. "We're getting good at that."

We were. And we would. But probably not tonight. All I wanted was to take my baby home, and batten down the hatches, and celebrate the fact that she was safe, and I still had her. The window could wait.

So we boarded it up, and shooed the remaining people out, and locked the doors, and went home. Charlotte to her kids and her parents, and I to my empty house and my dog.

Word spread about what had happened, of course, so I spent a lot of my time fielding phone calls. Mother called to make sure Carrie and David were all right. Dix and Catherine did, too. Grimaldi called to tell me that the girl, whose name was Jessica Lloyd, had been booked on kidnapping and stalking charges.

"It was a good thing she tried to take the baby," she told me, "because without that, we might have had to let her go. There's nothing illegal about taking pictures of people and posting them on social media. It happens to celebrities all the time."

Of course it did. And can't be much fun for them, either. "Rafe isn't a celebrity. He's a cop. And his safety depends on people not knowing too much about where he is and what he's doing."

"You and I know that," Grimaldi said, "but the law doesn't."

She let that sink in for a second before she added, "But because she took the baby out of the house and, we assume, tried to walk away with her, she not only demonstrated that she was a threat, but she committed a felony. So we can charge her with some things that are going to keep her locked up for a long time."

Good.

"There's just one thing."

"Uh-oh," I said. I had a feeling that I knew where this was going.

"She won't make bail. I'll make sure the DA sets it high enough that she can't meet it, and that's if they agree to bail at all. I'm going to push that they won't, and I'm sure between me and your brother and Bob, we can prevail on Todd Satterfield to prevail on his boss to deny bail."

Excellent. "So what's the problem?" I asked.

"Her public defender will most likely insist on a psychiatric evaluation. I would."

I would, too. "You mean, they'll discover that she's nuts."

"My guess is they will," Grimaldi said. "Sane people don't act that way."

No, they don't. "So what does that mean? They won't let her out, will they? She'll still be locked up, right?"

Grimaldi assured me that she would be. "It just won't be in prison. It'll be some psychiatric hospital instead. For inmates."

"I don't have a problem with that," I said. "I don't need her to suffer. I just want to make sure she can't come near my husband or my baby again."

Or David, but he was probably safe in Nashville by now.

"She won't," Grimaldi said. "I'll make sure of that."

"Thank you."

She sounded embarrassed. "No problem. Are you still willing to go investigating with me tomorrow?"

"Sure," I said. "What are we doing?"

And did she know that Rafe and Bob—and perhaps Dix—had plans to visit Art Mullinax to test out her theory that he'd killed Kent Jurgensson?

"I thought we'd take a walk around Mullinax's back forty," Grimaldi said.

Oh. "Um..."

I could hear her eyebrows going up. "Problem?"

"Not exactly. I mean…"

She waited, and since I'm just about the world's worst liar, and not much of a prevaricator, I broke within the first few seconds. "I told Rafe what you said. About Mullinax and Jurgensson's remains. And then we told Bob. And the two of them decided to go pay a visit on Mullinax tomorrow. Dix may be going with them."

Grimaldi sighed. I waited for her to start chastising me, but instead she said, "Good time to explore the back forty, then, while they're keeping him busy at the house."

That was one way of looking at it. "Jurgensson's been dead for almost thirty years. Do you really think we'll find any evidence lying around Daffodil Hill Farm?"

Even assuming she had a point about Mullinax and Jurgensson, Mullinax wouldn't have left the body just lying in the woods. He'd have buried it, surely.

"Unless he wanted to make sure it look like an accidental death if anyone found him," Grimaldi said promptly when I mentioned this. "Like Jurgensson had just stumbled onto Mullinax's property and accidentally broken his leg, far enough from the house that no one heard him crying for help. And then he, sadly, just died from exposure."

I suppose that might fly. It had flown for Katie Graves, who had been missing for fifteen or sixteen years when an ATF agent just happened to stumble across her remains up on the Devil's Backbone about six months ago. Rafe had ended up investigating that crime, and the question of exposure had definitely come up.

"I guess it can't hurt to look."

"Glad to hear it," Grimaldi said sarcastically. "I'll pick you up at eight-thirty."

I grimaced. "Yes, ma'am."

"Wear comfortable shoes." She hung up before I could respond. I made another face at the phone before I put it down.

Rafe made it home around nine. After leaving the house on Fulton Street, he'd taken David to see Audrey and Mrs. Jenkins before driving him home. Once there, Ginny and Sam had asked him to stay for dinner, and then it sounded like there'd been some discussion afterward. Ginny had a tendency to blame Rafe for making David run off, even when Rafe has had nothing to do with it.

Suddenly discovering, after twelve years of parenthood, that her son had another father, couldn't have been easy. I tried to imagine bringing Carrie up for twelve years, having her be mine, and then suddenly finding out that she had another mother, and because that mother hadn't known she existed, she had the right to sue for custody.

Rafe never had, of course. David was settled with Sam and Ginny, he was happy and healthy and loved. It wouldn't have been in David's best interest to change that. But I could well imagine Ginny's fear that it could happen, and her feeling that Rafe (and I and Carrie and Mother and everyone else) were taking something away from them. David would never be fully hers and Sam's again. From that moment when Dix and I knocked on their door a year and a half ago, to tell them about Elspeth's death and Rafe's existence, she'd always have to share him with us.

"Everything OK?" I wanted to know when Rafe ambled into the bedroom after putting the Harley in the garage.

He nodded, and his lips relaxed as he took in the tableau of me feeding Carrie and Pearl curled up on the rug (because I felt safer having her nearby than downstairs, where she usually sleeps). "David's grounded for a week. No electronics. He can't believe he's being punished for saving his sister's life."

"Let me guess," I said. "He isn't being punished for saving his sister's life—"

"He's being punished for running away from home and

making me spend several hundred dollars on cab fare. If he hadn't saved his sister's life, it woulda been two weeks."

He sat down on the edge of the bed next to me and looked at Carrie.

"I'll give her to you when she's finished," I told him. "If I do it now, she's just going to be upset."

He nodded. "She wasn't in any danger, you know. We had the house surrounded before you even pulled up."

"I figured that out," I said, "when I came out and saw you. I had no idea you were there until then. I had no idea *she* was there, either. I didn't notice her. Or recognize her. Not until we were outside."

"It was David's idea," Rafe said. "He thought you mighta mentioned the open house over dinner on Friday night, at Beulah's, and that she mighta heard you. So he talked me into providing backup, just in case she showed up."

"It was a good thing he did," I said, "or she might have made it out of there with Carrie."

He didn't say anything, and I added, "I only took my eyes off her for a few seconds. I swear."

"Nobody's blaming you, darlin'." After a second he added, "But that was too damn close."

Much too close. "I guess Grimaldi updated you on what's going to happen next."

He nodded. "Not somebody we have to worry about again. There were enough pictures and other things in her apartment to shut the cage door tight for a long time."

"You went to her apartment?"

"Figured I might as well get the full picture of what we're dealing with," Rafe said coolly.

"And did you?"

He shifted his weight, looking—as he rarely does— uncomfortable. "She had a lot of pictures. A lot more than she posted online. Not of you or Carrie, but of me. She had the intake form for the vet clinic for Pearl, when we brought her there, with my signature on it..."

"Your signature? Why?" What could she have done with that? It wasn't like she could pretend to be him.

"I think she just wanted it," Rafe said. "She had a used napkin from Beulah's—mine, I guess—in a plastic baggie, and a T-shirt—I have no idea where she got that—folded on top of her bureau. Tammy said it was mine. I couldn't tell." He shrugged.

"That's really creepy." I glanced around, at the bureau with his clean clothes and the hamper with the dirty ones. "You don't think she got into the house, do you?"

"I can't imagine how," Rafe said. "And I think Pearl woulda torn her limb from limb if she'd tried."

True. "I guess it doesn't matter, now that she's been arrested. Grimaldi told me she's going to make sure she won't get out on bail."

"Believe me," Rafe answered, "there ain't no chance of that."

Good to know. I shifted Carrie away from me and held her out. "Here. She's full of milk and all yours. Make sure she burps."

He grabbed her while I buttoned myself back up, put her against his shoulder, and patted her back. Cheek against her small head of curly hair, he closed his eyes. And didn't open them again, even when our small daughter let loose with a belch that wouldn't have sounded out of place coming from him. Although his lips did curve.

Eighteen

By the time Grimaldi came and picked me up the next morning, he was long gone. I had no idea what he and Bob were planning to do about Agent Yung—whether they were bringing her to Daffodil Hill Farm with them, or letting her cool her heels at the sheriff's office without telling her what they were up to—and I had refrained from asking. I did not expect Leslie Yung to be sitting in the passenger seat of Grimaldi's official SUV when it pulled up in front of the mansion.

I blinked at her. She ignored me in favor of my—Mother's—house. "Wow."

I pulled open the back door of the SUV and went to work attaching the base for Carrie car seat. "Yep."

"This is where you live?"

"This is it." I made sure the base was secure before I snapped the rest of the seat, with Carrie inside, to it.

"You're not planning to carry that through the woods," Grimaldi said. It was more statement than question, but I answered anyway.

"No. I have a sling. I'll strap her to my chest or my back when I get out of the car."

She nodded. Agent Yung, meanwhile, was still gaping at the house. "It looks like a museum."

I crawled into the back seat next to Carrie and answered,

"It is, pretty much. Built by one of my ancestors between 1839 and 1841. We have stuff inside from almost as long ago."

She had the visor down on her side of the car, and I wasn't sure whether it was to block the sun or so she could look at me in the makeup mirror. Maybe she'd been touching up her face. "Your husband lives here?"

"Of course." Where else would he live?

"That must be interesting," Leslie Yung said blandly.

I decided to pretend I didn't understand what she was getting at, since I found the implication insulting. "He grew up in a trailer on the other side of town, so I don't imagine he ever thought he'd be living here. But a lot of things have happened since then. To both of us."

Grimaldi smirked, but didn't say anything.

"Speaking of that," Agent Yung said. "I heard what happened yesterday. That must have been scary."

"Not as scary as certain other events we've been involved in. I'm sure, by now, you've familiarized yourself with my husband's file." I met her eyes in the mirror. "You probably know it better than I do."

A few of the events that had been among the scariest weren't part of any file, of course. But she didn't need to know about those.

"I didn't expect to see you this morning," I added, when she didn't answer immediately. "This little excursion falls outside your purview, doesn't it?"

"Outside the Classicist case, you mean? Your husband and Sheriff Satterfield informed me that Mr. Mullinax was likely to respond better to the two of them than to me." She sniffed.

"I feel your pain," I said politely. "I wanted to come, too. They said no. Was my brother there, by any chance?"

"The lawyer?" She nodded.

"Typical. They took him and not me."

"If you'll pardon me for saying so," Agent Yung said, in a

tone like she didn't give a damn—darn—if I pardoned her or not, "he looked more professional than you do."

"He probably wasn't planning to be hiking through the woods. And besides, there's something to be said for showing up in jeans and sneakers and with a baby in tow, you know. Everybody relaxes and nobody suspects you of being a spy. You should try it sometime."

She sniffed. I did, too. Grimaldi grinned. "Children," she intoned, "no arguing."

Yung gave her a fulminating glare. I smirked. "Yes, ma'am."

When we got to the rear of Daffodil Hill Farm, though, and Grimaldi pulled off to the side of the road into a little graveled patch, the sensibility of my attire became apparent quickly. I strapped the baby to my chest and set off in my jeans and sneakers. Yung, meanwhile, had to keep her wool from snagging on branches and her heels from sinking into the ground. It must have been annoying enough that after a few minutes, I took pity on her and decided to be nice. "You probably didn't expect to be doing this today."

She gave me a glare. "You think?"

"You don't have to be here, you know. Or so I assume." She didn't say anything, and I added, "You could go back to the car and wait. It isn't so hot yet that you'll perish without the air conditioning running."

It was hot enough, though. Or must have been quite uncomfortable for her, anyway, even without the crazy heels. I was fairly content in my jeans and long-sleeved T-shirt—which I had had the foresight to wear because I thought there might be brambles, and because I knew I'd be responsible for keeping whatever it was off Carrie.

She fell asleep in her sling covered with pictures of zoo animals, legs dangling and her cheek against my chest. As time passed, I felt a wet spot spread across the front of my shirt from her drool.

By then, we had been walking—or cutting our way through the woods—for about forty minutes. We had yet to see any sight of civilization—of the buildings at Daffodil Hill—but we were far enough from the road that the sound of passing cars had faded.

"Remind you of anything?" I asked Grimaldi.

She gave me a sardonic look over her shoulder. Like me, she'd dressed for the occasion, in a pair of heavy-duty khakis and what looked like hiking boots. "I assume you mean that trek through the woods in South Nashville when we were looking for Hernandez's victims."

I nodded. That was exactly what I meant. There had been more of us then: Wendell Craig and the three young men from the TBI had been with us, along with Rafe. And we'd been near the airport, so every minute or two we'd had to deal with the sound of a jumbo jet coming in for landing practically on top of our heads. But otherwise it had been a similar experience. Hotter, though. It had been June, and the heat and humidity hadn't made the task any easier.

And this time, as far as we knew, we were looking for a single set of remains. Back then we'd been looking for several. I'm not sure whether that made it easier or the opposite.

"Hernandez?" Yung glanced between us. I left it to Grimaldi to explain.

"Eugenio Hernandez. One of Hector Gonzales's associates. He was in prison when Agent Collier took down Gonzales's SATG. By the time Hernandez heard what had happened, and got out, it was June. He grabbed Collier off the street, spent the best part of a day torturing him, and then left. Agent Collier freed himself and made it home."

Yung nodded. "I read about that."

Neither of their voices gave any indication that they understood what that had been like, and the strength of will it had taken. Rafe still had scars all over his chest and stomach from Hernandez amusing himself, not to mention the one on his arm, where Hernandez had pinned him to the table with a knife through the forearm. But since that wasn't what this conversation was about, I swallowed both the nausea that the memory produced, and the need to point out how heroic my husband had been, and let Grimaldi carry on.

"Collier suspected that Hernandez was responsible for the disappearance of several young women. We went looking for them."

"And did you find them?" Yung wanted to know. She swatted irritably at a strand of something sticky that tried to attach itself to her pants.

Grimaldi nodded. "In the woods behind the house he lived in at the time. It was a situation much like this one. But they'd been gone less time. Five years, instead of twenty-five."

"Bones don't disappear," Yung said.

Grimaldi ignored this sage comment. "Have you ever done this before?"

"Looked for remains?" Yung didn't look up. "Yes. It's easier when it's bones."

No question. "Harder to see, though." I kicked at a dry, brittle stick that could have been a bone or just something that had fallen off a tree. (It was a twig, or I wouldn't have kicked it.) "Jurgensson's remains could be five feet away from us, and we'd walk right by them."

"Maybe we should spread out," Yung said, with no enthusiasm whatsoever.

Grimaldi shook her head. "No point. I'm not expecting to find anything. This is just something to do because I can't sit still."

Yung slanted her a look. "You're not expecting to find anything because there's nothing to find? Because you don't think the remains are here? Or—"

"I don't expect to find anything because the remains could be five feet away from us and we'd walk right by them," Grimaldi said. "This isn't the way to do a proper search. We'd need more people, and dogs. And permission. As it is, we're just three women taking a walk in the woods."

"On private property."

Grimaldi shrugged. "I'm not too worried about that. If he comes and warns us off, it's just confirmation that he has something to hide."

"And he won't be coming anyway," I added, swatting at a clump of leaves. "Rafe and Bob are keeping him busy."

"And your brother."

Right. And my brother. Because you never know when you might need a lawyer.

"How far from here to the house?" Agent Yung wanted to know.

Grimaldi glanced at me. I shrugged. "I've never been here before. I have no idea."

Yung looked from one to the other of us. "Did neither one of you think to consult a map?"

"It's not like we're walking the Appalachian Trail," Grimaldi said. "We're never more than twenty minutes from civilization."

"We've walked a lot longer than that and seen nothing!"

"That's because we're walking parallel to the road," Grimaldi said. "If he's going to dump a body on his property, and he didn't want to bury it in the pigsty or under the rose garden, chances are he'd put it as far from the house, and as far from the road, as he could. At the same time."

I nodded. That made sense to me. "Less chance someone would stumble over it accidentally."

"Less chance anyone would find it at all if he'd buried it in the rose garden," Leslie Yung grumbled.

"And he might have done that. That's what Sheriff

Satterfield and Agent Collier are trying to ascertain. Meanwhile, we're here looking at the terrain to see where someone might have left a body."

We walked another few feet in silence.

"Is he a big man?" Yung wanted to know. "Mullinax?"

I glanced at Grimaldi. "He isn't small. Not as big as Rafe, but no shrimp. And would have been in better shape at fifty-some than he is now, in his mid-seventies."

"What about the victim? Jurgensson?"

It had never occurred to me to wonder, so I waited to see whether Grimaldi knew. As I might have expected, she did. "Per his most recent driver's license, thirty years ago, he was five feet, ten inches tall, and weighed a hundred and ninety pounds."

So not super-sized, but as I'd said about Mullinax, no shrimp, either. Hefty enough that it might have taken two people to get him out here. It's one thing to carry a woman twenty yards, from a truck to a dumpster, and quite another to haul almost two hundred pounds on a twenty minute hike into the woods, over downed tree trunks and rough terrain. The weather might have been bad too, for all we knew. It was too long ago for anyone to remember, most likely, especially since we didn't know exactly when he'd disappeared.

"Maybe he had help," I said, pushing aside a branch and holding it until Yung, behind me, could get a grip. "Maybe Noah Trent helped."

"The victim?"

"The kid Jurgensson supposedly molested," Grimaldi confirmed. "Mullinax's nephew. His sister's son. No way to ask him. He's dead, too."

We walked forward in silence. Until my phone rang and the Hallelujah Chorus rang through the trees. Grimaldi snorted, as she usually does when she hears my phone go off with this particular ring tone. Yung, who wasn't in on the joke, just looked politely inquisitive.

"Hi," I told Rafe.

"Darlin'. Where are you?"

"Walking through the woods, somewhere between Mullinax's place and the road."

"Nothing yet?" His tone told me clearly what he expected the answer to be.

"If we'd found remains," I told him, "I would have called you."

"Right. Well, I'm calling to let you know we've been and gone. We're in the car on our way back to Sweetwater."

"Already? Wasn't he there?"

"Sure he was. We talked to him for fifteen minutes and left. You didn't think it was gonna take all day, did you?"

Well, no. I guess we'd been out here longer than I thought. On the one hand, it felt like we'd been stomping through the trees forever. On the other, it didn't seem as if he'd had enough time to properly interrogate Mullinax.

"Did he say anything you didn't already know?"

"No," Rafe said. "But then I didn't expect him to come out and confess."

"Do you think he might have done it?"

"Killed Jurgensson? I wouldn't rule it out."

So that was something, anyway. Grimaldi met my eyes across the phone—we were standing in a huddle around it, with the speaker on—and I knew she felt vindicated. If Rafe also thought Mullinax might have killed Jurgensson, at least Grimaldi wasn't imagining things.

"What about the women?" Yung asked.

Rafe hesitated a second, as if he hadn't expected to hear her voice. "That you, Yung?"

He went on without waiting for an answer. "Ain't nothing to suggest he's any kind of a serial killer. Don't drive a truck, has what looks like a normal life with a wife, a couple kids, and grandkids."

"But?"

He chuckled. "Can't put nothing past you, can I, darlin'? He does own an RV. Somebody's out here working on the engine right now."

An RV? "Like a Winnebago? A motor home? Did anyone see a Winnebago at the truck stop the other day?"

"Nobody mentioned one," Rafe said, "but they do stop at truck stops. Some stops even have designated overnight parking for RVs. Somebody in an RV'd look less outta place than someone in a regular car."

Interesting. "So we might not be looking for a trucker at all. We could be looking for a family man with an RV."

"As long as the family wasn't with him," Rafe said. "Most wives ain't gonna be OK with their husband bringing prostitutes home and strangling them."

"Maybe the husband brings the prostitute home and the wife strangles her."

He chuckled. "You wouldn't say that if you'd seen Mrs. Mullinax. She looks like your mama, only about ten years older."

Yes, I had a hard time imagining Mother strangling anybody, too. And if Mrs. Mullinax was seventy, give or take, the chances that she could actually squeeze the life out of a woman half her age were probably slim to begin with.

"But it could be Mullinax," I said. "On his own."

"Might could," Rafe agreed.

"Are you going to get a search warrant for the RV? To see if there are any traces of anything inside?"

"Bob's gonna work on that. Anything on your end?"

"We're standing in the middle of the woods," I said, "with nothing around us but trees. I'm surprised we have cell service. And it's really hard to tell the difference between a dry twig and an old bone."

"Tell me about it." I'm sure he, too, remembered that outing through the brush, looking for Hernandez's victims. "We've headed out, so from now on, there's nothing to keep him here. He was talking to the mechanic when we left, but if he gets the idea you're back there, he might decide to come root you out."

I looked around, at the wilderness we were standing in. It was hard to believe we were only a quarter mile or so from the road and the houses. "Does he have anything that'll drive cross-country? Because there are no trails back here."

"He has an ATV," Rafe said.

"One of those little four-wheelers?" I met Grimaldi's eyes over the phone. She grimaced.

"That's it," Rafe said. "Man likes his toys."

He paused for a second before he added, "My advice? Get on outta there. The chances you were gonna find anything were slim anyway. It's a big area, and what you're looking for is tiny."

No argument here. "I'll see you at home," I said, and hung up. "Guess we'll make our way back."

Grimaldi nodded. It was totally without enthusiasm. Yung, meanwhile, seemed delighted. "About time," she said.

"Tell you what," I told her. "We're not that far from the road. Like Grimaldi said, we're walking parallel to it. Since you're not enjoying this, and you're not really dressed for it, why don't you strike out that way—" I pointed, "on your own, and you should get to the road in a few minutes. Then you can walk back to the car from there. It's the same distance we've already covered, but at least you won't have to deal with the rough terrain."

And we wouldn't have to deal with those frequent little sighs and muttered curses.

Not that I blamed her. For being a federal agent in a designer wool suit and high heels, she'd held up remarkably well. Much better than I would have under the circumstances. But if all we were doing were going back, there was no need to put her through it. And this way, Grimaldi and I could have a private conversation, too.

Not that I had anything I wanted to say that Yung couldn't hear. But the group dynamic was different with an FBI agent in our midst.

Yung looked at once elated and suspicious. "Are you sure that's the right direction?"

"Pretty sure. Grimaldi?"

She nodded. "We went due west from the car, and then south. The sun's up there." She pointed it out, as if it hadn't been slanting fingers of light through the leaf canopy for the past hour. "If you keep it at roughly the same angle, you should be able to go straight that way and hit the road in ten or fifteen minutes. Then you can follow it back to the car."

Yung nodded. "I'll see you there. You have my number if you find anything?"

Grimaldi assured her she did, and then we watched Yung navigate away from us through the trees, until her black-clad figure was gone from sight. Grimaldi turned to me. "You OK moving ten or fifteen feet in one direction, and I'll go ten or fifteen in the other, and we'll walk a parallel track back the way we came?"

"Sure." Twenty or thirty feet wasn't enough that we'd lose each other, but we could cover more ground that way.

So Grimaldi paced off to the west, and I paced off to the right, in the direction Leslie Yung had disappeared, and we headed back toward the car at a more than polite distance. The sounds of Yung's passage—the swishing of leaves, and the occasional cracking of a dry branch or muttered curse—had faded now, so she must be making good time toward the road.

Grimaldi and I shuffled northward. Carrie stayed asleep, and I kept one arm up over her small body to keep her from any accidental harm. I used the other to push aside branches and vines that got in my way.

"Are there rattlesnakes around here?" I called out to Grimaldi.

She gave me a look, potent even across the twenty-five feet that separated us. "You're the local. Shouldn't you know?"

"I never spent much time in the woods," I said. "You're more of the outdoorsy type. Besides, this was your idea."

She sighed. "Yes, there are rattlesnakes here. Timber rattlesnake and pygmy rattlesnake. Also cottonmouths and copperheads. They all bite."

"Lovely." I started to look around even more carefully, and lifting my feet higher. I probably looked like a majorette—minus the twiddlestick. "Is it the right time of year for venomous snakes?"

"They hibernate when it's cold," Grimaldi said, scanning left to right as she shuffled, "but it's warm enough by now that I figure they've come out. So the answer's probably yes."

"Lovely."

I found myself looking more for snakes than for bones, and told myself to stop. There's being cautious, and then there's being afraid enough to forget what your job is.

I widened my area of inspection, though, so I'd see any snakes coming, and it was because I did that I saw it. "Hey!"

"What?" Grimaldi's voice said.

"Come here. I think I may have something."

She changed direction and came toward me.

"Look out for snakes," I added, as she crashed through the underbrush.

She gave me a look, but didn't comment. Just stopped beside me. "What?"

"That." I pointed. "Over there, past that log. Is that a rock? It looks very smooth and regular to be one."

And just in case it wasn't—just in case it was what I

thought it was: the top of a skull—I wanted someone else to go over and touch it.

Grimaldi looked at it. Her eyes narrowed and her lips tightened. "Stay here," she told me.

"No problem." I had no need to go any closer. But I watched carefully as she made her way forward, observing the ground closely before she put her foot down. I didn't think she was looking for snakes.

She scrambled over the fallen log—it sported some moss and a colony of fungi on top—and bent over the... let's be charitable and call it a rock.

It wasn't a rock, though. I'd known it as soon as I caught sight of it. And Grimaldi's body language—the set of her shoulders, like she'd half expected and half dreaded it—was confirmation.

But I asked anyway. "It's him?"

She glanced up at me. "It's somebody. Definitely a skull, and I see some other bones, too."

"I'll call Yung," I said, lifting my phone.

"You have the number?" Grimaldi kept poking at the ground with the toe of her boot.

Of course I didn't. "You call Yung. I'll call Rafe. And tell him to tell the sheriff to add a search warrant for the property to the warrant for the RV."

Grimaldi nodded, fishing for her phone. "Either one of us is going to have to stay here with the remains, or we need some way of marking the spot."

I nodded, and then held up a finger as the phone was answered in my ear. "Darlin'."

"Rafe," I said. "We found bones."

There was a beat. "In the woods?"

"Of course in the woods. Where else would we be?" I didn't wait for him to answer. "And if you're planning to ask me next whether I'm sure they're human..."

"I wasn't." I could hear the smirk in his voice. "I figure you can tell the difference between a human and a deer. Where are you?"

"I told you. In the woods. We're trying to come up with some way to mark the spot. If not, one of us will have to stay behind."

"I'll let Bob know that we need the warrant to include the rest of the property. Hang tight."

He hung up before I could say anything else. I stuffed the phone into my back pocket and told Grimaldi, "They're working on it. Why can't we both stay?"

"One of us has to go tell Yung," Grimaldi said. "She's not picking up. And it could take hours for them to persuade a judge to get the warrant and get the personnel and equipment together and back here. We can't let her sit there by the car until they do. She doesn't even have the key to open the door."

"Oops." Guess we should have thought of that before we let her go off on her own.

"Let's just find some way of marking the spot," I said. "I don't suppose you have a helium balloon in your pocket?"

"No," Grimaldi said. "Do you?"

She went on without waiting for my answer. "If you want to go back to the car, I don't mind waiting here."

"I'd rather we went back together. You said it yourself. It could take them a while to get out here."

"So what do you suggest?" Grimaldi asked.

"That we take this blanket—" It was Carrie's and it was bright yellow, "and hang it from a handy tree branch. It's big enough and bright enough that anyone who comes this way should be able to spot it. And then, if we go straight east from here, we may be able to mark the spot in the road where we come out, and maybe some of the path, too."

"Path?" Grimaldi said, eyeing it. I gave her a look, and she shook her head. "Fine. We'll do it your way. Give me the blanket. I'll climb this handy-dandy tree and hang the flag."

She suited action to words: hauled herself ten or fifteen feet up into the air and onto the branch of a scraggly pine tree.

"Is that branch strong enough to hold you?" I wanted to know, watching it bow under her weight.

"Are you calling me fat?" She was inching out, one careful step at a time.

"Of course not." Only someone severely nearsighted would. She was tall and lean and well-muscled. And probably weighed quite a few pounds less than I did. "I just don't want you to fall."

"I'm not going to fall." She draped the blanket carefully over the next branch up, and tugged it into place. "There. Hopefully that'll stay there long enough to be a good signal."

It was eye-catching, anyway. Nice and bright against the dark green of the pines and the lighter green of the fresh spring leaves around us.

Grimaldi skinned down the trunk and came toward me. "Got anything we can use to mark the way?"

"If she were a little older, we could have used teething biscuits or Cheerios." I patted my pockets. "I don't think I do."

Grimaldi nodded. "Guess we'll just do the best we can. I'll film the walk."

"I'll walk behind you," I said, since I didn't want my too-big derriere in the shot, and since I'd rather she get us through the woods than me.

Nineteen

Grimaldi must have had a better sense of direction than me, because after about five minutes, the trees started to thin out as we approached the edge of the woods. Grimaldi, who had been breaking twigs as we'd been walking along, in an effort to mark the path, stopped just shy of the road and began to undress.

"What are you doing?" I inquired.

She glanced at me over the top of her T-shirt before she continued to pull it over her head. "What does it look like?"

The question was muffled inside the blue cotton.

"It looks like you're stripping."

"I want to leave this here to mark the spot." She draped it over a branch before shrugging back into her overshirt and buttoning it up. That done, she proceeded to tie the navy T-shirt around the trunk of a sapling on the edge of the vegetation. "Come on."

She scrambled into the ditch and up the other side. I slid down, more carefully—the last thing I wanted was to fall and crush Carrie—and while I did, Grimaldi gathered a bunch of little stones and formed them into a small cairn on the gravel edge of the blacktop. "Just in case the T-shirt blows away."

There wasn't much chance of that, from what I could see. The sun was high, the sky was cloudless, and the breeze was practically non-existent.

On the other hand, Mullinax's back forty consisted of a lot of trees, and if we lost our spot, it could take a lot of time and effort to find the bones again. It was mostly just luck that we'd found them the first time.

"Let's go," Grimaldi said, hauling me up the last few feet to the road. "You all right?"

"Just winded. The car's this way, right?"

Grimaldi nodded. "I can run ahead and come back for you, if you want."

She was obviously raring to go, and not discomfited at all by the hike through the wood.

In my own defense, I'd like to say that I was still carrying a little baby weight, not to mention the weight of the baby herself, and that I'd never been in the kind of condition Grimaldi was. "Sure. If you want."

She was practically twitching with eagerness, so it didn't surprise me when she took off like a rocket down the road. I bent my arms and picked up my speed, power-walking, while I watched her disappear into the distance, and then around the nearest bend in the road.

It was a lot easier to walk along the road than through the trees, and took a lot less time, too. I'll be honest, I figured I'd see Grimaldi's SUV come toward me pretty quickly, because I had a feeling we hadn't covered all that much distance back there in the woods.

But that didn't happen. Eventually, though, I got to the spot in the road—or on the side of the road—where I was pretty sure we'd parked. The car wasn't there. Nor was Grimaldi.

I looked around. It looked like the right spot, but one set of trees looks very much like another, so maybe I'd been mistaken. I kept walking.

A few minutes passed, and then I heard the car engine. A few seconds later, the SUV rounded the curve in the road and pulled to a stop beside me. The passenger window rolled down. "Get in," Grimaldi said."

I peered into the back seat. "Where's Yung?"

"Not here," Grimaldi said.

"Didn't we park back there?" I gestured with my thumb over my shoulder.

She nodded. "She wasn't by the car when I got there, so I drove up the road looking for her."

"Maybe she got lost?" I opened the back door and prepared to transfer Carrie from the sling to her seat.

"Don't worry about that," Grimaldi told me. "Just put the seatbelt around both of you. I want to get going."

Sure thing. I crawled into the front seat and buckled in. Carrie had slept through everything so far, and kept sleeping through this.

Grimaldi had the car moving practically before I'd shut the door, and I turned to her. "You look worried."

"I don't like it," Grimaldi said. "It should have been an easy walk from where we were to the road. It didn't take you and me long. A bit longer for her, maybe, since she wasn't dressed for hiking. But even if she veered off course, she should have hit the road before we did. And she's nowhere."

The car was picking up speed as she was talking. I scanned the trees along the side of the road for any sign of Yung, or sign that she'd been there, and didn't see any. The small cairn of stones and Grimaldi's blue T-shirt flashed into view and then out again as we zoomed past.

"How far did we walk after Yung left us?" I wanted to know. "Five minutes? Ten? A football field or two?"

"No more. It was heavy going through the woods." She kept her eyes on the road as we traveled back toward town. "She ought to have hit the road right around the time we stopped to look at the bones. God, what was I thinking to send her off on her own in that suit and those stupid heels?"

"That she's a federal agent who's used to taking care of

herself?" I suggested. "Besides, you were trying to do her a favor, so she wouldn't have to walk back through the woods in those heels."

Grimaldi nodded, but she still looked grim. After another minute she glanced over at me, with reluctant amusement curving her lips. "When I got there this morning, your brother was looking at her like he liked what she looked like. Guess I thought it wouldn't hurt to make her look a little less pretty."

And a little more sweaty and disheveled. I nodded. I got it. "What's going on with you and Dix?"

Normally, when I ask that question, Grimaldi tells me it's none of my business. This time, maybe because it took her mind off Yung, lost in the woods, she sighed. "I'm not sure."

"What do you mean, you're not sure?"

She glanced at me. "It means I'm not sure."

Obviously. "Can you be, maybe, just a little more specific?"

"When your sister-in-law first died," Grimaldi said, driving the car down the road toward town, "your brother was mourning. Then he had to learn how to be a single parent to two girls who were going to grow up without their mother."

I nodded.

"I lost my mother young. Not as young as Abigail and Hannah, but young enough that I felt the loss."

I nodded.

"We talked a lot during the first six months or so after Sheila died. And it felt like—I don't know—like things were moving forward. But very slowly, because Dix was in mourning for his wife and not ready for another relationship, and then there were the girls, and what kind of stepmother would I be to two little southern girls, anyway?"

"A fine one," I said firmly. "You gave them Police Barbies for Christmas that first year." And it had freaked my mother out, which had been lovely to behold. Almost as lovely as her reaction to Rafe, when I informed her he'd be spending the night in my room. "You'd open up possibilities that I certainly didn't get to see when I was their age. You'd be good for them."

She shrugged, as houses started to crowd in around the car as we got closer to town. I kept watch, but there was no sign of Agent Yung.

"I don't think he's ready for another relationship," Grimaldi said eventually. "It hasn't been that long since your sister-in-law died."

"A year and a half."

"Less than the shrinks usually say it'll take." She scanned the road and changed the subject. "No sign of her. God, I hope she's not back there with a broken leg."

"Maybe we should have stopped and called out," I said. "We could go back and try to find her."

She shook her head. "We were close enough that we would have heard her if she'd yelled. And she had her phone. And my number. She could have called."

"Maybe she got lost," I suggested. "Not in the woods, but when she got out. Maybe she got turned around and started walking the wrong way."

"If she had, we'd have found her by now. Unless someone picked her up."

"And gave her a ride?" Someone might have. This is the south. People are friendly here, and a young, pretty woman in a fancy suit and high heels walking down the road away from a stopped car would rouse the protective instincts in everybody. "She might be back at the police station with her feet up, sipping a Coke."

"Let's hope so," Grimaldi said, and put her foot on the brake to slow down as we hit the first stop light in Columbia proper.

She wasn't, though. Yung. Sitting in the lobby at the police station with her feet elevated and a cold drink. And no one had seen her, either.

Grimaldi, looking quite grim now, dialed Bob. "Have you heard from Agent Yung?"

"Not since she left with you this morning," the sheriff's voice came back over the speaker. "Something wrong?"

"Not sure yet. We lost her in the woods. She was supposed to walk to the road and up to the car while Savannah and I made our way back through the woods, but she wasn't there."

Bob hesitated for a moment. "You look for her?"

"Not in the woods. Along the road, yes. But we figured, since we'll have to take a team in there anyway, we'll find her if she's there. It isn't cold enough to worry about exposure, and I doubt she's suffered anything worse than a twisted ankle."

Or a broken leg, possibly, but I wasn't going to say it. I focused on Carrie, who had woken up, finally, and indicated that she was hungry. At the moment I was sitting in Grimaldi's office feeding her, while I listened to the plan.

"I'm getting a team together to retrieve the skeleton," Bob said. "We'll make sure we bring medical supplies. And an extra stretcher, in case we come across her and she can't walk."

"That'd be a good idea," Grimaldi agreed. She was sitting behind her desk doing her best to look and sound calm, but one hand was tapping a pencil against the tabletop in an increasingly rapid rhythm. "I'll go back out there with you and show you the way."

"I've got Collier going back to Daffodil Farm with the crime scene crew and the warrant," Bob added. "He'll take care of the RV. The warrant's limited to that, and to the woods. With what we've got, we can't search the house."

"There's not likely to be anything in the house, anyway."

Grimaldi tapped for another second before she added, "I'll meet you out there."

Bob said he'd be on his way in a few minutes, and they

both hung up. Grimaldi turned to me. "I don't have time to take you back to Sweetwater. Can you call someone for a ride?"

"Sure," I told her, since I could tell she was twitching with nerves and a guilty conscience. "I could call Charlotte, or my mother, or anybody of about a dozen people who'd come pick me up. But you're not getting rid of me that easily. I feel bad about Yung, too."

"You weren't the one who sent her out in the woods by herself."

"Actually, I was. It was my idea originally. And we sent her toward the road, with instructions on how to get there. She should have found it in five or ten minutes, the direction she was going." We hadn't had any problems.

"So why do you think she didn't?" Grimaldi wanted to know.

"I have no idea. It was a straight shot through the trees to the road. And she had her phone. I spoke to Rafe while we were in the woods, so we know there's coverage."

"If something happened to her?"

"What, though? I mean, think about it. It's a matter of a quarter mile, at most. There aren't any ravines or waterfalls she could have fallen into. The weather's good. There wasn't enough wind for a branch to come loose and hit her on the head, or anything like that. And there aren't any wild animals to worry about."

"There are those rattlesnakes," Grimaldi said.

I felt myself turn pale, until I thought about it. "But if she got bitten, she wouldn't have passed out immediately. She would have had time to call for help. You, or Bob, or 911. Besides, she would have yelled. And we would have heard her. We weren't that far away."

"Maybe she got turned around. Maybe she started off in the wrong direction."

"How? You told her to keep the sun at the same angle. If

she did, she would have hit the road. If she didn't, she still would have made it to the road, just farther up or down. There was nothing between her and the road that would have been likely to stop her, and if anything had, and she called out, we would have heard her. It was quiet in there."

Grimaldi nodded. "So let's say she got to the road. What could have happened once she got there?"

"She got turned around and walked in the wrong direction? Somebody picked her up and gave her a lift?"

"If so," Grimaldi said, "shouldn't she have been here by now?"

"If she was headed here. She might have been going to the sheriff's office or home. Wherever home is while she's in town."

"She's staying at the Hampton Inn by the interstate," Grimaldi said. "We can run out and check her room before we go out to meet Bob and his team. We have time."

"Or you can send someone else to check the hotel while we go meet Bob." She had a whole police department at her disposal. And if Yung wasn't at the hotel, going there was a huge waste of time. Let someone else waste it, not us.

"Bob might have a deputy out that way." She reached for her phone again. "Excuse me a minute."

I nodded, and focused on feeding my daughter while she spoke to Bob and was assured that he would tag the deputy nearest the interstate and have Yung's hotel room checked. "We're about to head out," he told her.

She glanced at me. I held up two fingers. "We need another couple minutes here."

"It'll be fifteen before we even get to your neck of the woods," Bob said comfortably, "so take your time."

They hung up, and Grimaldi turned back to me. "She would have made it to the sheriff's office by now, I think, if she was going there."

I nodded.

"So if she isn't at the hotel…"

"You're thinking something," I said. "What is it?"

She looked at me. Looked like she was thinking, and then thinking better of it, whatever it was. Finally, she opened her mouth. "She fits the victim profile."

"The…? Oh." The serial killer's victim profile. "Not really."

"Sure she does. She's the right age and size. She has long, dark hair and medium skin…"

"She's Asian," I said.

"Part Asian. And he's killed blacks, whites, and Hispanics so far. No reason to think he'd turn his nose up at an Asian woman if one fell in his lap."

Maybe so. "How would she fall in his lap, though? She was miles from the truck stop…"

It was my turn to trail off.

"On Art Mullinax's property," Grimaldi said.

"He was over by the house, though. Talking to Rafe and Bob."

She shook her head. "Not by then. By then they'd left. He called you, remember, to let you know they were done and leaving? Mullinax could have been anywhere by the time Yung came out of the trees."

Maybe so. "Where would he take her? Not to the farm."

"Depends on whether he suspected they were coming back with a search warrant or not." She pushed to her feet. "You ready?"

"One more minute." I burped Carrie and stuffed her back into the baby sling. "You'd better call Bob and let him know we'll be going to the house instead of the woods."

Or at least that's what I assumed we'd be doing.

"I'll call from the car," Grimaldi said and strode out, leaving me to scurry along behind.

Rafe was there, with a crew of crime scene techs, by the time we made it back to Daffodil Hill Farm. Grimaldi had phoned Bob again to tell him her concerns, and he had agreed that she could go hunt down Art Mullinax just as soon as she'd met him and his retrieval crew, and told them where to go. So we sat on the side of the road and waited for Bob to show up.

Or more accurately, I sat on the side of the road and waited. Grimaldi had walked back to where she thought Yung might have come out of the woods, and had examined the ground for any signs of accident, struggle, or anything else.

"I'm pretty sure I found where she came across the ditch," she told me when she'd made her way back to me. "Something pushed through the branches recently, and slid into the ditch and climbed back out. I saw what looked like a heel mark in the bottom of the ditch, where it's just wet enough for the ground to hold an impression. I couldn't testify to it being her, not without a plaster cast of her shoe for comparison, but I'm pretty sure it's the imprint of a high heel."

"Well, then I'm sure it was Yung," I said. "Who else would have been out here in the last day or two in high heels?"

"I imagine not a lot of people." Grimaldi shaded her eyes with her hand as she gazed down the road in the direction of town. "At least we don't have to worry about searching the woods for her. She's not hurt and helpless in there somewhere."

No. But she might be hurt and helpless somewhere else. And I'm sure it was that same thought that caused Grimaldi's next outburst. "What's taking them so long? I could have jogged to Sweetwater by now!"

"Not really. And I'm sure they're coming as quickly as they can. But it's not like *he*—" I nodded in the direction of the woods and the skeleton they contained, "needs help in a hurry."

Grimaldi nodded reluctantly, and started to pace back and

forth in front of the car instead.

I put up with it for about two minutes, and was just about to tell her to knock it off when I heard the sound of a car engine coming closer. "That must be them."

I scooted off the hood of the SUV and peered down the road. "Yes. There they are. Blue lights and everything."

But no sirens. It wasn't that kind of hurry.

Bob pulled his sheriff's SUV up on the shoulder across the road from us, and got out. The crime scene van made a U-turn and parked behind Grimaldi's car. Bob came toward us. "This the place?"

Grimaldi nodded. "That's the cairn of stones. That's my T-shirt. The body is a five or ten minute hike straight back."

"One of Carrie's blankets is draped over a branch up above," I added. "It's bright yellow. You can't miss it."

"I don't imagine we will." Bob scratched behind his ear. "I heard from Cletus Johnson. Agent Yung hasn't turned up at the hotel so far."

"We think we found the place where she came out of the woods," Grimaldi said, including me in the discovery even though I'd been sitting here with the car while she'd done all the work, "so I don't think it's a case of her still being in there."

"We'll keep an eye out," Bob told her, "and holler as we go. But if she made it out, and she isn't with you, or with me, and she hasn't gone back to the hotel, I'd say we probably have cause for concern at this point."

I'd say so, too.

"You girls run along." He waved us off down the road, metaphorically. "We'll gather up the bones and anything else we might find in the drop zone. You go look for Agent Yung."

Grimaldi nodded, "Come on, Savannah. Let's go."

She hustled to the car door while I hurried to keep up. Behind us, two sheriff's deputies in stout boots and with big bags of paraphernalia prepared to follow Bob across the ditch and into the woods.

"I feel kind of bad for leaving them to get there and deal with it on their own," I said, as they faded away in the rearview mirror.

Grimaldi glanced over. "It isn't your job. If anybody should feel bad, it's me."

"Don't you?"

"Not about Jurgensson. Assuming it's him in there, and I guess we have to assume it is."

I nodded. It was probably safe to assume that, under the circumstances. "I can't think of anyone else it's likely to be."

"But I do feel bad about Yung. If she got picked up by Mullinax, it's my fault."

"Of course it isn't," I said, in spite of feeling a little like that myself. Logically we had no reason to. "She's a federal agent. She's trained. She's probably armed. She's supposed to be able to take care of herself. And we have to assume she isn't stupid. She wouldn't be in this job if she were."

"So what happened?"

I shrugged. "I have no idea. But I know it wasn't your fault. Or mine. All she had to do was walk for fifteen minutes and then wait for us. If something happened to her, it's tragic, but it isn't our fault. If you'd walked back to the road and been grabbed by Mullinax, would it have been her fault? Or my fault?"

"Of course not," Grimaldi said. "But she'd never even seen Mullinax. She wouldn't know him from Adam if he rolled up next to her and offered her a ride. He looks like such a harmless old man…"

I shook my head. "She didn't need a ride. She was waiting for us. And she wouldn't take one if he offered. She isn't five years old."

"Well, something happened," Grimaldi said, her lips tight

and her hands white-knuckled on the wheel. "Maybe it was Mrs. Mullinax. Maybe the old lady's picking up victims for her husband, and Yung went into the car because she thought it was safe. Or maybe it was Mullinax himself, and he shot her…"

"We would have heard the shot. And I'm not saying that nothing happened. Something did, or she would have been there, waiting for us. Something is keeping her from answering her phone." Hopefully it was just unconsciousness or ropes, not death. "But beating yourself up over it doesn't help. She's a grown woman, and a federal agent. She can take care of herself. If something happened, it was her fault and not yours."

I waited a second to see if she'd argue again. When she didn't, I went on. "The best thing we can do right now is focus on finding her. And what we're going to do once we have."

Grimaldi nodded. "Well, we're about five minutes from Daffodil Hill Farm. Once we get there, I figure we use the search warrant to go through every room in every building, and every vehicle in the place. If Mullinax isn't there, we figure out where he is and what he's driving, and we put out a BOLO on the vehicle."

"What if he is there?"

"Then we make him tell us where he put her," Grimaldi said. "Hopefully he hasn't had time to kill her yet. He doesn't keep the women long, but usually longer than just an hour."

I nodded. "There's the turnoff. See it?"

Grimaldi took it on two wheels, and we barreled down the track toward Daffodil Hill Farm.

Twenty

Rafe was there when we reached the parking lot, directing sheriff's deputies to the left and right like he was born to it. When Grimaldi pulled up with a spatter of gravel, he arched a brow. "Problem?"

"Looking for Yung," Grimaldi told him, assessing the property.

It had been a working farm at one point, so there were several outbuildings. A big barn sat at the far end of the property, closest to the trees, and looked mostly ready to come down. The three-bay garage looked like it had started life as a carriage house, same as at the mansion. The silver SUV was gone today, but the golf cart and darker gray sedan was still parked outside. And there was a brown and tan RV parked off to the side. A couple of crime scene techs were making their way toward it.

"That warrant doesn't cover the house or outbuildings," Grimaldi said, "does it?"

Rafe shook his head. "With what we had, this was all we could get. There's gonna be no evidence of Jurgensson's murder, so many years later, and there's no evidence he took the women here before he killed them."

"Yung's missing," Grimaldi said. "Would that make a difference?"

"Not less'n you have some reason to think she's here."

Grimaldi went over the reasons we thought she might be here, and Rafe nodded. "You can go talk to the judge. But with what I've got, all I can do is search the RV. All Bob can do is search the woods."

"Damn." She thought a moment. "Does Mullinax know that?"

"He has a copy of the warrant, so I imagine he does." He glanced at her. "You know the rules. He gets a copy."

She nodded. Rafe took her acquiescence as an excuse for greeting me with a quick kiss, and Carrie with a tickle. "Hi, pretty girl."

She gurgled and kicked her feet, back in the car seat again. "I think she's happy to be out of the sling," I confessed. "She's spent a lot of time being strapped to my chest so far today."

"She'll be all right." He kept one eye on her and the other on the door to the RV, where the two crime scene techs had disappeared.

"I'm going to go talk to him," Grimaldi declared. "Maybe he'll let me look around if I ask nicely."

If he had Leslie Yung stashed somewhere, I wouldn't count on it, although if he knew we were looking for her, and knew we suspected him, maybe he'd think twice about killing her.

And on the plus side, he was here, not wherever she was. So that was one positive thing we could focus on.

"I guess I should go with her," I told Rafe.

He nodded. "Leave the baby with me. If he does something crazy, I don't want her over there."

No argument here. I transferred the carrier from my hand to his, and jogged after Grimaldi.

I got there in time to hear her greet him, politely enough. "Mr. Mullinax."

He nodded. "Chief Grimaldi. Is this your doing?"

"The sheriff's. Although we're working together." She paused a second before added, "I'm hoping you will cooperate, too."

Mullinax gave me a distracted look as I appeared behind Grimaldi. It didn't seem to occur to him to ask what I was doing there. "I'm cooperating. Nothing else I can do when you're waving a warrant in my face, is there?"

"We found bones in your woods," Grimaldi said, point blank. "The sheriff and a couple of techs are back there retrieving them now."

Mullinax hesitated for a second. "I imagine there are a lot of bones in the woods."

"Not this kind," Grimaldi said. "Or at least I hope you haven't killed more than one person and left him out there."

Mullinax stared at her.

"The warrant only covers the RV and the woods," Grimaldi added, "but if you want to cooperate, maybe you'd give me permission for a quick look through the house and the other buildings, too?"

It took a second, and I could practically hear the gears moving inside Mullinax's skull, but he must have come to the conclusion that he had nothing to lose. "I don't suppose I should, without a warrant. But I have nothing to hide. Look all you want."

"Thank you." Grimaldi headed for the door. I scrambled to catch up.

"She won't be here," I said as Grimaldi reached for the doorknob.

She shook her head. "Not if he let us in that easily. But just in case we're wrong, and he's got her drugged or tied up so she can't make any sounds, let's look carefully."

I nodded. "And even if she isn't here, maybe there's some clue as to where he's taken her."

"Mrs. Mullinax is away from the house," Grimaldi said, as we walked into the foyer. "Yung could be with her."

"Put out a... what did you call it? BOLO?...on her car. If

she's doing something legit, it's probably parked at the spa or the country club."

Grimaldi nodded. "Go that way." She pointed with the hand that held the phone. "I'll go this way. Open all the doors, look into all the closets."

"You don't have to tell me how to snoop," I told her. "I'm an expert at this."

Looking through other people's houses has always been a guilty pleasure of mine. It's why I went into real estate, so I'd have an excuse to go into other people's houses to see how they lived.

This was the first time I'd searched a house looking for a missing person, though. I opened all the doors, including the ones of the wardrobe in the spare bedroom, and even lifted the lid of the heavy steamer trunk that sat in the middle of the parlor with a flower arrangement and a stack of magazines on it. But the gravity of the occasion didn't keep me from enjoying the experience. Mrs. Mullinax, or maybe it was Mr. Mullinax, had great taste, and enough money to indulge it. I grew up with antiques, so I'm used to seeing them. I'm also pretty well versed in assessing how much they're worth, and Mrs. Mullinax hadn't spared any expense. Daffodil Hill Farm was a lovely specimen of Victorian farmhouse.

But it didn't contain Leslie Yung.

"She's not here," I told Grimaldi when we met on the upstairs landing. "I checked under the beds and everything."

She nodded. "Would this place have a basement?"

"You didn't come across it in the kitchen?" The access stairs are usually there. I guess in the old days, before refrigeration, the cook probably kept things like potatoes and onions in the cool darkness below the house. "Then there's most likely just an outside hatch somewhere. Let's look."

Art Mullinax gave us a look when we came back out of the house empty-handed, but he told us, nicely enough, that the access to the area under the house was on the side. "Look out for the spiders," he adviced us, with a semi-malicious smirk.

I'm not a fan of spiders, and part of me wanted to call Rafe over so he could do the honors. But Grimaldi wasn't the type to let fear of a few creepy crawlies keep her from doing her job. She pulled open the small door in the foundation and went down on all fours to go through.

"Do you see anything?" I wanted to know, bent in half as I tried to peer through the low aperture.

"Too much. A lot of rotted planks, some old windows, an old plastic tarp—we might want to take that with us, just in case he wrapped Jurgensson's body in it for the trip into the woods—what looks like a raccoon skeleton…"

"No sign of Yung?"

"No," Grimaldi said, crawling back through the hole. "It's all open under there, so nowhere to hide anything. It doesn't look like anyone's been there in decades."

"It doesn't seem like a good place to hide an abduction victim, anyway. Too exposed, with all these people here, and if she woke up, or got free, she could just crawl away."

"He didn't know the place would be crawling with cops," Grimaldi said, brushing herself off. "I'm sure Bob didn't warn him they were coming back with a warrant. But you have a point."

"The outbuildings next, then?"

"And the trunk of the car," Grimaldi said. "I should have checked there first."

Well, yes. That was the logical place to look. If Mullinax had been driving the gray car when he picked up Leslie Yung, the trunk of the gray car was probably where he would have stashed her.

"Would you mind opening the trunk of your car, Mr. Mullinax?" Grimaldi called up to him.

He stared at her a moment, and I thought he was going to

refuse. Then he shrugged, and pulled a keychain out of his pocket. He pointed it at the sedan and pushed the button. The car beeped, and the lid unlocked.

Grimaldi headed for it. I scurried behind, and even Rafe moved over to us to see.

"Nothing in the house?"

Grimaldi shook her head. "There's an old tarp in the crawlspace that could be related to Jurgensson, though. It looks old enough, and I imagine they must have wrapped him in something for the trip into the woods. But that's just a guess."

She grabbed the bottom edge of the car door and lifted.

We all leaned forward.

"Empty," Grimaldi said. As if either Rafe or I needed it spelled out.

Art Mullinax must have had enough, or maybe he was curious. In either case, he had left the porch and was coming across the grass toward us. "Can I ask what you're looking for? If I knew, maybe I'd be able to help."

I glanced at Rafe. He glanced at Grimaldi.

She squared her shoulder. "I believe the bones the sheriff is currently removing from the woods—your woods!—belong to Kent Jurgensson, and I believe you killed him and put him there."

Mullinax didn't say anything for a few seconds. Then he opened his mouth. "Kent's been gone almost thirty years. Even if I did have something to do with his disappearance—and I'm not saying I did—why are you looking for evidence in a car I bought three years ago? Or for that matter—" he looked over his shoulder, "in an RV my wife and I have owned for seven years? These vehicles both post-date Kent by a decade or two."

"Where have you driven the RV, Mr. Mullinax?" Grimaldi wanted to know. "On I-65?"

Mullinax blinked. Hard to say if it was because of guilty conscience or just surprise. "Of course on I-65. It's the closest interstate to us." He didn't add, *'you twit,'* but it was clearly implied.

"Indiana?" Grimaldi asked. "Kentucky?"

"We mostly take it down to the Florida Keys. We have a piece of land there, where we plug in for a few weeks and enjoy the water. Although we've taken it out west once, to see the Grand Canyon. And up to New England two years ago, for the fall colors. We drove up through Virginia and New York, though. Not Kentucky and Ohio." He looked from one to the other of us, and if he had any idea what we were getting at, he showed no sign of it. "What's any of this got to do with Kent?"

"Nothing," Grimaldi said. "We're missing a federal agent."

Mullinax blinked again. "Excuse me?"

"An FBI agent named Leslie Yung," Rafe told him. "Pretty. Long, black hair. Went into the woods with the other two this morning. And vanished."

"In my woods?" Mullinax chuckled. "They're not that big. She couldn't have gotten lost. Either she'd have wound up here, or she'd have found a road or a field."

"She found the road," Grimaldi said. "Someone picked her up."

Mullinax shook his head. "Wasn't me. I've been here all morning."

"Can you prove that?"

He looked at me, since I was the one who had asked. "My word isn't good enough?"

I opened my mouth to explain that under the circumstances, it really wasn't. But before I could, he'd continued. "I had breakfast with my wife. Then Jacob stopped by to work on the RV. It was making a sort of grinding noise on the way home from Key West last week. Then *you* showed up with the sheriff..." He glanced at Rafe.

My husband nodded. "You were in Key West last week?"

"Came home Thursday afternoon," Mullinax said, and

moved on to the next thing. Or maybe in his mind it was the same thing. "I understand about Kent. There are bones in my woods, and there's the connection to Noah, and you gotta ask questions. But why'd I want to make an FBI agent disappear? That'd be stupid. And wouldn't do much to help my case anyway. The bones are still there, right?"

Probably not anymore, but I got what he was saying. And what's more, if he'd been in Key West last week, he couldn't have been in Nashville picking up Ramona Mitchell.

But just for form's sake I asked, "Which way do you travel to and from Key West?"

"I-65 to Montgomery," Mullinax said promptly, "331 to I-10, and I-10 across to I-75."

I nodded. Much the same way Rafe and I had traveled on our honeymoon, as it happened.

You'll notice Nashville wasn't mentioned. That's because it's in the opposite direction, north of Columbia. But just to make sure… "You didn't go by Nashville?"

He gave me a look like I'd lost my mind. "No. What kind of fool would do that?"

Rafe's lips curved, and he put his free hand on my shoulder. "The body of a prostitute was dumped at the truck stop out by the interstate Wednesday night."

Mullinax nodded. "Heard about that. Saw the crime scene tape when we drove by."

"We think the killer might be local," Grimaldi said. "Someone who travels up and down I-65. Someone with access to a truck or a motor home."

She avoided rather ostentatiously looking at it, but Mullinax got the point.

"Oh, no." He took a step back and lifted his hands. "No, no. You're not pinning that on me. Kent, that's one thing. I get why you have to look at me for that. Noah was my nephew, and what Kent did to him was terrible. Ruined the boy's life. But not this other thing. And not the FBI lady. I had nothing to do with that. You ask my wife. She was with me in Florida, and on the way home. She'll tell you we didn't go by Nashville, and that we didn't pick up any hitchhikers."

None of us pointed out that the dead woman hadn't been hitchhiking.

"Where can we find your wife?" Grimaldi wanted to know, and Mullinax turned to her.

"She went to do her volunteer work at the homeless shelter. Every Monday and Thursday when we're here, she and Bonnie go to the homeless shelter and cook and read to the kids."

"Bonnie?" Grimaldi said.

"Drimmel. Jacob's wife."

Of course. She hadn't mentioned her first name when we'd been there on… must have been Friday.

"So that was Jacob Drimmel," Grimaldi said, "who was here, working on your RV?"

Mullinax nodded. "He left about an hour ago. Needed a part before he can finish the job, and it won't be in for a couple of days."

"His wife told us he's a diesel mechanic. That's a diesel engine, I assume?"

Mullinax nodded. "Much better mileage with diesel."

"That's what I hear." She smiled at him. "You two go back a ways, don't you? Was it Jacob who helped you carry Kent Jurgensson's body into the woods back then?"

Mullinax took a step back, and she added, "You were golf buddies, right? You and Jacob, Kent Jurgensson and Sid. I don't think Sid helped you dispose of the body—"

I shook my head.

"—and I don't imagine your wife would have been able to, even then—"

Rafe shook his head.

"—but you must have had help. You were younger then,

but he wasn't a small man. And dead weight—pardon the expression—is heavy."

"I don't know what you're talking about," Mullinax said, but his voice was hoarse, like he had a hard time getting the words out.

"No?" Grimaldi tilted her head. "Maybe Jacob Drimmel can help us."

Mullinax cleared his throat. "He isn't here. I told you, he left. Needed a part."

"Where would he have gone, do you think? Home?"

"How am I supposed to know?" Mullinax demanded. "Probably. He would have stopped somewhere to order the part, and then yes, he'd probably have gone home. He's got this old car he's working on fixing up…"

"Thank you, Mr. Mullinax." Grimaldi turned to me. "Let's go."

She strode off toward the SUV, leaving me, Mullinax, and Rafe behind. Mullinax didn't seem to mind—he stood there and stared after her, but didn't make any move to follow. I scrambled to keep up, and behind me, Rafe didn't bother to scramble, but managed to keep up anyway.

"What?" he asked Grimaldi when we were far enough from Mullinax that the latter wouldn't be able to overhear. "There ain't no hurry. Jurgensson died decades ago."

Grimaldi shook her head. "Jacob Drimmel left here about an hour ago. He might have driven down the road where the car was parked while we were in the woods."

Might have. But— "Why would Jacob Drimmel kidnap Agent Yung?"

And then the picture realigned in my head, and I added, "Oh, my God. But no… he couldn't have raped and killed his own daughter. And besides, he's not a truck driver. He's a mechanic. He wouldn't be driving up and down the interstate."

"He would be if he worked for a trucking company," Rafe

said. "Some of'em keep mechanics on staff to work on the trucks between trips. And sometimes, if a truck breaks down on the road, the mechanic'll drive out and try to get it started again."

"Trucks have diesel engines?"

"Same as RVs."

"But Laura Lee was his daughter. He wouldn't…"

"Some men do," Grimaldi said, her voice even. "But he needn't have raped her. He might have been there, at the truck stop, for some reason, to talk to her or just because he was passing through. And he could have seen that she was turning tricks. If it made him angry, he could have killed her. She'd refused financial help, it was Frankie's fault and he didn't like Frankie, she wouldn't listen to reason and come home with him… the motive doesn't matter. He could have found a reason to kill her. And that could have been the trigger for the others."

I suppose it could have. "So she had sex with someone else. But her father raped and killed the others."

"It's a theory," Grimaldi said. "More to the point right now, is that he was here this morning, and drove home around the time Yung went missing. That's reason enough to talk to him. If he didn't take her, he might have seen something."

Of course. "The outbuildings…"

Grimaldi didn't even glance at them. "I like this better."

I liked it better, too. "Let's go, then."

"I'm coming, too," Rafe said, in a tone that brooked no argument. "I need a minute to let the team know I'm leaving."

He handed me the baby and walked away. Grimaldi opened her mouth, and then closed it without speaking. I guess she wasn't any more keen on seeing what would happen if she left without him than I was.

Besides, if what we suspected was right, and Jacob Drimmel did have Agent Yung, we might need help getting her away from him in one piece.

And anyway, there's no one I'd rather have with me on an errand like this than Rafe. I don't mean to disparage Grimaldi in any way, she's very capable, but she isn't Rafe.

By the time he came back, we had sorted ourselves into the SUV. I had crawled in next to Carrie and left him the front seat, partly because it was more comfortable, and partly because this was an official trip and he was more official than me. It wouldn't look good for the lead investigator on the case to crawl out of the backseat while his wife lounged in the front.

Also, his legs are longer than mine.

"You sure you don't want me to drive?" he asked Grimaldi when he slid into the front seat. "I can get there faster."

She was already revving the engine. "I've got it."

"Suit yourself," He pulled the strap across his chest and had barely had time to buckle it before the SUV rocketed down the drive and into the trees. "Whoa."

"Told you."

She didn't say anything else, just concentrated on driving. It wasn't possible to speed down the narrow track, but Grimaldi did her best. Once we hit the paved road, she picked up speed. "Tell me where to go."

"They live in Sunnyside," I said, before Rafe could ask. "If you know a shortcut, now would be the time to say so."

He nodded. "Turn right at the next intersection, then left, then right again. There's not really a quick and easy way to get halfway around town, though. It takes the time it takes."

"If we're lucky," Grimaldi said, turning right and left and right again, "he had to wait for his wife to leave before he could bring Yung into the house."

"If he's there at all. He could have taken her somewhere else."

Grimaldi glanced at him. "Where?"

"How would I know? He didn't bring the others home,

though. And if it was him, he didn't have an eighteen-wheeler with a sleeper cab where he could take'em, either."

No, he hadn't. "Any way to figure out who he worked for and what he drove? And whether he even did travel? We're spinning this out of air, after all."

"Not completely outta air," Rafe said calmly, swaying with the motion of the car as Grimaldi made the second right on two wheels. We were on the backroads now, without having to deal with the traffic of downtown Columbia, and she could let the car go faster. "Remember what your uncle said? He played golf with Mullinax and Jurgensson—and Jacob Drimmel when he was around."

"Meaning Jacob wasn't always around."

Rafe nodded. "Meaning Jacob mighta been traveling for work."

"Why didn't we ever suspect him before?"

"'Cause there was no reason to suspect him," Rafe said. "He was the first victim's father. No reason to think he'd be involved."

"When she walked out of the restaurant with the trucker," Grimaldi added, as she kept the SUV zipping around the curves, "Drimmel was at home with his wife. The DNA on her body was no match to anyone she knew. And of course nobody came forward to say he'd slept with her…"

"I wouldn't have either," Rafe said, "if I'd known she'd been murdered."

Grimaldi nodded. "Hard to prove a negative. He'd had sex with her. Who'd believe he hadn't killed her, too?"

Not many people, I imagined.

"Right at the next intersection," Rafe said. "So Drimmel left Daffodil Hill and started home. He ran across Yung a few minutes later. Somehow he convinced her to get in the car with him…"

"I'm sure he had a good story," I said. "She might not have

been suspicious. Not of an old guy on a quiet country road and with us so close."

"Leaving for the moment the question of how he did it," Grimaldi said, "he got her into the car or truck. I'm guessing she was unconscious at that point. Or got that way pretty quickly. If he gave her even half a chance, she would have taken him out."

We drove another few seconds in silence.

"The question is where he took her," Rafe said. "And it mighta been home, if he knew his wife was gonna be gone."

"He's friends with Uncle Sid," I said, "but he wouldn't have taken her there. I don't care if he's my uncle; I refuse to believe he knew anything about this. Any of it. Jurgensson or this other thing."

The other two nodded. "Left down here," Rafe said.

I continued, "He's friends with Mullinax, but he isn't there. And I didn't get the impression Mullinax knew that his buddy Jacob has been killing women, or that he would approve of it if he did."

"Would he have called Drimmel after we left?" Grimaldi wondered.

"If he did, we'll deal with it when we get there," Rafe said. "Right here. Go on, Savannah."

"I don't know that I have a lot more to say," I answered. "Jurgensson's dead, Jacob isn't at Daffodil Hill Farm, and he wouldn't have gone to Uncle Sid's. His daughter's dead, and he didn't like his son-in-law. His granddaughter's away at college—not that he'd be likely to involve her—and his grandson's in high school, and would be there this time of day. If he spent his time working on trucks and traveling, he might not have any other friends."

"So he'd take her to the house," Grimaldi said. "And plan to be finished with her by the time his wife or Curtis comes home."

"We're close," Rafe said. "Right here."

Grimaldi took the right, and two minutes later the fields and woods gave way to the winding roads and large lawns of Sunnyside.

"Do you remember where to go?"

She nodded. "It's just around the corner from here."

It *was* just around the corner. Grimaldi took it like Jeff Gordon, narrowly escaped clipping the postman's truck that was idling there, and gunned the engine up the street. Twenty seconds later we powered up the long driveway and came to a quivering stop outside the garage.

There was a moment's pause.

"No vehicle," Grimaldi said.

"Prob'ly inside the garage."

Maybe. Although last time we'd been here, Jacob had been working on a different car inside the garage. "He wasn't driving anything with fins when you saw him at Daffodil Hill, was he?"

"Fins?" Rafe repeated. "No, darlin'. He was driving a pickup. Blue and rusty."

That might fit into the second half of the garage, then. "Go look," I said. "See if the pickup and the car with the fins are in there."

Rafe slipped out of the SUV and pulled his gun. Grimaldi got out on the other side and did the same, bracing her hands on the top of her open door to cover him as he made his way toward the garage.

"There are windows on the side," I called out.

Unlike last time we'd been here, it was quiet. No big band music seeped out of the garage. But maybe Jacob didn't like to rape and kill women to the standards. Maybe he needed something different, or the sound of silence, for that.

Rafe made it to the corner of the house and crept along the brick over to the nearest window, shoulders against the wall behind him. He did a neat a hundred and eighty degree turn, and looked in the window. And ducked back out of sight. After a second, when nothing happened, he leaned over and peered again. "I see the fins. The other bay is empty."

"He isn't here."

It was Grimaldi who said it, as she holstered her weapon, and her tone hit somewhere between resigned and hopeless. I knew just how she felt. If Jacob Drimmel had taken Agent Yung, we were the only thing that stood between her and being murdered, and we didn't know where he'd taken her.

Twenty-One

Rafe was halfway down the path toward the SUV when the front door to the house opened. Grimaldi had already holstered her weapon, but Rafe hadn't, and when he saw the realization on her face, he swung around and brought it up in firing stance.

"Whoa!"

Curtis—for he was the one who had opened the door—jumped back, eyes wide.

"I didn't do nothing!" he called out. "Don't shoot me!"

"It's all right." Rafe had already tucked the gun out of sight, in the holster at the small of his back. Out of sight if not out of mind. "Sorry," he added. "I didn't think anybody was home. Why aren't you in school?"

Curtis's face fell. "Oh. Um…"

Rafe waited, and eventually Curtis tried what he obviously thought was a charming smile. "You're not with the truancy department, are you?"

"There's no truancy department. Get over here."

Rafe gestured. Curtis looked like he was thinking about jumping back inside and slamming the door, but he moved forward. Slowly. Dragging his feet with every step.

"We're not looking for you," Rafe told him when he'd finally made it halfway down the walk, to where Rafe was standing. "We're looking for your grandfather. Any idea where we can find him?"

"He went out to the old Mullinax farm this morning," Curtis said, readily enough, "to work on a rig."

"He's not there anymore," Rafe said. "We thought he'd come back here."

Curtis shook his head. "I ain't seen him since this morning."

It finally, belatedly, dawned on him that the police, that Rafe, was here for a reason that didn't have anything to do with him, and he turned pale. "What's wrong? It it my gramma? Did something happen to my gramma?"

"Your gramma's fine. Gone to the homeless shelter with Mrs. Mullinax, her husband said."

Curtis nodded. "Mondays and Thursdays. She OK? You sure?"

"I'm not sure," Rafe said, "I haven't talked to her, but I have no reason to think she's not OK. That's not why we're here."

"Why're you here? Other than looking for my granddad?"

Rafe hesitated. And seemed to decide that he might as well put the cards on the table. "We have a missing federal agent. An FBI agent who came here from Memphis to work with us on a case. She was out at the Mullinax place this morning, and now she's gone, and we can't find her."

"You think my granddad saw her?" Curtis sounded intrigued rather than worried, at least so far.

"Something like that," Rafe said.

Curtis must have heard something in his voice, or maybe seen it on his face. I don't know what; Rafe had his back to me. But Curtis's face hardened, and I saw his hands curl into fists. "You think he took her. That's why you're here. Isn't it?"

Rafe hesitated, and it was hard to blame him. "We think he might know something. If he isn't involved, he might have seen her."

Curtis shook his head. "You think he took her. Just tell me the truth. That's what you think. Isn't it?"

"We think it's possible," Rafe said.

It was Curtis's turn to hesitate. For just a second before he said, "I lied, OK? You're the cops, and I didn't know what you wanted, so I lied."

"About what?"

Curtis gazed up at him. "That I hadn't seen him since he left this morning. I did. He was here. About thirty minutes ago. Just long enough to walk in and see that I was home."

"You didn't expect him back?"

"I didn't not expect him back. That's not the point, OK? He was here. He walked in, looking to see if the house was empty, and when it wasn't, he left again."

"Did he tell you where he was going?"

"He said he was gonna go fishing," Curtis said, with a glance up at the sky, where the sun was burning down on us. "Like I'd believe anybody'd go fishing in weather like this."

"Where'd he go, then?" Grimaldi wanted to know.

Curtis looked at her. "My boss," Rafe told him.

Curtis gave Rafe a look, gave Grimaldi another one, and shrugged. "Not sure. Coulda been anywhere."

"Surely you must have some idea. If he had an unconscious woman in the trunk of his car…"

"He drives an old pickup truck," Curtis said.

"And he wanted to take her somewhere where he could…" Grimaldi trailed off, probably not quite sure how to frame the rest of the sentence for a seventeen year old boy.

"Don't sweat it," Curtis told her. "I'm not stupid. I watch TV. I've seen the kinds of skin magazines he keeps in the garage."

Ewww.

"I'll take you to a place where he might be. Although I guess maybe I oughta get a pair of shoes first."

He turned around, brushed past Rafe and into the house.

"Think he's going to call his grandfather?" Grimaldi asked, softly.

Rafe hesitated. "Nothing we can do about it if he is. We'll just have to wait and see."

Grimaldi nodded. Curtis came back outside less than a minute later, with a pair of Nike's on his feet and a set of keys in his hand. He might have had time to make a call or send a message, but maybe not.

"It's gonna be tight," Rafe told him as they came toward the car. "You'll have to share the back seat with Savannah and the baby."

"I'll sit in the back." Curtis moved to the rear of the car, yanked up the hatch and crawled into the cargo space in the back of the SUV.

Grimaldi shrugged. I guess the fact that he wouldn't be strapped in worried her less at the moment than getting to where we were going. "Take the wheel," she told Rafe. "And you—" she glanced into the back at Curtis, "find something to hold onto."

Twenty seconds later we took off like rocket down the driveway and took the turn onto the road on two wheels. Curtis let out a whoop as he tumbled sideways like an overturned beetle, but it sounded more like excitement than pain.

"Told you," Grimaldi said over her shoulder. She was holding onto the door handle for all she was worth.

I'm used to the way Rafe drives—even if he only rarely drives like this—so I just swayed back and forth with the motion of the car. "You're taking this pretty calmly," I told Curtis, after he had gotten himself back into an upright position and was kneeling on the floor of the car with his arms braced on the back of the seat.

He gave me a sideways look. "He's always been a bastard."

It's a long way from bastard to serial killer and rapist, but OK. "Rafe's grandfather wasn't much to write home about, either. He shot Rafe's dad because he didn't want his daughter involved with a black man."

"My granddad wasn't big on my dad, either," Curtis said. "He never shot him, though. Just told him he couldn't come around after my mom died and dad got outta prison."

"That must have been hard," I said.

Curtis shrugged. "My gramma, she's all right. She took care of Christie and me. She didn't let granddad beat on us too bad."

Not exactly a ringing endorsement. "I think Rafe's mother probably tried. But she was just a girl herself, when he was born. Old Jim beat her, too."

"If we can stop talking about that for a second," Rafe interrupted from the front seat, and his eyes met mine in the mirror, "mind telling me where we're going, Curtis?"

"Not sure," Curtis said. "He has a fishing hole down on the Duck River. He coulda gone there."

"I don't think he's fishing," Grimaldi began, and Curtis gave her a look.

"I know he ain't fishing. But it's private and out of the way."

"That's what we're looking for," Rafe said. "Where?"

Curtis told him where the fishing hole was located, and Rafe figured out the directions in his head while the car was moving down the suburban road at sixty miles an hour. Once we hit the bigger road, he pushed it up to eighty. "Got any flashers on this thing?" he asked Grimaldi, who leaned over and flipped the switch. The rearview mirror lit up with blue lights.

"Let's leave the sirens off for now. We don't want to warn him we're coming."

No, we didn't. If we gave him warning, there was a chance

he'd kill Yung and dump her in the river before we got there, and if he did, it might be hard to prove he'd had anything to do with it.

"How far is it?" I wanted to know.

Curtis shrugged. "Twenty minutes?"

"I can get us there in fifteen." Rafe's tone was grim, and I got the impression that if he did, it would be from sheer force of will.

"Better hold on, then," Grimaldi advised. We all took a better grip on whatever was near us.

He was right, though. It was fourteen minutes and a little more by the time Curtis said, "It should be along here somewhere."

He sounded a little breathless, so maybe the excitement of driving with a madman at the wheel had worn off. But we were all in one piece, and nothing worse had happened than that a car that hadn't gotten out of the way fast enough when we approached had ended up nose down in a ditch. It was a small ditch, so the driver should be able to get up on the other side without much problem. Or so it seemed to me. It hadn't seemed important enough to either Rafe or Grimaldi to stop. Clearly the car in the ditch was a less urgent problem than Leslie Yung.

"You're taking this pretty calmly," I told Curtis as we moved along at a much slower pace now, looking for the entrance to Jacob Drimmel's fishing hole. The road was thickly forested, it had been several minutes since we'd seen any sign of habitation, and from the somewhat vague map in my head, I knew we were close to the river.

He gave me a look. "That my grandfather might be a serial killer?"

None of us had mentioned that, as far as I could recall, and I had my mouth open to say so when he added, "He's been watching the news about that woman at the truck stop all week. And reading about it in the paper. When I asked him if he hadn't been at the truck stop on the day she was found, he told me to mind my own business."

"That's the case Agent Yung came here to consult on," Rafe said, peering out the window at the trees. "That it?"

He nodded to a slim opening between two trees that made the entrance to Daffodil Hill Farm look practically opulent.

Curtis nodded. And then qualified it with an, "I think so."

"Better cut the lights," Grimaldi said and reached for the switch, but Rafe had already done so.

The SUV crept along the narrow track, with leaves brushing the windows and branches scraping the roof. "Doesn't look like anyone else ever comes down here," I said.

Curtis shook his head. "That's why he likes it. He likes his privacy."

"That why he told you to mind your own business?" Rafe glanced at him in the mirror.

Curtis shrugged. "I suppose. He's always liked being alone. Whenever somebody's truck broke down three states away, so he could be gone for a couple days, he was always excited about it."

If those trips provided opportunities for him to stalk and kill women, I could well understand the excitement. "Was he on a trip that day last week when the dead women's body was found at the truck stop?"

"Just up to Nashville," Curtis said. "He don't go out on the road like he used to when he was working. But that car in the garage? He went up to Nashville and picked it up."

"And stopped by the truck stop on his way home?"

"He knows people at every truck stop in the country," Curtis said. "He goes over to the one by the interstate and has lunch there at least once a week."

So nobody would think anything of it if they saw him there. Especially if he was towing an antique car with fins behind the pickup.

I was going to ask Curtis about his mother, but before I could, Rafe said, "Looks like it's opening up ahead. We got a plan for what we're gonna do when we get there?"

"If Yung's there," Grimaldi said, pulling her gun out and checking it for bullets, "find and secure her. If she isn't, take him into custody. Alive."

Rafe nodded. "You want me to stop here so we can go the rest of the way on foot, or keep going?"

"Let's take him by surprise," Grimaldi said. "Keep going."

The SUV rolled forward. The path opened up into a little clearing by the side of the river. The water was muddy and sluggish, the way the Duck River usually looks: an unpleasant sort of greenish-brown.

Jacob Drimmel's truck was parked in the middle of the clearing. The engine was off and there was no sign of life.

Rafe glanced at Curtis in the mirror. "He carrying?"

"He keeps a gun in the truck when he goes on the road," Curtis said. His voice was hushed, small, like either the place or the situation had finally gotten to him.

Rafe nodded. "Stay here," he told me in the rearview mirror. I nodded, and watched as he pulled the gun from the waistband of his jeans and made his way toward the truck. Grimaldi slid out on the other side of the SUV and left her door open. I guess they didn't want to startle Jacob, if he hadn't heard the car pull up.

While Grimaldi made her way around the SUV, gun out and ready, Rafe sidled up to the rear of the truck and glanced into the bed and through the window before he made it to the front, where he could put his hand on the hood. It must have been warm, because he nodded to her.

Both of them turned and scanned the area.

I did, too, from where I was sitting inside the SUV.

There was nothing to see or hear, just the soft rippling of

the water as it brushed along the edges of the river.

Until a protesting shriek cut through the silence, and was abruptly shut off.

Rafe took off running. Grimaldi did, too.

"Move," Curtis told me, his voice panicked.

I scrambled out of the car as he slid, snakelike, over the back of the seat and oozed through the door and onto the grass. He took off after the others.

I hesitated for a second before I ran around the car and started wrestling Carrie, protesting at the rough handling, out of the seat.

Then a gunshot rang through the air, blasting my eardrums, and my fingers fumbled.

Rafe and Grimaldi both had guns. Jacob Drimmel had a gun. Hell—heck—Agent Yung had a gun. That bullet could have come from any of them, and could have hit any of them, but my first thought was that Rafe had been shot. Again. He wasn't wearing body armor today, and a bullet now—unlike last month—could have killed him.

There were sounds from the woods, as if a body—or more than one—was crashing through the trees.

I ducked down behind the car, still trying to unfasten Carrie, but the straps and buckle were fighting me, probably because my fingers were shaking.

Then Jacob Drimmel burst out of the trees and I saw him for the first time.

There was absolutely nothing of Curtis in him, although Laura Lee might have had his height, if nothing else. He was a big guy, and looked something like an overgrown, aging Howdy Doody. The hair must have been flaming red at some point, and there were still streaks of faded ginger among the silver. His face was ruddy and broad, fair-skinned, and I imagined as a young man, he'd probably had freckles. At the moment, the color was florid, and he was baring his teeth in a snarl. He was wearing a pair of jeans and a plaid shirt with the sleeves rolled up, and his forearms were still muscled in spite of his age.

He ran for the truck, but when Rafe burst out of the trees on the left, Jacob changed direction and made for cover behind the truck instead. At the same time, Curtis came out of the woods a few strides behind Rafe. "Granddad!"

I didn't see Grimaldi, so I figured—if I were thinking clearly at all at that point, and I'm not sure I was—that she was taking care of Leslie Yung. Hopefully that meant that Yung was alive, and that Jacob hadn't had time to kill her.

He hesitated for a second at the sound of his grandson's voice, just long enough to look in Curtis's direction. That in turn caused him to notice me standing there on the far side of the SUV. When he moved toward me, I shoved the lock down and slammed the door, shutting Carrie inside. It took a couple of crucial seconds, but it put a locked door between him and her. Then I did the same with Grimaldi's door, that she had left open.

All this locking and shutting only took a couple of breaths, but it was long enough that Jacob was on me before I could get away. He reached out and twisted a hand in my hair, and yanked me backward.

I shrieked—being pulled by the hair like that hurts—and then my back slammed into his chest and drove the rest of the breath out of my lungs. He wrapped a meaty arm around my torso, pinning my arms to my sides. With the other, he pressed the muzzle of the gun in his hand to my temple.

"One more step and she gets it!"

It was such a horrible movie-cliché, but I didn't doubt for a second that he meant it. I froze, and everyone else did the same.

"That's my wife," Rafe told him, and his voice had that same soft rumble a big cat's growl has just before it jumps.

Jacob chuckled, and I could hear the edge of excitement in it. It made all the little hairs on my body stand up. "Then you'd best be careful what you do with that weapon."

He met my eyes, and I knew what he was thinking. He was a good enough shot to put a bullet in the middle of Jacob's forehead from where he stood—or anywhere else in Jacob's body, too; at least the parts of it he could see above the car—but if he did, Jacob might squeeze the trigger of his own gun by reflex, and where he had it aimed, I'd be dead before I hit the ground.

"Granddad," Curtis tried, "you don't have to do this."

Jacob looked at him. I could feel the slight movement when he turned his head. "What do you know about it, kid?"

"I know you killed Mom," Curtis said, and swallowed. I could see the movement of his throat. "I figured it out in the car on the way over here. You killed Mom, and you killed the woman last week, the dead one, at the truck stop."

"I've killed a lot more than that." Jacob's voice hit somewhere between irritated and proud. I guessed he wanted acknowledgement. "Eighteen of them."

He gave me a little shake. "Guess you'll be number nineteen, since I didn't get a chance to finish up the other one."

So Yung was alive. That was good, although at the moment I couldn't find it in myself to care a whole lot. "Too bad you couldn't make it an even twenty," I managed, although my teeth were chattering.

He chuckled. "Isn't it?"

"So you didn't have anything to do with Kent Jurgensson," Rafe said. His voice was conversational, but he still had the gun up and I knew that at the least sign of distraction on Jacob's part he'd fire.

"We found the bones in Mullinax's woods this morning," I added, to do what I could for the cause. I assumed the goal was to distract Jacob enough that Rafe could get a bead on him.

"We thought maybe you'd helped Mullinax get him out there."

"Art did that on his own. Him and that nephew of his, I guess. Or maybe the kid's father. The kid might not have had it in him."

He said it like it was a bad thing, and to him I guess maybe it was.

By now there were sounds from the woods opposite the car, and after a few seconds Grimaldi appeared between the trees.

"I called for an ambulance," she told Rafe, calmly, as if she couldn't see me standing here in Jacob's embrace with the muzzle of a pistol pointed at my head. "She's not walking out of here. And since you both ran off…"

She turned to Jacob. "Mr. Drimmel. I'm Tamara Grimaldi. Police chief of Columbia. You killed my mother."

As I waited for what sounded like the obvious end to that sentence, "Prepare to die," I wondered, slightly hysterically, whether I was losing my mind.

Jacob didn't seem to have heard anything funny in the statement. Maybe he wasn't familiar with *The Princess Bride*. "Which one was she?" he asked, with every indication of interest.

"Her name was Maria Grimaldi. Number three."

Jacob thought about it. "I think I remember her," he said finally, as if pleased with himself. "Pretty woman, but she looked tired. Not a hooker."

"No, she wasn't. She worked the night shift at a motel near the interstate. That's why she was tired. She'd just come off a work shift when you picked her up."

Jacob nodded. I waited—we all waited—for him to say something else, but he didn't. And to be honest, I'm not sure what he could have said. He wasn't sorry, and nobody would believe him if he said he was. And I certainly didn't want to hear any of the details of the crime. I'm sure Grimaldi didn't, either.

"I've been looking for you for a long time," she told him. Still calm, as if they'd met in much more pleasant circumstances than across the roof of an SUV in the middle of the woods. "It's thanks to you that I became a cop. I wanted to figure out what happened to my mother."

Jacob didn't say anything to that, either, and Grimaldi continued, "I'd like to know about the numbers. The Roman numerals. That's why we started looking at Kent Jurgensson and found the remains, you know. We thought it might have had something to do with the Latin classes at the school."

Jacob giggled, and all the little hairs on my body rose again. "I got those off those old books of my wife's. In the living room at the house."

"The Encyclopaedia Brittanica." I'd noticed them—a lot of volumes in leather bindings—but hadn't gotten close enough to see the Roman numerals stamped on the spines. I knew them, though. We have a similar set at the mansion. There's stuff at the mansion from generations back.

"Always thought she was better than me, with her la-dee-dah ways. Lunching with Debbie Mullinax and volunteering at the homeless shelter, like there isn't plenty of work to do at home."

He turned his head and spat, an eloquent opinion of his wife's airs. I braced myself for Rafe to shoot him while his head was turned and his attention wasn't on me, but it didn't happen.

"You killed Laura first," Grimaldi said. "Your daughter. You want to tell me about that?"

Jacob stared at her. "Why'd I wanna tell you anything?"

"It might be the last chance you get to tell your story."

Jacob chuckled. "You gonna shoot me dead right here? I don't think so. Not while I've got this."

He wiggled the gun at my temple. I gulped.

"Then maybe you owe it to your grandson to let him know the truth," Grimaldi said. "He's been without his mother a long time. Don't you think you ought to tell him how it happened?"

Jacob glanced at Curtis, standing still and pale on the other side of the car. "You wanna know what happened to your whore of a mother, son?"

He didn't give Curtis a chance to answer, and it was just as well. "Your good-for-nothing father had gotten himself arrested, finally. I told her from the start that he was no good, but no, she had something to prove, so she married him. And look where it got her. Alone with two kids, one barely out of diapers and the other one just a baby. I figured she'd come crawling back then, but no. She took a job serving food at the truck stop. I had to run out that night—had a broken-down truck an hour and a half north, in Kentucky—and I stopped in to see her on my way past. Got there just in time to see her crawl into the cab of some trucker looking for a lot lizard while his wife was at home…"

The injustice of that was rather breathtaking, considering what he'd been doing while his wife was at home, but it didn't seem like a good idea to mention it.

"Too proud to take money from her parents," Jacob said bitterly, "but not too proud to sell her body for twenty bucks at a truck stop."

Curtis had, if anything, turned even paler, but he didn't say a word, just stared at his grandfather, his eyes like black holes.

"So you waited for her to come out," Grimaldi prompted.

Jacob gave a little shudder. I could feel it in the arm that held mine pinned, and felt the pistol shiver against my skin. "She didn't expect to see me. Gave me lip, the little bitch. Stood there smelling of this man, telling me it was none of my business what she did. That I gave up the right to tell her what to do when she married Frankie. So I slapped her."

He said it like it was something that happened every day,

like it wasn't momentous. And maybe it wasn't. From some of what Curtis had said, it might have happened all the time.

"She fell and knocked herself out," Jacob said. "Hit her head against the side of the truck and fell. I couldn't leave her there, so I picked her up and tossed her in the truck and took her with me. She woke up halfway to Nashville, and tried to get out. I was afraid she was gonna hurt herself, so I tied her hands. And before I got to the broken-down rig, I gagged her and put her in the back. Couldn't have the trucker see her."

No, he definitely couldn't. The unknown trucker might have thought it was a little strange that Jacob had his daughter bound and gagged in the car.

"She was in there kicking her feet, trying to get attention. So when I had the rig moving again, I opened the truck and I tried to get her to stop. But she wouldn't, not even when I hit her again. So I put my hands around her throat and squeezed…"

His voice trailed off, and it had an almost dreamy quality to it. I fought back a shiver. Nobody else said anything, for a moment. Curtis looked ready to drop. Rafe still had his gun up, pointed at Jacob's head, his eyes black and hard. If the story had affected him, it didn't show. I wasn't sure he'd even been listening. The only thing he was focused on, was the right moment to pull the trigger.

"So you lifted her out of the car and left her there," Grimaldi said, and Jacob came back to himself.

"I didn't wanna take her back with me. You never know when someone might pull you over. And I knew we'd get her back eventually…"

He trailed off again. No one else said anything, either. Like me, I guess they didn't know what to say.

I wasn't aware of movement behind me until the very last second. I heard the sound of rushing footsteps, what sounded like a war cry, and the next moment Jacob smacked face first into the side of the SUV. I heard a crunch. The gun fell from his hand and bounced off my shoulder on its way to the ground. Jacob slid to the grass in a boneless jumble, and was handcuffed by Yung—Yung?—almost before he'd come to a stop.

It was over.

Epilogue

The elegant FBI agent from this morning was a thing of the past. Her perfect sheet of black hair was a straggling mess past her shoulders, decorated with leaves and twigs. The sleeve of the elegant suit was ripped half off, her makeup was smeared, and she had the beginnings of a black eye and a streak of blood at the corner of her mouth, and her bottom lip looked like she'd either bit it or been punched in the face. I figured it could be either.

But her eyes were flinty and she didn't hesitate or wince when she flipped Jacob over on his back and shoved him up against the tire of the SUV. But where I would have expected her to go right into the Miranda warning, she glanced over at Grimaldi. "You want to do the honors?"

I expected Grimaldi to say yes, she did. She'd told me as much: that Leslie Yung was welcome to join the team, but Grimaldi wanted the prerogative of slapping the handcuffs on her mother's killer herself. I guess maybe Yung's experiences made Grimaldi feel differently. She shook her head. "We got him. That's good enough."

Yung nodded. "You're under the arrest for the murders of Laura Lee Matlock and Ramona Mitchell," she informed Jacob, "with more charges to follow. You have the right to remain silent..."

By that point, Rafe had holstered his weapon and was

holding me in an embrace so tight it was hard to breathe. I didn't mind, though. That had been a little too close for comfort. "I need to stop doing this," I murmured into his chest.

He buried his face in my hair and breathed in. "That'd be good. Keep me from losing my mind so often."

"Sorry," I said.

"Don't mention it. Nothing I haven't done to you before."

True, that.

He let me go with a pat, and went to let Carrie out of the SUV. I took the opportunity to survey the scene.

On the other side of the car, Grimaldi was dealing with Curtis. The kid was obviously distraught—who wouldn't be?—and he kept repeating, "I gotta see my gramma. I need to go see my gramma."

"We'll go see her together," Grimaldi told him. "Just as soon as we're done here. I'll go with you, and we'll explain it all to her."

Curtis glanced at her. "He killed your mom?"

"A long time ago," Grimaldi said. "Couple years after he killed your mom."

Curtis shot a look across the car. He couldn't see his grandfather, who was still sitting down and still mostly out of it, but his voice rang with defiance. "I'm glad you caught him. I'm glad he's going to prison. I hope he dies there."

I hoped he did, too. And at Jacob's age, that was more likely than not. There was no need to spell that out, though.

Yung left Jacob where he was, head and shoulders against the metal of Grimaldi's SUV, and went to talk to them. She was limping, so she'd either hurt a leg or lost a heel at some point today. I still wanted to know what he'd done to get her into the truck with him, but since all's well that ends well, I figured it could wait.

"Here comes the cavalry," Rafe said, as he dropped Carrie into my arms. His ears, sharper than mine, had picked up the sirens. It took another second before I heard them, and a minute or two after that before the ambulance roared into the clearing and came to a stop.

Behind it, like an afterthought, came a blue SUV. I blinked at it. "Is that Dix?"

It was Dix. My brother got out of the SUV, still in the fancy suit he wears to work—probably the same suit he'd worn to go with Rafe and Bob to Daffodil Hill Farm this morning.

While the two paramedics scrambled down from their vehicle, and converged on Yung and Jacob Drimmel, checking pulses and doing triage, my brother stood there beside the SUV taking in the scene. After a few moments, he focused on Grimaldi, and I could hear the crackling from where I was standing. She could see it, too, because she fell back a step when he started toward her.

"Uh-oh," I said. The corner of Rafe's mouth turned up. And then we both fell silent as my brother grabbed Grimaldi, shook her once, and kissed her. And kissed her. And kept kissing her.

"About time," Rafe said after a few seconds had passed.

I nodded. Yes. It was.

And then things got even better. Dix let Grimaldi go, and dropped down to one knee, right there in the middle of the crime scene. And while I couldn't hear what he said, it was obvious to everyone what he was doing.

I held my breath while I waited to see Grimaldi's response. And while I couldn't hear that, either, I saw her nod. And saw Dix surge to his feet and grab her, and plant another kiss on her.

Rafe slung an arm around my shoulders. "Congratulations," he told me, dropping a kiss on the top of my head. "You lost a friend and gained a sister."

"You, too."

After a second, I added, "I can't wait to see how Mother responds to this one."

He smirked. "It'll be nice to have someone else take some of the heat off me at the Thanksgiving table."

"Grimaldi might be used to lasagna for Thanksgiving. I wonder how Mother will handle that?"

"With her usual finesse," Rafe said, and gave me a nudge. "C'mon. Let's be the first to welcome your brother's fiancée to the family."

"Don't mind if I do," I answered, and stepped forward.

# # #

About the Author

New York Times and *USA Today* bestselling author Jenna Bennett (Jennie Bentley) has written more than 40 books, most of them in the genres of mystery and suspense. For more information, please visit Jenna's website:
www.JennaBennett.com

9 781942 939375